Dimwater's Dragon

By

Sam Ferguson

This is a work of fiction. All of the characters, organizations, and events portrayed in this book are either products of the author's imagination or are used fictitiously.

Dimwater's Dragon

For Dana T. and Juvi G.
Thank you for your continued support.

Other Books by Sam Ferguson

The Fur Trader

The Dragon's Champion Series

The Dragon's Champion
The Warlock Senator
The Dragon's Test
Erik and the Dragon
The Immortal Mystic
Return of the Dragon

The Netherworld Gate Series
The Tomni'Tai Scroll
The King's Ring
Son of the Dragon (Coming Soon)

The Dragons of Kendualdern
Ascension

Haymaker Adventures
Jonathan Haymaker
Brothers Haymaker

The Sorcerese of Aspenwood
Dimwater's Dragon
Dimwater's Demons
Dimwater's Dagger

Contents

CHAPTER ONE

Cyrus grabbed Janik's left shoulder and stopped him mid-step. Janik turned around to regard the old wizard. Cyrus stroked his beard and narrowed his eyes on a far distant point.

"You aren't backing out now are you?" Janik asked.

Cyrus casually shook his head. "When we approach the lair you must remain vigilant. Lady Caspen will be well guarded, and her captor will have minions of his own to throw at us."

Janik nodded his head. His hand went down to the battle axe tucked in his belt. "Yes, well I have a few tricks of my own."

"Don't get too cocky there, warrior," Cyrus said. The wizard adjusted a sapphire ring on his left ring finger so that the gem was in the direct center of his finger. He then reached back and took his staff from a holster near his saddle. The horses whinnied and shied away, pulling at their guide ropes. "It appears as though the horses don't want to be here any more than I do."

Janik shrugged and started his way through the forest. The early morning air was cool, but warming by the minute. The silvery light of dawn had just begun to break the blackness of the night. Janik and Cyrus walked through the forest as quietly as they could, stealing their way up a large hill and winding between pine trees and aspens. There was no breeze, nor movement of any kind. The area around them was silent, devoid of any signs of life.

When they crested the hill they could only see a narrow entrance to a cave next to a very shallow stream. Cyrus pointed to the cave. Janik nodded, he knew that was the lair. Lady Caspen had been abducted several weeks before, and it fell to Janik and Cyrus to save her.

Janik pulled his axe free from its holster and made his way out by the stream toward the cave entrance. The closer he got to the entrance, the more he could feel a warm, putrid breeze. It carried with it a strange odor, something like iron and sulfur mixed together. Janik paused at the entrance, peering in and leaning side to side to gain a vantage point as he tried to spy further down the tunnel. In the blink of an eye Cyrus was at his side again. The old wizard stopped, pointed his staff into the cave and muttered a simple phrase. A yellow spark leapt from the end of the staff and hovered in the air before them. The spark grew to the size of a man's fist and then floated into the cave, illuminating the tunnel and laying bare its secrets.

With the aid of the spell, Janik could see that the cave was narrow for perhaps fifty yards ahead before it disappeared around a curve to the left. Jagged rocks of gray, brown, and black jutted out from each side, promising to gash any unwary traveler who was careless in his advance through the cave.

"Have you ever hunted a shadowfiend before?" Cyrus asked.

"I have hunted two," Janik replied. "However, both times I was in a party of twelve warriors."

Cyrus nodded. "Well, I suppose that had the previous parties sent to rescue Lady Caspen not all vanished, perhaps we would have found ten others to join us." Cyrus motioned for Janik to enter the cave first.

"Age before beauty," Janik said with a smile.

"Beauty before brains," Cyrus replied with a welcoming gesture. Janik ceded the point and entered the cave. Cyrus remained two yards behind Janik at all times. Janik knew this would allow the wizard to wield the staff not only to cast spells, but as a melee weapon as well. The two of them rounded the corner to the left only to find that the cave ended in a small chamber spanning three yards across and four yards high, with jagged stalactites dripping a green, algae filled water from their points.

"This doesn't make any sense," Janik said. Janik took his hands and pressed into the wall. The stone was cold and damp to the touch, worn smooth from years of weathering. Janik followed a rivulet of water with his eyes upward until he found a small fissure in the ceiling above. Algae grew around the sides of the crack. "There isn't anything here. There should be a cave here. It should be right here. There should be a cave that goes all the way into the lair."

Cyrus patted at the air with his left hand to quiet Janik while he studied the stone intently with his eyes.

"Give me a moment." Cyrus muttered as he raised his staff and tapped on the stone before him. *Tap tap tap.* Everywhere he knocked his staff, the stone clicked and clacked, creating an echo in the small chamber. Cyrus let out a small sigh and then tapped his staff to the floor three times.

"I told you, there's nothing here." Janik threw his hands up in the air and started to turn around to leave.

Cyrus raised his staff one more time and then slammed it on the floor. A great wave of golden light shot out from the top of the staff. The light filled the room and then vanished through the stone. After the golden light had radiated through the stone, a small red circle on the wall shone brightly.

"This is it," Cyrus said with a nod. The old wizard moved to the piece of stone and touched his staff to the red spot. Without a sound, the stone wall on the north side of the chamber vanished as if it had never really been there at all. "A vampire's illusions are among the strongest, save for those made by a dragon." Cyrus smiled and then pointed down the newly opened tunnel. "As I said before, beauty before brains."

"I thought we were after a shadowfiend?" Janik asked quickly.

Cyrus laughed and shook his head. "A vampire is similar. Now go, he will know we have come before much longer."

Janik snickered at the old man and brushed past. The new tunnel was not nearly as rough as the first portion of the cave had been. There were no jagged rocks jutting out from the sides, and there were no more stalactites either. The cave went straight out for roughly a hundred yards before a stairway dropped down sharply. The steps descending downward were carved from the gray granite meticulously. Each stair was level and as tall and wide as the last before it. The walls on either side were smoothed, but had not been polished for a very long time. Instead, they were left dull and dark, without decoration or garnishment of any kind. The air continued to get warmer the further down they went into the lair. The little golden orb of light conjured by the wizard went before them faithfully, illuminating the path.

When they finally reached the bottom, the walkway opened up to become roughly fifteen feet wide. The floor spread out smoothly before them. Janik noticed the slabs of granite were carved to resemble tile flooring, cut into large squares.

The two heroes walked forward cautiously. The golden orb flickered and flashed, struggling to pierce the darkness around them. Cyrus twirled his staff in its direction and the light was strengthened, but it managed only to illuminate roughly ten feet before them, and only just dispelled the shadows from the walls at either side.

"I am afraid that is the best it can do for now," Cyrus commented dryly. "We are deep enough in the lair that the vampire's magic is already countering my own." He flashed a confident grin and winked at Janik. "Not to worry though, when it comes to a battle, he will find that I am the better magician."

Janik sighed and shrugged off the comment entirely. "Let's just get a move on."

As they continued to walk along the path, the darkness closed in on them. The walls faded out of view and the way before them became murky as if covered in dark, thick fog.

Janik felt Cyrus' staff tap him on the shoulder. He stopped and turned to regard the old wizard.

"Perhaps it is best if we walk side-by-side now," Cyrus suggested. "The light is not faring so well."

Janik nodded.

A high-pitched squeal sounded in the darkness and the two froze immediately.

"What was that?" Janik asked

Cyrus put a finger to his mouth and leveled his staff before them. As they stood, waiting for the source of the shriek to reveal itself, the golden orb grew dimmer by the second until it barely illuminated the area immediately before their faces.

"Can't you strengthen the light again?" Janik whispered.

"No time for that. If you are ready, the enemy is about to test your mettle," Cyrus told Janik. "It is time to earn your pay." Cyrus raised his staff and shouted loudly, "Aka eek es eser!"

"What language was that?"

The old wizard didn't answer. A great flame burst out of the staff and encircled the two adventurers. A pair of winged beasts swooped in from above. Janik barely caught a glimpse of their leathery bodies, sharp fangs, and crooked claws before he was forced to swing his axe. His first strike hit true, sinking deep into the neck of the first beast. Blood sprayed out, landing droplets onto Janik's leather armor. As the vile liquid connected with the leather, it hissed and smoked as it burned through.

A flash of lightning jumped out from Cyrus' staff and struck the second winged beast. The foul monster exploded into a puff of smoke. The third monster managed to circle around behind Janik and came in for an attack. It screeched loudly as it dove for him, but Janik rolled away safely while Cyrus flipped his staff over and used it as a club to smash the top of its head. The beast fell to the ground and Janik jumped in quick as a snake to drive the killing blow down through its spine.

The two heroes looked around, studying the chamber they were in for any sign of other foes. Even with the circle of fire around them, the darkness was too thick to see into very deeply.

Cyrus summoned seven orbs of light and set them in a rotating fashion above them to push back the shadows and allow the heroes a greater field of vision.

"The enemy surely knows we are here now," Cyrus said. "That was likely only the first challenge."

Janik didn't say anything. He nodded with his head and moved forward. The two of them walked for another ten minutes, taking their time to allow the seven orbs of light to pierce the shadows before them as they walked. Fortune smiled upon them, and there were no other creatures that attacked them before they finally came to the lair's entrance.

Cyrus poured more magic into the orbs until the entire chamber was illuminated fully. Janik let out a hushed whistle of amazement as he studied the structure before them. The chamber spanned forty yards from where they stood to the front of a castle standing at the far end of the cavern. The front wall itself spanned the entire width of the chamber, roughly twenty-five yards across, and stood tall, stretching from the floor all the way up to the ceiling some thirty feet above.

Two towers stretched from floor to ceiling, standing at each edge of the wall. Large, arched windows broke the stone towers in the middle and again at the top. The windows were not filled with glass, but rather they were left as open passageways. Between the two towers, a large skull stood out from the center of the wall.

Fashioned from polished granite, it was black as night and shinier than any gem Janik had ever seen. It shimmered as the seven orbs of light spun overhead as though it were a black diamond. The two eyes of the skull made up the only windows in the main portion of the castle's front. The end of the nose was broken off short and the jagged pieces stood out from the face, rigid and grotesque. The door, Janik presumed, must have been in the back of the mouth. The mouth was filled with sharp, curved fangs longer than a man was tall, and stood as ever-watchful sentries before the entrance.

"The entryway is closed," Janik said.

Cyrus nodded. "I had expected as much."

"Perhaps we can use the windows in the towers," Janik offered.

Cyrus scoffed and shook his head. "I intend to live to see tomorrow," he said. "Just wait a moment and I will open the door." He raised his staff. A soft, red glow emanated from the staff's top as Cyrus began to chant in a whisper that Janik could not fully understand. The red glow stretched out from Cyrus' staff toward the large skull façade.

A voice, at once deep as thunder over crashing waves and shrill as the hiss of a snake, called out to them from the castle, "I have not invited you here. What have I to do with you?"

"We come searching for Lady Caspen, of course," Cyrus replied.

The voice in the castle cackled and laughed. "Oh, but you lie."

"We are here for Lady Caspen," Janik insisted. "Open the doors now and I will make your death a quick one. Resist, and we will enter anyway and we will destroy you."

The laughter grew until it echoed off of each wall in the large chamber.

"Foolish warrior, it seems that only one of you is here on a noble quest. The other has ulterior motives at heart, or can you not see that with your simple mind?"

Janik glanced at Cyrus.

"Vampires are masters of cunning and trickery," Cyrus cautioned.

"Oh are we?" the voice inquired from the castle. "I can smell the truth of the situation from here," the voice said.

Cyrus gestured to get Janik's attention. "I can open the door.

However, you should know that as soon as that door opens, we are not going to make an easy time of whatever comes out."

Janik nodded his understanding and fixed his grip on his axe. Cyrus stamped the butt of his spear onto the ground four times and then shouted in a language that Janik could not understand. The red light reached in toward the castle, flowing between the closed fangs and causing the mouth of the skull to glow brightly as though a great, glowing ruby sat within the mouth. Thunder broke the silence as bolts of lightning flashed inside the closed jaws and blasted the granite teeth apart.

As Janik watched the stone shatter and fly every which way, he saw a dark mass moving behind the red glow of Cyrus' spell. It took him a moment to fully realize the mass was not really one moving thing. It was a multitude of moving things. Out they came, flowing out of the mouth as if the great skull had opened its maw and retched. There were more beasts like before, their dark wings curved over their slick backs. Those with wings took to the air, while other beasts with large arms and wickedly spiked tails ran upon the ground. The monsters running upon the ground used all four limbs to propel themselves forward at an amazing speed. As they ran, their front arms made a strange, loud clickity-clack upon the floor.

That was when Janik realized that the beasts without wings had large, horn-like hooks instead of hands on their arms that extended all the way down from their elbow joints. Janik wasn't sure how many there were. Maybe fifty, maybe seventy, it was hard to tell as the darkness was closing in again.

Cyrus sent a whirling tornado of fire directly at the monsters. Janik charged ahead, taking on a few that were able to evade the tornado of fire. He dropped two of the flying beasts before one reached down and grabbed his shoulder with talons sharp and strong as any saber Janik had ever seen. The talons ripped through his armor and pierced his flesh, enabling the flying monster to fling Janik thirty feet away. As he landed on the stone floor, the experienced warrior tucked and rolled to minimize the impact. He pressed up to his feet and scanned around him.

Janik was not about to give up. He saw a trio of winged monsters flying toward Cyrus that he could intercept if he moved quickly. He rushed in to reengage the enemy. In a matter of seconds he crossed the five yards between him and the enemy and using his right hand to wield his axe, he brought one of the three flying beasts down with a solid chop to the middle of its skull. He jerked his weapon free just in time as one of the grotesque beasts on foot ran directly for him from behind. Janik dodged to the left as the large monster swung its wicked claws at him. Then Janik deftly jumped up and over the creature's whirling tail. The mighty warrior let out a yell and brought his axe down, severing the tail in half. The monster howled in agony, but it did not let up its attack.

It snarled at Janik and came on. Janik swung his axe horizontally, but the beast dove under it and grabbed the back of the axe with its left claw. It raised its right arm over its head, preparing to chop down and hook Janik's head, but Janik ran forward, using the shaft on his axe as a bar with which to push the beast back. When he got in close enough, Janik deftly kicked the monster's front knee in backwards. The cracking bone could no longer support the monster's weight, and the beast fell to the ground. Janik kicked the beast twice in the head and brought his axe down to sever its neck.

Janik whirled around in time to see a spear of ice run through three similar monsters that were charging him and had come within only a few yards of striking. Janik nodded his thanks to Cyrus and then continued on. There were a lot of monsters, but they were not coordinated in their attack. Each monster tried to fight on its own and cared little for the other, fallen monsters around. None of the creatures attempted to protect each other's flanks, which made it much easier for Janik and Cyrus to work through the group.

Within five minutes the battle was over and all of the ghastly creatures were dead.

Janik surveyed the scene. He had taken down ten, or perhaps twelve of the creatures with his axe. Cyrus had done the rest. Scores of creatures lay upon the stone floor. Many of them smoldered from magical fire attacks, while others were pinned to the wall or floor with great spears that had been fashioned from magical ice. The scene of carnage was far beyond anything that Janik had ever witnessed a wizard do before.

"I do believe the battle goes to you," Janik said.

Cyrus looked at Janik questioningly.

"You have the higher body count," Janik explained. "That

means I buy you a round at the nearest pub."

Cyrus smiled appreciatively and offered a nod. "If you survive, then you can buy me a beer."

Janik frowned, but the old wizard only laughed and began walking toward him.

Cyrus concentrated once more on the door and cast another spell like the first. A red glow expanded in the doorway and sizzled and cracked with bolts of lightning streaking over it. After a few moments, the door shattered and crumbled to the floor.

"Time to move," Cyrus said.

In the two ran through the entrance to the castle, Cyrus' spell still crackling and popping inside the entrance, holding the granite jaws open. The two only just made it inside when then the jaws snapped shut. Inside they were confronted by mirrors lining the walls, making it hard for them to know which way to go.

"I will handle this," Janik said. He swung his axe into the nearest mirror, shattering it into a thousand pieces. "I hate these kinds of tricks."

The old wizard let the warrior break a few more mirrors before finally growing impatient. Cyrus summoned a whirlwind with his staff that shattered all of the remaining mirrors before them and sucked the sharp shards of glass into a swirling cyclone. Cyrus then caused the cyclone to disappear, along with the shards it carried. Afterward he summoned two more orbs of light.

Janik glanced to Cyrus.

Cyrus shrugged. "My way is faster." He then pointed to the orbs of light above them. "These are not just to light our way, they will help us find the right path to the vampire."

"How can they do that?"

"They are designed to sense the vampire's magic. Come on, try to keep up." The two of them walked through the main entryway and then down the corridor on the left. A pair of disfigured creatures entered the hallway from an adjacent doorway. Cyrus was quick to catch them with a blast of fire that reduced them to a smoldering pile of gray ash.

"I am going to enjoy watching you both die," a voice taunted.

Janik glanced over his shoulder but saw nothing there.

"He is just trying to scare you," Cyrus said. "He is still far off. The orbs will turn red when we get close."

Janik nodded, but the statement did little to calm his nerves. He wanted to know how the vampire knew where they were.

The pair followed the orbs as they glided through a maze of halls and a staircases. The two turned up a stairway that was flanked by a pair of large, hulking stone gargoyles at the base of the stairs. Janik readied his axe, but Cyrus sneered and shook his head.

"These are made of stone," Cyrus assured Janik. "Save your strength and follow me up the stairs."

"How can you tell?"

Cyrus didn't bother answering the question and instead pushed beyond Janik and made his way up the stairs. Janik kept an eye on the stone gargoyles for a few moments before deciding Cyrus was correct. He made his way up the stairs as well, following Cyrus as the wizard turned into a corridor on the right. After several yards they passed under a large arch and stepped into a grand ballroom.

Everything up until now had been granite carved from the mountain, but the floor in the ballroom was made of pink, green, and blue marble tiles. Four massive, granite columns stretched from floor to ceiling. Each column held four sconces with burning torches. Above them, the underside of the cupola was painted with a macabre scene of a silver haired man raising the dead from a graveyard and subjecting them to his servitude.

Along each of the four walls were hung several tapestries. Some depicted beasts and monsters that Janik knew and was familiar with, such as werewolves, imps, large snakes, and ghouls. Other tapestries showed great horned beasts and monsters the like of which Janik had never seen before. His eyes fixed upon one such tapestry of a large, greenish humanoid. Small spikes grew out of the humanoid's shoulders, curving forward and out to the side. Larger, triangular spikes protruded out from the monster's back. Instead of hands, each arm ended in two wickedly sharp hooks, much like the creatures they had just fought before they entered the castle. The legs were thick and muscular, shielded with scales that ended abruptly above the sharp hooves. Three tails protruded out from the back of the beast, and small spikes jutted out from the end of each tail.

"That is a wylkin," Cyrus said, noting Janik's wide-eyed stare as they walked past. "Not to worry, though. As I understand it they mostly prey upon cows and sheep."

Janik nodded and the two turned toward the northern wall. There they saw a closed door of ebony wood. Brass straps encased the door, shining brightly in the torchlight. There was no keyhole, and no doorknob. Cyrus directed the two orbs toward the door. The closer they got, the more red they became.

Janik held out his axe and then gestured to the door. Cyrus shook his head. The wizard took a silver coin from his coin purse and flicked it across the room to hit the door. A great flurry of lightning bolts assaulted the coin, holding it suspended in the air for a moment before allowing it to drop to the marble floor. Smoke rose from the coin as it glowed red hot for a full minute before fading.

"That is the right way, but we will need to find the proper method for opening the door." Cyrus leaned upon his staff and stared at the door for a long while.

Janik stared at the wizard incredulously. "Shall I just wait while you catch your breath?" he asked.

Cyrus dismissed Janik with a wave. "Go stare at the tapestries and leave me be. I am thinking."

Janik huffed and thought of a clever retort, but it would have to wait.

The other doors leading to the ballroom slammed shut, echoing loudly in the chamber. Janik startled and held his axe up at the ready.

"It looks like we are now trapped," Janik said.

A wind suddenly rushed around the entire room, pulling the tapestries away from the stone wall and bringing with it the chill of death.

Janik looked up and his mouth fell open when a large snake fell from the tapestry that held its image. The serpent slithered toward the center of the room and flicked its tongue out. The tongue bounced in the air, tasting the scent in the room. Then it locked its eyes on the heroes and turned to strike.

"I hate snakes," Janik yelled. Janik ran forward and swung his axe just as the snake struck out at him. Its fangs dripped with an opaque liquid which dangled grotesquely from the tip of each point. Luckily, Janik was the first to connect and the axe tore through the snake's head.

"On your guard," Cyrus called out. "More are coming."

Janik's mouth fell open as all of the tapestries began to shake and tremble. One by one, monsters dropped out from the embroidered scenes into the real world. Janik was quick to engage them on the ground while Cyrus did his best to set fire to the tapestries before they could give birth to the monsters whose images they held. The wizard succeeded in burning more than half of them, including the werewolves and the ghouls and the imps. For good measure, he also set the tapestry of the wylkin ablaze.

"I thought you said they only attack cattle and sheep," Janik shouted as he battled with a giant wolf.

"I only said that so as not to scare you," Cyrus replied.

The two heroes slew another pair of large snakes, a trio of braindead zombies, and a dozen skeletons.

This time, the body count was tipped in Janik's favor.

"Now you owe me a round," Janik said with a wink.

Cyrus shook his head. "I almost got half of the monsters," he replied.

"Uh-uh," Janik said with a shake of his head. "The battle goes to me. I have more bodies."

Cyrus pointed up to the burnt tapestries. "Fine, then I am counting the ones I killed before they materialized. The battle goes to me, and now you owe me two drinks."

Janik frowned and opened his mouth to say something. He huffed and set his axe back in its place. There was no way for him to refute the wizard's logic.

Unfortunately, Cyrus was no closer to opening the door than he had been before the monsters appeared. Cyrus assaulted the door a series of spells. He tried lightning, fire, ice, and wind, but nothing so much as budged the ebony door.

"What do we do now?" Janik inquired.

Cyrus didn't respond. He stood still, and continued to stare at the door.

The voice taunted them again, "You have done better than the others, but you will die here."

The cupola above cracked and broke. Giant pieces of slab fell to the floor below, fracturing the beautiful marble floor and shaking the entire ballroom. Janik darted to the side while Cyrus threw up a magical shield to protect himself. Great columns of fire descended from the ceiling above with flames so intense, even Cyrus inside his magical shield had to shy away from it. Out from within the fire emerged a beast unlike any of the others they had fought heretofore in the castle. The demon had four muscular arms, each as large around as one of Janik's legs. The demon's legs, in turn, were larger around than Janik's chest. Sharp, thick talons clicked and scraped over the marble floor, scratching and breaking the stone as the demon walked toward them. The demon had no weapons, but it did have a long snout filled with sharp, jagged teeth. Its eyes were black as night in their centers, and burned with flames which leapt off of them. When it caught sight of Janik gaping at it, it snarled and walked slowly toward Janik.

Janik studied the demon's gait and then made his move. He ran forward, holding his axe up high, ignoring the pain in his left shoulder where he had been stabbed earlier. The demon turned his lower left hand out toward Janik and fireballs leapt from its palm. Janik only barely escaped the crackling fire as he jumped out to the left, but the demon had already lifted its lower right hand to lash out with a long whip of fire that it had conjured. The whip circled around Janik's axe and ripped it from the man's hand. The force of the blow was so intense that Janik fell to the ground with his arms singed and smoking. He looked up just as his axe melted away into molten steel and dripped to the floor below.

Cyrus sent in a series of magical ice darts, but none of them had any effect on the beast. The demon absorbed each dart directly into its chest and only grew larger and stronger. The demon then took both of its lower arms and clapped them together in front of himself, sending a shockwave out that flung Cyrus to the back wall and knocked him unconscious.

Janik knew he was in serious trouble without Cyrus there to help. He reached for the short sword hanging from his belt, hoping against all odds that the blade would somehow affect the beast. The demon cracked his whip and sparks of lightning exploded over it. A moment later, Janik was flying through the air as scorching pain seared through his left leg. He stretched out his left hand to break his fall, but his wrist and forearm snapped in three different places. He called out in agony, writhing on the floor as the burning made its way through his leg up into his hip, while radiating pulses shot through his chest and shoulder from his left forearm. His vision blurred and he gasped for breath.

He rolled over and saw the fiery whip coming down for his face. The weapon seem to unfold over him slowly, as if time stretched out, allowing him to watch his death for much longer than he should have needed to. Yellow and gold sparks leapt from the bright red whip, but he felt no fear. He lay still, watching the weapon soar down toward his face and then all went black.

Death was anything but what he had expected, for there was no bright light, and no imp to drag him down to hell either. In fact, he wasn't even sure he was dead, for he was still breathing, and from what he could tell, the sounds of battle still raged around. He tried to open his eyes, but they would not obey him, so he listened with his ears as Cyrus, apparently conscious again, threw spell after spell. He guessed that what he heard was lightning, or possibly spears of ice as he had seen before, but he had no way to be sure. He knew only that there were large, crackling sounds flying in the air around him, followed by gusts of wind and heavy thumps.

Janik had lost all feeling in his body. It was replaced by a cold numbness that left him confused and paralyzed. Then he felt a scorching heat on his right side. His eyes flickered open and a great flame stood before him. His left eye saw only red blood, presumably from his own face, but his right eye looked up at the demon from below with one leg standing on his right side and the demon's other leg standing on his left arm, which he could no longer feel. Instinctively Janik reached for his short sword that was still tucked into a sheath on his right hip and thrust it upward, driving the point of that sword into the demon's groin and twisting it as he pushed farther into the demon's body. The demon howled and cried out as sparks of fire jumped out of its mouth. Blood as yellow as liquid gold coursed down the demon's legs. The demon collapsed backwards, its four arms flailing and fire spewing out of its mouth. Janik saw a trio of blue spears strike down into the beast's chest and the demon was no more.

Cyrus walked over and stood next to Janik, looking down and shaking his head in dismay. "There's nothing I can do for you, other than to ease your pain if you are ready to die."

"I don't want to die," Janik said.

"Everyone dies," Cyrus said callously. "You fought well. You will be remembered as a hero."

"Khefir take you!" Janik spat. "I don't want to be remembered, I want to live! I want to live!"

Cyrus stiffened and arched a brow as he looked down at Janik. He tugged with his left hand on his gray beard and narrowed his eyes on Janik.

At that moment, a terrible burning overpowered Janik's body. His back arched up on the floor and his right arm trembled and shook. He had no way of knowing if the wet he felt on his forehead was blood, sweat, or both. He cried out incoherently as his body spasmed and cramped.

Janik didn't see the spell that Cyrus was weaving around him, nor did he comprehend the silver orb that encased him a moment later, all he knew was that he had been saved from his terrible torment and was now lying still and wet upon the ground.

"Your body is indeed broken, Janik. However, with a will as strong as yours, I can save you. I can end your torment and restore you to your body. It will not be easy, and I doubt I can fully save your arm and leg, but I can preserve your life."

"I thought you said there was nothing you could do for me."

Cyrus nodded his head slowly as he brought a hand up and smoothed his hair. He knelt down on to the stone floor on Janik's left side. He waved a hand over Janik's left eye and the blood was gone so that Janik could see out of both eyes again. With the vision in his left eye restored, Janik could see that the left side of his nose was gashed open and a bit of flesh from his eyebrow hung over his eye as well. The wizard brushed the flap of skin away, and to Janik's surprise, there was no pain as the flap was moved.

"There is nothing I could do for you unless you vowed to serve me." Cyrus brought up his left hand and pulled a small dagger from his belt. "If I offer you your life again, will you dedicate yourself to my service?"

"What would you want me to do?" Janik asked.

Cyrus sneered, stretching his thin lips across his face. "I have not come to save Lady Caspen. I am willing to give you the glory of saving Lady Caspen and restore your life to your body so that you may enjoy a comfortable retirement according to the ways of the Middle Kingdom. In return I want a wizard's oath that you will serve me and fulfill any request I shall make of you for the rest of your life. I should warn you that if you make this oath, your heart will cease beating should you ever decide to go against it."

Janik hesitated. He could tell by Cyrus' voice that the wizard had no good intentions. The fact that he had not outright said what he wanted Janik to do was more than a little unnerving. Cyrus must have sensed Janik's hesitance and reticence, because whatever spell was keeping his pain away weakened enough so that Janik got another taste of the horrible agony and fire. Janik spasmed and clenched his jaw.

"It would be useful for me to have somebody like you," Cyrus said. "I will not ask for much, mostly information and books. However, when the time comes there will be individuals who will need to be removed from the plane of the living. Do these things for me and I will take away your pain now. What do you say?"

Janik nodded. The pain was gone instantly. Cyrus drew a line horizontally across his palm with his dagger. It was not so deep that the flesh hung open, but it was deep enough that droplets of blood formed and started to run down his palm and wrist.

"Now repeat the words that I will say to you, and your life will be restored and your power renewed."

Janik held his right hand up, reaching out towards Cyrus' hand.

"I want magic too," Janik demanded.

"What would you do with magic?"

"I will serve you, wizard, but to do so I want to be more than what I was. If I am to be your servant, then I want enough power that I will not need to serve others around me anymore."

"That can be arranged. I will restore you, and I will give you a great portion of magic. Then together we will go and rescue Lady Caspen and return her to her family. You will take her back, while I remain here and look for something that the vampire has in his possession."

"What is it you search for?"

"That is none of your concern. It is something *I* am looking for; something personal. We will do this and you will complete your part of the job. When I need you I will call upon you. Otherwise, do not speak of me to anyone ever again."

"You are not Cyrus, are you?" Janik asked. "For Cyrus was recommended by the Academy to aid me, and I doubt they would have sent someone like you."

The wizard smiled wide. "No, my dear Janik. I am not Cyrus, nor am I a wizard who has ever dealt with Kuldiga Academy. However, my name shall not be made known now. It is enough to say that I am a warlock from a land far, far away."

"So you killed Cyrus to take his place with me? Let me see your true form."

The warlock shook his head.

"It is not so simple as that."

"Then at least tell me what it is you're looking for. If I am already bound to your service, I will further covenant not to speak of you to anyone without your permission on pain of death under this wizard's pact that you are giving me now. I must know what it is the vampire has."

"It is simple Janik, he has a book. The book is called Aikur's War. It is the story of a man who managed to infiltrate Hammenfein, and rescue loved ones who had been falsely imprisoned in hell."

"Who do you know that is in hell?" Janik pressed.

Cyrus bristled and his tone turned cold. "That is a question for another time. Come, let us finish the pact and our nasty business with this foolish vampire. Remember, you are now bound to me. Play your part as the valiant knight of the kingdom, but remember that I will and can come for you at any time to request your services. I swear to you now that if you ever betray me, your death will make the pain you suffered at the demon's hands feel as a warm, gentle spring by comparison."

The warlock took Janik's hand and the two made their binding oath.

"Come, we will destroy the vampire and you will be the hero, and I will get the items I came for."

Janik nodded and then paused as the wizard began to walk away.

Items? The wizard had only mentioned the book. What else did he want?

CHAPTER TWO

Five years later, Cyrus paid Janik a visit in his home late one night. The wizard had arrived suddenly, appearing at a time when Janik was alone.

"Why him?" Janik growled. "Why should my brother get the girl when I am the one who saved the mother?"

Cyrus grinned from across the table in the dimly lit chamber. "I know it has been a few years, but surely you don't believe that *you* actually had anything to do with Lady Caspen's rescue, do you?"

Janik huffed and folded his arms across his chest. "I only mean that it doesn't seem appropriate. Why should my younger brother be the one to wed the girl?"

Cyrus sneered and scraped a long fingernail across the table. "It isn't important," he said. "The simple fact is that your brother is closer in age to her. You are several years older than your brother. Beyond that, you are not publically viewed as a Master anymore. We will have to pander to Lord Caspen's greed, which will include throwing him a son-in-law that still has a proper title and fame."

Janik shook his head and hooked his finger into the loop on the ceramic jug before him. He pulled it up to his lips and pulled a long drink of whiskey.

"Fine. I will set my brother to marry the girl, but it won't be an easy task. I have to convince Lord Caspen, and my brother."

"How's that?" Cyrus asked.

Janik took another drink and then set the jug down. "My brother is a very honorable sort. He won't readily accept the offer. He will fight me on it and insist that I claim her hand. After all, as far as he knows, *I* was the one who rescued Lady Caspen."

Cyrus reached down below the table and brought his hand up

with a small leather bag clutched tightly in his fingers. "Make your brother drink this. You can mix it with anything. It doesn't matter what the drink is so long as it is mixed with this powder and goes down his gullet."

"What is it?" Janik asked.

"It is an enchanted blend; something of a proprietary secret, you might say. Get him to drink this, and then you should be able to control his mind. Come, I will teach you a charm spell. It won't take long to master, but it will enable you to manipulate him in almost any way once he drinks the mixture. The powder itself is odorless, and tasteless, but it might dissolve better in something hot. Once he has this in his body, you will only need to give him more every few weeks at most."

"I understand," Janik said as he reached forward and took the bag.

"You won't be able to force him to do anything, mind you, so do use caution while exercising the power. If you ask him to do something that wholly goes against his character, the spell will break."

"But it will be enough to get him to agree to marry the girl?" Janik pressed.

Cyrus sniggered and nodded. "That and much more, my friend."

*****

Kyra reached out to test the door to her father's study. She knew he was gone. He was meeting with another nobleman downstairs in the south parlor. The cold, smooth metal did not turn in her hand as she had hoped. She frowned and let out a small sigh. Her left hand went down to retrieve her lock pick set from a pouch that she normally tucked into her pocket. Her instinct to grab it was faster than her mind was in recalling the memory that her father had taken it from her the week before, after he had caught her in his study. It wasn't that she wasn't allowed to read books and study, but Father's library was always off-limits. Perhaps that was why she liked going there so much.

Certainly she could get many books just as good as the ones in her father's library in her own study, which was really just a small corner of her mother's library in the east wing of the manor. Frankly, her mother had many books that were more detailed about magic and the types of spells that she liked than her father would ever be able to collect in his own library. Still, she found herself drawn not only to the myths, legends, and the secret arts spoken of in her mother's works, but also to the myriad languages, histories, and chronicles of the peoples of Terramyr which her father had collected. That, and she liked the thrill of going to places where she knew she was not supposed to be.

She would have made a new lock pick set had her father not also followed her back to her bedchamber and taken her metal file and the other hairpins from which she had made the first set. But that was not about to stop thirteen-year-old Kyra Caspen. If the study was locked, then she would find another way in. She turned and walked quietly over the red, hardwood planks in the hallway. The next door on the left put her into a small sitting room with a large hearth and a cabinet filled with brandy. It had always seemed peculiar to her that her father's study should ever be locked when a room filled with liquor sat unlocked nearby. She moved through the sitting room, hardly more than glancing at the brandy in the cabinet, before throwing the window open and scampering out onto the side of the manor. She didn't need to be careful, for no one would see her here. She was on the northwest corner of the building, and from this side she was invisible to the road that led up to the main entrance. She slid her slender fingers into the grooves between the flat flagstone rock which covered the exterior of the manor as she also slid her feet along.

Slowly but surely she made her way back toward the study, but this time she would not enter through the door. She had long ago disabled the lock on the study's window for just such an occasion as this. She liked to pride herself on being one step ahead of her father. For instance, recently, when her father would tell her to go and play while he conducted official business, he had no idea that she knew the real reason for the noblemen's visits. In two weeks she would turn fourteen years old. That was the time her betrothal would be announced.

"That is the way of noble women in the Middle Kingdom," Kyra's mother had said.

"It is proper and right for a lady to be married to a

nobleman," her father had told her many times.

Neither had asked her opinion about it one way or the other.

Perhaps that was the real reason she had broken into the study more often in the last year. It was her way of getting back at him, showing him that she could control her own life, at least in part.

She slid her hand onto the window. Pressing against it, she lifted the pane of glass. She slipped under it into the study. Within seconds she was in the room and gently pulling the window down behind her. She couldn't have it slamming shut and causing a ruckus.

Kyra moved into the room and noticed that her father had left a book out on his reading table. She moved closer to see what it was he had been reading. She slipped her hand under the red leather book and picked it up from the table, turning it over to read the runes on the side. They were Elvish, written by the Sierri'Tai in fact. The Sierri'Tai were a race of drow, or dark elves as many others called them. She squinted at the runes, trying to decipher them. She had studied some Elvish books before, but the writings of the dark elf races still were difficult for her to decipher.

When she finally deciphered the runes, she almost retched.

"The art of selling carpets," Kyra read aloud. She knew that her father was not selling carpets, nor had he ever done so. More likely he was using the text on trade to become a better negotiator for selling her hand in marriage. She dropped the book and moved to the large, green armchair and flopped down inside it. She lifted her feet and snapped her fingers, magically calling a small footstool to place itself under her waiting legs. She relaxed down inside as she looked up toward the picture on the wall in front of her. It was a painting depicting two men fighting numerous winged beasts. One was a wizard and the other a warrior who held an axe. A brass placard at the bottom of the painting read simply, "The rescue of Lady Caspen." She looked at the man holding the axe in the picture and sighed in disgust.

Kyra already knew who her future husband would be. She had known since her fifth birthday, which was exactly five years and eight months after her mother had been rescued from a vampire's lair. The wizard in the painting, a man by the name of Cyrus, had disappeared after the rescue. No one knew whether he had made it out alive. Most presumed he had been killed, as had numerous heroes before the pair of them made their way into the vampire's subterranean castle. Only the warrior named Janik had survived. Kyra's mother had never spoken much of her rescue, nor of her captivity. Kyra's father, however, had spoken often of the hero's bravery, cunning, and strength.

It was on her fifth birthday that she met the warrior's younger brother, Feberik Orres.

Kyra's father did not know she had been listening that day, as she was playing with a pair of dolls at the far end of the table in the dining hall while the men chatted among themselves. She had nonetheless heard every word her father spoke that day, and she did not fail to catch the fact that Janik was demanding Kyra be wed to his younger brother as recompense for his heroism. Her mother had come to take her away then, before the conversation progressed too much farther, but Kyra still remembered her father's next words.

"Though I appreciate what you did in winning my wife back for me, what other tangible consideration can I expect for such a betrothal?" her father had asked.

As Kyra reflected on it now, she realized it was not long after that conversation she had started rebelling against her father. Still, her mother raised her to be a lady, and that meant bending to her father's will. That was exactly what she was going to do. Kyra would accept the announced betrothal, to whomever it may be, and then she would go off to Kuldiga Academy for four years. Her father had wanted her to choose the school of wisdom, to become an apprentice scholar and follow his footsteps. Luckily, Kyra's mother had intervened and instead insisted she join the School of Sorcery.

Kyra took her eyes away from the painting and shut the memory out from her mind. She twirled out of her father's chair and walked along the long row of cherry-wood bookshelves, scanning the titles as she walked. Her eyes browsed from the floor to the ceiling, not finding anything in particular she wanted to read that day. That is, until she came to an odd set of books. Surely she must have seen them before, for she had been in the study hundreds, maybe even thousands of times over the years, but she could not recall seeing this boxed set. Each book had black leather binding with gold letters stamped into the spine. The letters were an ancient hybrid of cuneiform and Peish, the language of the dwarves. More peculiar than this extremely rare language, was the fact that each of these books was locked into an ebony shell with a glass front.

Her hand almost instinctively went back for her lock pick, but this time her mind cut in more quickly and she stopped. She reached up to move the box and see if she might open it some other way, but the very box itself was secured into the bookshelf. She would have to settle for reading the words on the spines of the books and nothing more.

She studied the ancient hybrid language for several minutes, trying to remember what she knew of the dwarven language, which was even less than what she knew of the dark elves' languages. Not one to give up easily, Kyra turned around and moved toward the opposite wall where her father kept his language books. She traced along the shelves with her fingers. She glanced over the shelf filled with several manuscripts and books about the history and proper usage of Common Tongue. She grimaced as her eyes saw those books, for they had been instruments of torment for her. The proper use of Common Tongue was a subject that her father had painstakingly shoved into her mind from a very young age. She could remember many times during lessons with her father that she would ask if she could go to the bathroom or if she could get a drink, only to have her father reply with something along the lines of "I hope you can," or if she were terribly unlucky, she would receive a ten minute lecture on the difference between the use of the words 'may' and 'can.'

Other language references on the shelf included those for Terryn and Silamite, the various dialects and languages of the elves known as Taish, a couple of rare records on the Orcish languages, as well as one on the language of the goblins, and an extremely small record of giantish and ogretic. None of those were the ones that she was looking for. Kyra was looking for the language of the dwarves. She found more than half of an entire shelf dedicated to tomes and references about the dwarven history of language and finally the languages themselves. Like the elves, there were many different races of dwarves, all with their own complete language system, and many had more than one writing system. However, despite the vast amount of books kept in her father's study, there was only one book that addressed the hybrid language she was looking for. While all of the other books about the Peish language were extremely thick and complicated, this book was only sixty pages long. She pulled it from the shelf and open the first page to see an alphabet conversion chart. There was a list of cuneiform characters and symbols on the left page. On the right page was a corresponding list of dwarven runes.

She took the book back across the study to find the sealed books. Kyra set her finger to the first book and pointed to the first symbol. Then she looked down to her cipher, looking for what letter the complex symbol stood for. However, she found that instead of representing one letter, the complex character in fact represented an entire word, thus saving space upon the spine of the book.

Kyra flipped the page and found a similar list to the first, but this one translated the dwarven runes into Terryn letters or words. It had been a while since she had studied old Terryn, the predecessor of the Common Tongue, but she remembered enough of it and she started to successfully decipher the titles of the books in front of her. She found that the first symbol on the spine of each book was actually the same symbol. So in deciphering it, she would decipher part of each book's title instead of only one. After a laborious ten minutes, she settled upon the meaning of the symbol to be "Chronicles." She moved on to the next complex symbol.

Able to decipher this one faster than the first, she fell into a rhythm. The second symbol on each spine meant "Dragon." The third symbol was a word she had never heard or seen before. She could tell from its structure that it was a possessive formation of the word, but she did not know what the word itself referred to. Even when looking to the old Terryn, she could not find an appropriate cipher for it. So she moved on to the next symbol and discovered that the fourth character meant "world."

Kyra paused and looked at the book in front of her. She found the brain teaser quite exciting and deduced from the sentence structure that this series of books locked within a case upon her father's shelf was some sort of chronicle about dragons that belonged to the world. She had absolutely no guess as to what the mystery third symbol meant. It was not an adjective, she had checked all of those. She was almost positive that it looked nothing like any word that she could think of that should go in its place. Instead she believed the missing symbol to denote a name, which was quite an intriguing notion in and of itself. For if denoted a name, then perhaps it did not refer to her world, Terramyr. Or if it did, then it was certainly a name that she had never learned about before.

A key scraped into the study's lock. Whatever the symbols meant, they would have to wait for another time, as Kyra needed to leave now. Kyra rushed back to the shelf with the language references and slid the book about the ancient hybrid language of the dwarves back into its place. She then turned and started for the window but the door opened and she was discovered.

"Kyra, what are you doing in your father's study?"

Kyra breathed a sigh of relief. Her mother would not nearly be so difficult to deal with as her father would have been. Kyra turned around to see her lovely mother standing in the doorway with a quiet smile upon her face and her slender hands clasped in front of her waist. She wore a form-fitting green dress as she often did. It snugly hugged her neck and covered her all the way down to her ankles. Upon her feet she wore simple, yet elegant looking brown suede shoes that matched the color of her hair, which had been pulled back into a braid and lazily hung over her left shoulder.

"I was just looking," Kyra replied.

"You do have your own study, and within that there are more books than you can read in the time that you have left here before you go to Kuldiga Academy."

Kyra nodded. "I know, it is just that…" Kyra's voice trailed off. She couldn't think of an adequate answer to give to her mother. She never could lie to her very well.

Lady Caspen slipped her hand around the door and closed it behind her. She moved into the study and motioned to the window.

"I am going to have to ask you to lock the window. When we leave your father's study today, you should not enter by that way again. Better to get his permission and walk through the door like a young lady is expected to do."

"How did you know I'd gone through the window?"

Kyra's mother laughed softly. "Seeing as how your father took your lock pick and I replaced the lock on the door with a new one, that really leaves only one option."

Kyra nodded and moved to close the window. She reengaged the locking mechanism and pushed hard until it clicked into place. She turned back around to her mother and motioned to the lock with her right hand.

"Are you going to tell father?"

Lady Caspen shook her head. "No. But Lord Horatio would like to see you. He is here with his son, and they are speaking to your father about –"

"Buying my hand in marriage, I know," Kyra said. Had Kyra been outside she might have spat in disgust on the ground, but she knew better than to produce such a display in front of her mother. That being said, her tone did not conceal her contempt in the least.

"I was also betrothed," Kyra's mother said. "Your father is twenty years older than me, and for several years I felt as though I were nothing more than a doormat to his manor, or possibly a trophy he hung up on his bed when it pleased him." Lady Caspen walked to the large green chair and sat down. She motioned for Kyra to come and sit on her lap. Kyra feigned displeasure, as was appropriate for her age, but she really didn't mind sitting on her mother's lap. She enjoyed the feeling of comfort and security that it brought her.

"Did you ever learn to love him?" Kyra asked as she moved to join her mother.

Lady Caspen embraced her daughter and gently pressed Kyra's head down onto her shoulder as they both leaned back into the chair.

"I suppose I have in a way. It isn't anything like I dreamed about as a child. I come from a family of lesser nobles, as you already know. My father and mother loved each other very much, but they were struggling, and their lands had ceased producing. So they married me off to the highest bidder." Lady Caspen sighed and went quiet for a moment before continuing. A hand reached up to stroke Kyra's head. "Unfortunately, they both died before you ever got the chance to meet them. You would have liked them very much, and they would have loved you! I was their only child, and so the title to their lands went to me. Those lands now belong to your father. That is the way of the Middle Kingdom, Kyra."

"I don't want it. I didn't ask for it either."

"I know. That is why I have been working with you so sincerely to improve your talents. If ever there was a young girl who could change the traditions of the Middle Kingdom, it would be you, Kyra. However, if you are going to succeed in doing that, you must be able to master not only your studies at home and at the Academy, but the entire subject of sorcery itself. You have that ability within you, but it will take work and consistent effort. If you do well enough, then maybe, just maybe, you might be able to carve out your own future."

"Then why do you let father sell my hand in marriage?"

Lady Caspen sighed again. She pushed Kyra away from herself and looked deeply into her eyes.

"Because a lady must be smart. The men plot and scheme and push their muscle around to get their way. A lady must be cunning and shrewd. Hear what I say Kyra, for I am not telling you to be mean and ruthless. What I am saying is that open defiance will earn you more scrutiny in a man's world than quiet, feigned acceptance and obedience to the rules and traditions of the Middle Kingdom. If you can convince others that you are not a threat either to their personal authority or to the traditions at large, then the men will ignore you, or leer at you at worst, but that is preferable to open scrutiny and being stamped down by those in authority. You can use the quiet space to look for a way to get what you want. You may not know this, but even I use this very tactic with your father."

"And what is it you want, Mother?"

Lady Caspen smiled brightly. "I want my daughter to be happy. I also want for her to have every opportunity to succeed in whatever way she defines as success. You may not understand, but I am encouraging your father to reach a suitable negotiation for your hand not because I want to see you betrothed as I was, but because I have convinced him that it is proper to share a portion of the wealth with you upon your betrothal. We can discuss this more in depth at some other future point, but I thought a girl as smart and sly as you might find a way to put such a treasure to use to further her own ambitions. It might be enough to ensure at least a sliver of freedom, but I hope it will help bring much more than that."

Lady Caspen gently pushed Kyra off of her lap and rose to her feet. She motioned toward the door and started to walk, but

Kyra stopped and looked back to the bookcase where the sealed books sat.

"What are those?"

Lady Caspen followed Kyra's finger to the bookshelf and saw the black books sealed in a case.

"Those are the Chronicles of the Dragons of Kendualdern. They are the forerunners of the ancients that lived upon our lands until only a few generations ago. I don't know if you would enjoy reading all of the books, but there is one that you might find particularly useful. It is the history of a dragon by the name of Gorliad. Like you, the fates also dealt him a hand he would not accept. The first book on the left is titled 'Ascension', and it details Gorliad's struggle. If you promise to stay out of your father's study for the next few weeks until you go to Kuldiga Academy, then I will get that book out of the case and give it to you as a present for your fourteenth birthday. Do we have a deal?"

Kyra smiled wide. "Can I also read the others?"

"We will see," Lady Caspen said with a wink.

The two exited the study and Lady Caspen locked the door behind them. They walked down the hallway together and changed the subject from books to men.

"Have they come too?" Kyra asked.

"Who?" Lady Caspen replied.

"Janik and his brother Feberik," Kyra said.

"Ah, the Orres brothers. No, they have not come yet. I suspect they will be here next week."

"Mother, what was it like?"

Lady Caspen stopped walking and turned to look at her daughter. Kyra's stomach twisted into knots and instantly she regretted asking her mother that question. She had never asked it before, somehow knowing inside that it was too sensitive a topic. She wasn't even sure why she asked it now, except that they had mentioned Janik, the man who had rescued her, and Kyra had been looking at the painting in her father's study earlier.

Lady Caspen knelt down beside Kyra and put a hand on each shoulder. "It was terrible, and it was wonderful, all at the same time. I have conflicted feelings about it. In some ways it was extremely liberating, while of course in others it was the very definition of being a captive in hell. All you need to know at this time is that we are safe, both you and I. I will make sure that it remains that way. Now let's go, we really are running late and your father will begin to fret."

*****

A few days later, Kyra awoke slightly before sunrise. She had fallen asleep translating Ascension, one of the books about the dragons of Kendualdern that her mother had loaned her. As was typical of Kyra's mother, she had not been able to wait until her birthday to give it to her along with the cipher needed to transliterate the characters into Peish. She did, however, say that the others in the set would be her birthday present. In the meantime, her mother suggested, she should become more familiar with the characters and the language the book was written in.

Kyra pushed the black book away from her with a sigh. It would be a long process before she could read this book fluidly and fully enjoy the story. She rose to her feet and pulled her robe tightly about her as she shook off the cold, shivering against the goose pimples tightening her skin. It was then that she noticed her window was slightly open.

She went to her window to close it, but something down below caught her attention. There was a brief flash of darkness, something that was almost like a man's shadow standing near a tree. Could it be one of the noblemen? No, surely no nobleman would come calling before sunrise. The dawn had not fully broken yet, and the last shadows of night still clung to the outside world beyond her window. Perhaps it was the gardener, or maybe it was Fletcher, bringing fresh milk from the cows. Yes, that must have been it, it was Fletcher.

She turned and started to walk away, but then she turned back to the window and stared down at the ground right in the same spot where the shadow had been next to the large oak tree. Why would Fletcher be on the north side of the manor? The kitchen, and all the storerooms, were on the east side of the manor. The barns and pastures were even farther out to the east. There was nothing on the north side of the manor except for forest land.

Kyra tied off her robe, walked to the window, and threw it open. She cast a spell that she had practiced since she was three years old. She waved her left index finger before her face and then muttered a single word. In response, an egg shaped ball of light appeared in the air. She then pointed to the oak tree and the egg flew down with blinding speed. Just before the light reached the area where the shadows still stood, she caught a glimpse of a man's face. The skin was gray and the face was long and narrow with a starkly defined jawline under a pointy nose. Shoulder length black hair hung loosely around the man's face. He was dressed in dark garb, but that was all the more detail she could catch before he turned and vanished into the forest.

It was not Fletcher, nor was it anyone else in her father's employ.

She shut the window and locked it, then she threw the drapes closed. She ran quickly, yet quietly on the balls of her bare feet over the wooden floor to her door. She pulled the door open, preparing to run to her mother's room.

A large shadow stood in her doorway. Kyra's heart skipped and her breath caught in her throat as she slammed her door shut and went to lock it. She felt the handle turn against her hand. She slid her foot against the bottom of the door to keep it from being pressed open again. Quickly, as her mother had taught her to do when she suffered from nightmares in her early childhood, Kyra cast a ward on the door and used a spell to help close it.

A man groaned on the other side of the door and then there was a strange sound like water turning into steam and blowing away on a heavy wind.

She spun around and quickly put a ward on her window as well, lest whatever the intruder was gained entry that way into her room. She waited for several minutes before gathering the courage to look under her door. Her eyes could only see partly through the space between the door and the floor, but she did not see any shadows or feet. She stood again, slowly reaching for the knob and taking in a deep breath. She prepared a fire spell in her right hand. She was not quite as skilled as her mother of course, but she had practiced lighting torches with her magic, and she was certain that even a small flame would dissuade an intruder from attacking her.

Kyra ripped the door open and pointed her spell hand out the doorway. The figure was gone.

Satisfied that no one was there, she ran out into the hall and turned left for her mother's room. She couldn't see anything, nor hear anything, but she was certain that something, or someone, was following her. She ran as fast as she could, her bare feet slapping against the cold, wooden floor and echoing through the hallway. Her mother's chamber was another thirty yards down the hall. Something she could not see lightly swiped at Kyra's shoulder. The young woman ran faster, slinging her right hand back and letting her flame spell jump from her palm, hoping that it would hit and slow whatever was following her.

Something behind her hissed and screeched, making a sound like one might expect to hear after stepping upon a large rat. An invisible hand wrapped around Kyra's right foot and pulled her to the ground. She slammed hard on the wooden floor, scraping her knees and bumping her head. She turned over, preparing to fight whatever it was that had seized her, but she saw nothing there.

Then she saw the shadow at the end of the hall once more. She lifted her head to get a better look at it, but something pushed down upon her chest, holding her to the floor. She swung out with both of her fists, but caught only air. She started to weave another spell, but at that moment each of her wrists were caught and forced to the floor as well. As the weight upon her chest grew, she found it hard to breathe, and impossible to cry out for help.

The door to her mother's chamber behind her flew open and Lady Caspen stormed out with a red fireball hovering over her left palm and a ball of purple lightning gathering in her right. Her hair and robes flowed behind her as if a great gust of wind was blowing toward her. The woman's jaw was set and her eyes stared to the end of the hallway where the shadow was.

"You are not welcome here," Lady Caspen said. "Be gone!" The lightning shot out from her right hand, ripping the invisible force off of Kyra only a moment before the fireball soared through the hallway and blasted the shadow at the end of the hall. Kyra jumped up from the floor and ran to her mother. Lady Caspen swept Kyra behind her and slowly backed into the bedroom from the hall, warily watching for any additional sign of the intruder.

"What was that?"

Kyra's mother pushed her all the way to the bed and then set her down upon the mattress. Lady Caspen moved to the window and threw the curtains open, peering down to the ground below.

"He has found us again."

"Who found us?"

Lady Caspen shook her head and turned to Kyra and pointed a finger at her. "Not a word of this to your father, do you understand?"

CHAPTER THREE

Lady Caspen excused herself from the dinner table early that evening as she had previously arranged with Kyra to do. According to the plan, Kyra would take a bowl of hot soup from the dinner table to Lady Caspen's room under the guise of helping her mother feel better. In reality, Lady Caspen had prepared her room with wards that would allow only Kyra and herself in. She had thought to allow her husband as well, but she knew he would not likely come to her side of the manor. He rarely did anymore.

The sun had not yet fallen behind the horizon when Lady Caspen reached her bedchamber. She moved to a tall armoire, opened the door, and pushed in past the first line of clothes to open the hidden compartment. From that compartment she retrieved a pair of sturdy trousers, a tunic lined with fur, a pair of knee-high leather boots, and one pair of black shiny gloves. After she put them on, she reached into the compartment once more to pull a small dagger with a ruby encrusted hilt. She closed the armoire and moved to the center of her room.

Lady Caspen held the dagger in front of her face for a few moments, turning it over in her palm and studying the intricate metalwork in the engraved design spiraling up the blade. She held the handle firmly with the point facing down to the floor. She began to speak the words of a finding spell, focusing on the dagger itself. A light breeze, nothing more than a slight rustle in fact, began to swirl around her as she spoke the words of the spell. The breeze grew in intensity until it formed a vortex from floor to ceiling, spinning her hair around her face and ultimately lifting her from the floor. The floor fell away from below her and then she fell through the hole, vanishing into the portal.

When next her feet touched the ground she found herself

standing in the forest to the north of her home. At first everything was quiet. The trees stood as silent sentries over the area while a young fawn munched upon red berries from a bush a few yards to her left. The rubies in the handle began to glow, and she knew he was nearby.

"Come out from the shadows and face me," Lady Caspen said. She heard a rustling in the brush a short ways off, but she could not see anything. "Come out, I said."

"You know I cannot come out until the shadow of night covers the land."

It had been many years since she had heard that voice. At once it filled her both with anger and with desire. The memories of her captivity and the vampire's castle flooded her mind. Memories of pain and of loneliness mixed with memories of pleasure and love. No. It could not have been love, she knew. Lust perhaps, but not love. The vampire was a demon, nothing more than the spawn of evil itself. Such a creature could never love; it could only capture, charm, and seduce. That is all there had ever been, just the vampire's charm and his seduction spells.

"Why have you come?" Lady Caspen asked.

"You know why." Footsteps fell nearby and Lady Caspen shifted her gaze to look at a long shadow behind a grouping of trees. She could not see his form yet, but she knew he was there. Likely he had shifted into the form of a bat, or some other small creature to enable him to maneuver in the shadows before the sunset. "Have you not missed me?"

"You know I have not." Lady Caspen held the dagger firmly in her hand, staring at the shadows and waiting for the form to take shape. "I will ask once more, why have you come?"

The vampire laughed, not a maniacal, harsh laugh, but a soft one seemingly born of empathy.

"You loved me once," the vampire said.

"You ensnared me in your charm spells. I never loved you," Lady Caspen protested.

The vampire laughed again, "You and I both know there was more to it than that. Otherwise, you would not have helped me feign my death and escape the pair that stole you from me."

"You only fought to keep me because you had stolen me first," Lady Caspen said.

The shadows expanded enough that the man was able to take form and look at her. His dark hair framed his angular face perfectly. His dark eyes stared back at her, peering into her very soul it seemed. He took two steps toward her before she raised the dagger and then he stopped and put his hands in the air.

"As I recall, between myself and your husband, I was the only one willing to fight for you. Your little scholar would only send mercenaries to do his work. I thought not to keep something I had stolen, but to preserve the promise that we might have grown into something more. I can still offer you the gift I offered before, and we three can live in my castle forever. Your husband need not know where we go, and no other could ever force their wills upon us."

"Kyra is not yours to take either."

"She is born of me," the vampire said. "More than that, I have watched over her these last many years as she grew. You know the power stirs within her. She will never be accepted by the humankind."

"She is no vampire," Lady Caspen said. "She does not have the lust for blood, nor does she have any of your undesirable traits."

"Come now, Zana. You know that to become a vampire one must be turned. The child of a vampire is at best born with demon blood within them. I would not expect her to lust for blood, because I never turned her. That is only accomplished with an intentional act; a bite in which I can transfer my essence. However, you also know that the darkness within her will grow. If her true nature were ever to be discovered, her betrothal will be nullified and she will be expelled and exiled from the Middle Kingdom. All this work your husband goes through to sell her to the nobleman like some fancy chalice will be for naught. Even if she was not expelled and shunned, some hero will come looking for her, hoping to make a name for himself by taking her head. Within weeks she will be fourteen and she will be sent to Kuldiga Academy. I cannot let that happen. You know what will happen when she reaches her sixteenth birthday."

"I will prepare her for that when the time is right," Lady Caspen swore. "Besides, why would a monster such as yourself possibly care what happens to my daughter?" Lady Caspen asked.

"I know you saw them," the vampire replied. "There is a shadow, a demon that follows her. You may have thought that your wards and spells had kept me at bay these last thirteen years, but the truth is they have done nothing to stop me. I have come many times to strengthen your defenses and protect her from the others that seek her."

"Then why not come to take her before now?" Lady Caspen asked.

"Because until now the wards and spells did manage to keep the others at bay. That is, until last night when the shade was able to not only approach the manor but enter it as well. It seeks the darkness within her, and it will not stop until it has her. I can protect her, and I can protect you. I know you can tolerate the life you have here, but I also remember that you told me there was no love in your home. You may think me incapable of such things, but since the day you left me I have not been able to erase you from my memory. Come with me."

Lady Caspen felt a tug at her heart that she could not explain. There was indeed a part of her that was more than a little enticed by the offer. She also had to admit that the intruders that had come did not fit with anything she had ever known the vampire to employ in his service. Still, she knew that a vampire's words, no matter how sweet, were only a means to an end. These were not the sincere confessions of a loving heart. They were the manipulative words of a controlling monster, a selfish creature that cared only for its own pleasures. If he did want Kyra, it was certainly not to protect her and help her grow into a happy life.

She knew that she would regret what she was about to do. It would likely create a splinter within her that would worm its way into her heart for the rest of her life, but she also knew that it was the right thing to do. He was right, there was no love in her home. The fact that Lord Caspen had never personally gone looking for her when she had been kidnapped those many years ago had certainly never been lost on her. Nor had his lack of interest shortly after Kyra's birth. For a while she had hoped that Kyra would help them rekindle something that had really never been there in the first place. For whatever reason, whether Lord Caspen suspected that Kyra was not really his, or perhaps he had been disappointed by the birth of a daughter instead of a son, the child did little to pull them together. Still, the life she and Kyra had now was better than any life they could have hiding and skulking about with the vampire. So, while she knew in her heart that she would always regret her decision, she knew what she had to do.

Lady Caspen flipped the dagger over in her hand and sent it flying toward the vampire's heart. The vampire vanished into a cloud of smoke and the dagger flew through the air harmlessly. A moment later he reformed with a long sword in his hand.

"So, I have your answer, then?" he asked with a hiss.

"How quickly your temperament shifts," Lady Caspen noted.

"I will have her, with or without you."

Lady Caspen sneered, "As I thought, a monster like you is incapable of love." She rushed forward, calling down a maelstrom of fire from the sky that blasted into the trees and forced the vampire back. He tried to flank her to get close enough to use his sword on her, but Lady Caspen knew how he fought. She had not only watched him while he defeated the many rescuers who had come to save her, but she had studied and memorized his moves. When he appeared next to her and chopped down with his sword, she ducked aside and flicked a small bolt of lightning from her wrist to his eyes. It wasn't lethal of course, the vampire could easily shake off such an attack, but it left him blinded for a moment. In that moment Lady Caspen called back the dagger she had thrown and sent it flying straight into the vampire's heart.

The vampire smiled wickedly, exposing his two long, curved fangs as he dropped his sword to the ground. "You kept my dagger," he said. "Then that is what the others hunt."

Lady Caspen ignored the vampire's words as she finished what she started.

"You may have forgotten," Lady Caspen began, "but every time you offered to give me the gift, as you called it, you also explained that only an enchanted weapon, such as this very dagger, could ever end our lives. So on the day that I helped you escape, I stole it and replaced it with an illusion. You were always so sure of your own intelligence that you never suspected I might try to trick you." Lady Caspen snapped her fingers, and fire engulfed the ruby encrusted handle of the dagger and spread into the vampire's chest.

"Then I curse you, witch." The vampire raised his right hand and made a couple of swift movements in the air. "Inasmuch as the one I love has been kept from me, so too shall Kyra be kept from the one that she loves. And as my child is the reason I am dying, should Kyra ever conceive a child, it will destroy her from the inside and she will die."

Lady Caspen moved in quickly to counter the curse, but the vampire waved his hand and a magical force knocked her to the ground. As flames consumed the vampire, the glowing rune in the air solidified the demon's curse.

*****

Lady Caspen returned to the manor quickly, but she did not go into her room. Instead, she went straightway to her study. She walked up to the third bookshelf from the far window and tapped the top of each book as she counted seven books in from the end. Her fingers fell upon a large book and she pulled it out hastily. She knew she should finish setting wards about the house, but only now was she hearing what the vampire had said when he had seen the dagger.

"That is what the others hunt," he had said.

What could that mean? Why would anyone want this dagger? It was powerful enough to kill a vampire, but there were other such weapons in existence. She turned the blade over in her hands, marveling that there seemed to be no soot or dirt staining any part of it. The dagger was as pristine now as it was when she had first seen it on the vampire's desk in his large library. Whatever it was for, she had to get rid of it. She couldn't risk demons hunting the blade and imperiling her daughter.

She turned around and slammed the large, red book on the nearest table. She opened it hastily, fumbling through the pages until she came to the middle of the book.

"Web of fate and silk of destiny, suspend this offering in your grasp and release it not. Hoon'do ro'kimith. Habera bon'des derion, cul hemeth." Lady Caspen placed the dagger on the pages and then shut the book. A sickly vapor emerged from the magical book and a green light poured over it. The book shrank and fell away into a large rift that tore through the fabric of the air in front of her. A great, black hole opened up and swallowed the book and the dagger.

After the rift sealed itself, Lady Caspen went to her desk and pulled out a small piece of paper. She hurried to write her message and then cast a spell over it to change the words. The true message was meant only for Kyra's eyes. To any other who opened the letter, it would appear as a plain letter from home, written by a mother who missed her child. She slipped it into a small envelope and then hid it in a drawer.

A sudden scratch at the glass startled her and she whirled around to see a gaunt figure with narrow eyes staring back at her as it scraped its long fingernails over the glass in an effort to raise the window. Lady Caspen didn't waste any time. She cast a spell to blind the creature. It screamed and fell back into the night.

Lady Caspen rushed to the window and threw it open. The pale, thin man writhed on the ground below. A quick bolt of lightning ended his life. She glanced around, checking for any other sign of intruders. If the vampire had been telling the truth about adding his protection to the manor, then she knew there was a good chance that many others could be lurking about in the shadows now that he was dead.

She had always been prepared for them to come for Kyra. It seemed that monsters spawned from demons and hell always hunted out their ilk, even if they were only half-bloods, as Kyra was. She had been so careful to hide and protect her. How was it that the monsters seemed to have found her now? Or was it truly the dagger they sought?

Lady Caspen closed and locked the window. She took in a deep breath and calmed her nerves. If they were after the dagger, then surely they would stop coming around the manor now. If it was possessed by some evil enchantment, then the scent of its magic would no longer taint Caspen Manor.

Lady Caspen heard a scream from down the hall. It was one of the servants.

She rushed out and nearly threw herself down the main stairs, but when she reached the entryway she saw her husband standing with a perplexed look on his wide-eyed face holding a poker from the fireplace. To his right, Hilda, the maid, was standing on top of a chair and flinging her fingers about as she nervously chewed on her lower lip.

"What is it?" Lady Caspen demanded.

Lord Caspen pointed with the poker to a rather large rat cornered against the wall.

Lady Caspen was so relieved that she broke out into a soft laugh and turned to go back up the stairs. Her husband could deal with a rat. She had wards to finish that would ensure no more monsters came to the manor.

"Are you feeling better?" Lord Caspen called out after her.

Lady Caspen shook her head and continued back up to her room.

CHAPTER FOUR

A week after the incident with the vampire, Lady Caspen found herself in the south parlor offering tea to the very man who had come to rescue her from the vampire those many years ago. Janik was a handsome man, albeit now disfigured. His left leg dragged behind him stiffly, and his left hand was curled backwards at the wrist like a fleshy hook. Perhaps that was why he wasn't asking for Kyra's hand himself. Instead he was negotiating with Lord Caspen to arrange the marriage between Kyra and Janik's younger brother Feberik. If Janik was handsome with his dark hair and green eyes, Feberik was more so with eyes the color of the sky and dark brown hair with streaks of reddish blonde running through it. Feberik was large, and much wider at the shoulder than most other men. His black silk shirt only barely managed to cover his chest and shoulders without ripping at the seams. His smile was soft and kind and his voice was so deep that it almost resonated inside Lady Caspen's chest when he spoke.

He was a fine catch for any woman, Lady Caspen knew, but it was highly unlikely that he would be suited for Kyra. For starters, although he was several years younger than Janik, Feberik was still twenty years older than Kyra. It wasn't highly unheard-of for matches to be made with such differences in age, but Kyra was anything but the average young woman, and she was not going to like it one bit. Still, Lady Caspen kept her mouth closed, knowing that in this instance her silence would serve Kyra better than any protest she could offer.

Janik scooped a small teacup into his right hand and brought it up to his lips.

"I do love mint tea," Janik said just before taking a small sip.

"Yes, my wife has a way with mint tea." Lord Caspen reached

up to push the gold rimmed spectacles higher on the bridge of his nose. He then flattened the front of his shirt with his left hand and brushed a pair of crumbs off his left leg that he had somehow inadvertently dropped while eating a biscuit.

"I must say that just last week we had several suitors come by," Lord Caspen said in his nasally voice. He shook his head as if doubtful an arrangement could be made and then he leaned forward placing his empty teacup on the mahogany table before him. "The offers that were presented were, substantial."

"More substantial than rescuing your wife?" Janik asked.

Feberik put a hand on Janik's shoulder, and even from a distance Lady Caspen could see that Feberik was squeezing his brother's shoulder to quiet him.

"Of course we have an offer to make as well," Feberik said.

Janik slipped out from under his brother's grasp and nodded. "Yes, of course, I only wish to remind Lord Caspen that some connections are deeper than gold."

"It is true we go back quite a long time," Lord Caspen agreed. "In part one could say that I owe not only my wife's life to you, but my daughter's as well. However, I should like to remind you that you were paid for your task. You do recall that I gave you title and deed to all of my wife's properties that she brought upon our marriage, do you not?"

Lady Caspen hated sitting through these negotiations listening to her husband, the one man who should still be overjoyed at her return, casually talking about her as if she were nothing more than an artifact, or perhaps a book that had been lost and then returned to him. No, she knew that was an unfair comparison. If he had a book lost and returned, he would likely have spent more time with the book after it had been found. Still, she reminded herself that she wasn't here to support him. She was here for Kyra. As smart as Lord Caspen thought he was, he needed her help negotiating a proper dowry.

"Yes, actually I remember the property very well. I had thought that the property itself might make a good gift." Janik said.

"No, that won't do. Why, my husband had planned on giving those lands to our child, don't you remember dear?" Lady Caspen offered a soft smile to her husband accompanied with a short, sly wink.

Lord Caspen nodded. "Quite right, I had intended that those lands would go to our future child from the day that I married my wife."

Janik was about to say something, but before he could get the words out Feberik jumped in.

"Then it is settled, the lands shall be returned in full to Kyra, as they had always meant to be. That is not the only thing that we offer, is it brother?"

Janik bristled, his face reddening slightly. He took another sip of tea and set the half empty cup on the table in front of him. "No, it is most certainly not the only thing we bring to offer."

"I do hope it is something fairly substantial," Lord Caspen said. "Because Lord Higbee was here last week and he made an offer that I cannot in good faith refuse, except you are able to match it. Surely if you can match what he offered, no one can deny the balance to be tipped in your favor for services rendered in the past to House Caspen."

Services rendered in the past. Lady Caspen stifled her emotions as she had learned to do, taking in a deep breath through her nose and letting it out quietly so that nobody could see nor hear her displeasure.

"I can do better than that," Feberik said. "Whatever Lord Higbee offered you, I will offer you an additional fifty percent more."

Lady Caspen saw her husband's nostrils flare and his eyes went wide for a fraction of a second. The only thing he loved as much as his books was gold. Lord Higbee had offered a lot of it. Still, Lady Caspen was not here to sit idly, she was here to broker a good deal for her daughter. So, under the guise of a sly, supportive wife she continued to bargain before her husband could open his mouth and accept the offer as it was.

"So if I understand correctly, you are offering to put the title and deeds to the property that used to belong to my family into Kyra's name. Then you will pay one hundred and fifty percent of the offer Lord Higbee offered." Lady Caspen smiled and took a small sip of tea, making sure her pinky stuck out from the cup as is proper. She then gently rested the cup back into the saucer and held it in her left hand. However, as she brought the cup away from her mouth, she whispered the words of a minor charm spell.

All three men turned to listen to her.

"It is a handsome dowry to be sure, but I wonder if it is a little dry. Kyra has four years at the Academy before she will be able to wed. It might be prudent if her future husband were to contribute to her expenses directly as well. Perhaps if you could find it in your ability to double Lord Higbee's offer, then the additional fifty percent that I'm suggesting could be given directly to Kyra." Lady Caspen looked to her husband and smiled sweetly before continuing. Then she glanced back to Feberik.

"It is proper that the lady of the house should be able to administer all matters of the house. This additional amount to her dowry could be paid now in an effort to help her learn how best to manage funds of such a nature. Then, naturally as she is going to be your wife, whatever remains from her portion of the dowry by the time you wed returns back into your home and your treasury. It will show Kyra how much she means to you, and in turn it will help your wife become trained in the matters of home economics."

Lady Caspen slid closer to her husband and placed a gentle hand on his knee. "I know that our finances have certainly benefited from me having a proper education on how to handle such matters. It leaves the husband free to work his profession without worrying about a steward who is unrelated. Isn't that right, Darling?"

"Quite right," Lord Caspen said. The greedy dog was almost salivating.

Even with the charm spell over the room, it took several minutes for Janik and Feberik to agree to the terms. In the end it was Janik, and not Feberik, who finalized the arrangement.

"I'm sure it will not be a problem," Janik smiled and rose to his feet, thanking Lady Caspen for the tea and Lord Caspen for the hospitality. "We will send the portion of the dowry that is meant for Kyra upon our return home, including the titles and deeds to the land."

Lord Caspen stood and nodded his head with a slight bow. Lady Caspen remained seated and smiled as she nodded farewell. She watched her husband slowly show them to the door, accommodating Janik's terrible limp. She couldn't help but feel pleased with herself, for Lord Higbee's offer was one of the largest dowries that had ever been negotiated in all of the Middle

Kingdom. As much as Lady Caspen hated the thought, she knew that a beautiful young girl with magical abilities was a rare find among the nobility. The fact that she managed to not only double the monetary gain, but include the lands she had lost when she married Lord Caspen, made the negotiation very successful indeed.

Lady Caspen smiled wide and finished her tea, congratulating herself on Kyra's behalf.

*****

Kyra stepped out from the coach and waved goodbye to Lucas, her family coach master. She turned a longing eye to the inside of the coach and wished that her mother had come with her. Kyra had never envisioned going to Kuldiga Academy alone. Her mother had assured her that her inability to attend the first day with her was due to events beyond her control.

Kyra thought back to the previous evening when her mother had helped her pack the last of her things into her trunks before Lucas and his son would take them to be loaded into the coach.

"Are you sure you really need this at the Academy?" her mother had asked, holding up Kyra's wide leather belt which had a concealed pocket for a small lockpick set.

"You don't think it will go nicely with all these black school dresses?" Kyra had responded evasively, picking up the nearest dress between two fingers with a wrinkled nose.

"I'm not asking you about how fashionable it is, Kyra. I'm wondering what places in the school you think you'll be breaking into." To drive her point home, her mother had removed the lockpick set from the concealed pocket and waved it at Kyra. "I understand that you get bored from time to time here at home, but there will be studies to keep you busy, and plenty of other apprentices with whom you can make friends and spend your free time. I don't need to receive word from the headmaster every second week informing me that Kyra Caspen was found wandering around a forbidden room at school." Her mother's tone was playful, and there was a smile on her face, but she knew that her mother did worry about how well Kyra would keep the rules while at school.

"Studies? You mean the ones listed in my school papers?"

Kyra retrieved the small stack of parchment she had already packed into one of her trunks and began to read aloud,

> *"Dear Miss Caspen,*
>
> *We look forward to having you in our class this year. You may look upon this as a marvelous opportunity of becoming acquainted with all of the young ladies who will be matriculating into Kuldiga Academy this year. It is a priority of the administration to ensure that all female graduates of the academy are instructed in the proper graces and customs befitting noblewomen of the Middle Kingdom."*

Kyra had given her mother one of her special, *significant* looks as she readied the next parchment. Though Lady Caspen had taken in a breath to comment on, likely even justify, the excerpt which Kyra had read with obvious disdain, Kyra held up a finger and immediately began reading the next letter.

> *"Dear Miss Caspen,*
>
> *Enclosed you will find a list of the supplies necessary for our class this upcoming year,"*

Kyra held up the enclosed list as she continued on.

> *"Please note that it is important to purchase your first wand from a reliable tradesman, as many of the spells we will be learning this year will be challenging, and the use of an appropriate enhancement tool will be of vital importance in mastering the spells that will be found on your exams. There is nothing more disappointing than finding yourself unable to conjure light when you need to know in what direction a ward should be cast.*
> *With respect,*
> *Lady Priscilla Campton."*

Kyra had read out that final sentence with particular emphasis, and then flopped onto her bed with an exclamation as though she had been struck by an arrow. She had glanced briefly at her mother and then covered her eyes with her forearm.

"Kyra darling," her mother had begun gently, but obviously trying to stifle a laugh, "I know that you will find many of the subjects you will encounter this year... underwhelming -"

"I haven't needed a wand for basic spells since I was *four!*" Kyra had mumbled into the crook of her arm, but her mother continued on as though she hadn't heard.

"- but that doesn't mean there will be nothing for you to learn. It is important that you go into this year with a good attitude."

"Are you sure you can't come with me?" Kyra had asked without uncovering her eyes. She knew from the long pause that her mother had been upset, trying to manage her own disappointment at not being able to accompany Kyra, while still making the best of it for her daughter. Kyra had almost withdrawn the question rather than listen to the silence as her mother searched for words.

"My darling, you know that I would never miss this day unless there really were... business matters of the utmost importance that only I am able to tend to. Please trust me, and know that I will send you letters as often as you will be able to endure them." She had gathered Kyra up in her arms then, which at this age was quite a feat. Kyra had not made it easy either, taking this one last moment of childhood to reward her mother with a display of bonelessness. By the time her mother had managed to drag her onto her lap, and had arranged her uncooperative knees and elbows so that she could hold her properly, the both of them were giggling.

Kyra was torn from this bittersweet memory suddenly when a pair of porters approached to take Kyra's luggage. She hastily retrieved a small leather satchel from among the bags, and watched as the rest of her things were whisked off to some place through a side entrance in the great, stone building before her. She finally looked at the façade of Kuldiga Academy with her eyes and her mind fully engaged, and realized that she really was on her own now.

She looked around and saw scores of young apprentices rushing about. Some with their parents, and others obviously returning to the academy after summer holiday and fully aware of where they were going.

The sea of students might have swallowed her if Feberik had not found her.

"I have been waiting for you," he said with a warm smile.

Kyra returned the greeting with a forced smile. The man was huge. Each of his arms was larger around than her waist. Without warning or reason, the image of her being crushed under him on their wedding night exploded into her mind and caused her stomach to flip. She must have frowned or grimaced, because Feberik was there in a second, putting his arm around her.

"Are you alright?"

Kyra nodded and slid out from his embrace. "I am fine," she said, placing the strap of her bag over her head and adjusting it for longer than necessary as she gathered her manners to speak to Feberik civilly. "Just a bit tired from the road." Feberik nodded empathetically and motioned to the large, open doorway.

"Come, I will show you into the auditorium. The headmaster will give the formal welcome soon." He placed his massive hand across her shoulder blades, covering far more of her back with his giant paw than allowed her to feel comfortable. "I won't be able to stay long. I have some matters I need to attend to, but I should be back in the morning to check on you and make sure you are settling in alright."

Kyra maintained a stoic expression on her face, but inside she was screaming for air. Couldn't he wait until after she graduated to smother her? Was she to be watched and guarded for the next four years to ensure she was safely delivered up to the altar?

At least he had stopped talking. He finished guiding her to the auditorium in silence and then bade her farewell after showing her to a seat in the very front row, staying with her just long enough that she was more than certain everyone coming into the auditorium saw it. It was all she could do to look at the podium a few yards in front of her and pretend as though she were somewhere else.

She didn't bother listening to, or even looking at the headmaster during his welcome. He wasn't really saying anything she didn't already know anyway. He started by explaining that Kuldiga Academy was founded to train a corps of wizards to fight necromancers and shadowfiends many centuries ago. It was then expanded to train scholars, healers, swordsmen, and archers as well. Every child in the Middle Kingdom knew that. It was the subject of many bedtime tales and ingrained in every noble. Kyra slumped forward and leaned her head onto her hands and waited for it to end. She was probably as well versed in the history of Kuldiga Academy as the headmaster himself, maybe even more so. Her mother had always made it a point to recite the training program to Kyra ever since she had shown an aptitude for magic.

Kyra reached into the bag which now sat in her lap, reaching for the Peish cipher she had been working to memorize. When she pulled the small book out, she was surprised to see that it was not the cipher at all, but a book she had never seen before, and which had no title. She opened it curiously and found a note from her mother waiting inside the front cover.

> *My Darling Kyra,*
> *As promised, here is the first of so many letters, you will not be able to endure them. I know that you are worried about your studies this year being less than you might have hoped. When you feel yourself in need of a stretch, have a look at the spells which you will find here. Be careful not to let your professors find you with this book; they will most certainly disapprove.*
>
> *Love,*
> *Your Mother*

Kyra smiled when she read that the professors would disapprove of her having this book, and knew that her mother had picked it precisely to provide Kyra an approved way to rebel. She quickly glanced at the first few pages and found a spell to summon a whirl wind, one to summon a column of fire, and several that summoned a variety of unfriendly creatures. These were well beyond her skill level, and she tried to suppress a wicked smile as she imagined all the hours she would spend with this book instead of practicing the "grace and customs of noblewomen in the Middle Kingdom."

Then suddenly her smile vanished. All those years she had waited to share this moment with her mother, and now she was here alone. Except she wasn't really alone, she had a giant fiancé chaperoning her around like some prized animal taken in a grand hunt.

This was not how it was supposed to be.

It wasn't about to get any better for her either.

Over the first couple of days there, news of Feberik's betrothal to her spread through Kuldiga Academy faster than a wildfire in dry brush. The apprentices who didn't outright ignore her teased her mercilessly. It was more than difficult to maintain control over her anger. Kyra had always had a problem with her temper, but now she was finding it harder than ever to regulate. She kept thinking on her mother's words that she had often repeated during Kyra's early childhood. Even when she was able to put on a stoic expression and let the teasing roll off her back, she found herself imagining blasting the snobby brats into a wall.

She tried to tell Feberik about the others, but he seemed not to hear her complaints. She asked him to give her some space, but every morning he came with flowers to her room, and every night he came to make sure she had found her way to her dorm. His routine only served to fan the rumors of impropriety.

On the last day of her fourth week, she decided she was going to let Feberik have it. Once and for all she was going to end the rumors and demand her space. She knew she was betrothed, but that didn't mean she was shackled to him, not yet anyway.

Kyra paced back and forth in her dorm, mumbling to herself as she recited the words she was going to say. The other three girls in her room just watched her silently, sitting on their beds.

The door opened. Kyra spun around and pointed a finger at Feberik. Her face flushed with anger and her mouth opened to let out the barrage she had planned, but she stopped when she saw two other Masters standing with Feberik in the doorway. She recognized Lady Gerigan, one of the instructors from the School of Healing, and Master Lorry, the man who had worked with Lady Caspen to have Kyra placed in the School of Sorcery to begin with. Behind them was the Headmaster. Each of them wore somber expressions and looked directly at her.

Without anyone saying a word, she knew something was wrong.

"Girls, out," Lady Gerigan said. "We need to speak with Kyra alone."

The other girls scrambled to exit the room. Kyra stood in the center of the floor and waited as the adults filtered in and closed the door behind them.

"Kyra, I am afraid we have some bad news," Lady Gerigan said. Though Kyra had always thought she looked kind, knowing that Lady Gerigan often was the first person students were referred to when they were having personal troubles at school made her presence disconcerting.

"You may want to sit down, child," Master Lorry added.

Kyra looked to each of their faces and shook her head. "Just tell me," she said.

Feberik sighed and his large head hung low as his shoulders drooped. In his hand was a letter.

"Kyra, it's about your mother," he said softly.

Kyra's heart stopped and her tongue caught in her throat as she tried to swallow down her fear.

"My mother?" she squeaked.

Lady Gerigan moved in quickly and guided her to a bed and sat her down on it. She knelt in front of her as the others gathered around.

"This isn't easy," Master Lorry said.

Lady Gerigan nodded and looked up at Kyra with teary eyes. "Did you know that I was friends with your mother?" she asked. "We both graduated the same year from the academy."

Kyra's mouth hung open and her brow drew together as water gathered at the corners of her eyes.

"What do you mean you *were friends* with her?" The words barely left her mouth. It was almost as if some unknown force pushed them out for her.

Lady Gerigan reached for the letter and placed it in Kyra's lap. "There was an intruder at your home, Kyra. Your mother was killed."

Kyra's world collapsed around her. Tears fell as the adults all swooped in to hug her and tell her everything was going to be alright. Her body was numb to their embraces, and her mind rejected their assurances. How could it be alright? Nothing was the way it should be. Kyra sat still, letting the adults take turns holding her and pulling her close to console her. She hardly noticed when they stepped away from her. The door opened and closed, but she couldn't say who left first.

Feberik was the last to stay with her. He sat on the floor in front of her silently as she let the tears fall from her face. She glanced down to the letter and reached for it, but her fingers fumbled it and it fell to the floor. Feberik gently picked it up and held it out for her.

"Shall I read it for you?" he asked.

Kyra shook her head and took the paper from him. She opened it and her eyes traced the words on the page. She must have read the first line more than a dozen times, but she couldn't comprehend it. None of the letters made any sense to her. After several minutes of trying unsuccessfully to focus on the letter, she dropped the paper to the floor and let herself fall onto her side on the bed.

Feberik rose up from the floor and placed the letter beside her.

"I will arrange to find you a private dorm, if you like," he offered. "Usually they don't do that until you are a fourth year and working on your own research, but I think we can make an exception."

She didn't respond.

"Is there anything I can do for you?"

Again, Kyra was silent. She closed her eyes and rolled away to face the wall. A moment later she heard footsteps followed by the sound of the door opening and closing.

She cried until her body had spent all of its strength, and then she gave in to sleep.

*****

Janik closed the door to his small room and began to unbutton his shirt. He stopped suddenly, now aware of the fact that he was not alone. He turned toward his bed and waited for the man sitting there to speak.

"Lady Caspen is dead," Cyrus said in hushed tones.

Janik nodded. "My brother told me," he said. "Was that your doing?"

Cyrus snapped his fingers and the candles on the nightstand

burst into flame, their yellow light chasing the shadows away. The old wizard shook his head and tugged on his beard with his left hand. "I was there, but not until after it had already happened."

Janik nodded, not sure if he believed Cyrus. "Who was it?" he pressed.

Cyrus turned a fierce eye on Janik and pointed a bony finger at him. "I want you to go to Kyra's room and look for something," Cyrus said, ignoring Janik's question.

Janik sighed and nodded. "What am I looking for?" he asked.

"A dagger. You will know it by the three rubies set in the hilt."

"A dagger?" Janik echoed. "What do you want with that?"

Cyrus rose slowly from the bed and moved close enough to Janik so that he could whisper. "That was the other item I sought when we fought the vampire. All this time I thought he had taken it with him when he escaped from us, but now it appears he no longer has it."

Janik narrowed his eyes on the old wizard. "How do you know that?"

Cyrus put a finger to his nose and sneered. "Because the vampire is dead. He was slain with the dagger for which I search. More than that, it seems that someone else is hunting the item as well."

"If I find it?" Janik asked.

"Then bring it back to your room. I know where to find you," Cyrus said.

"What is so special about this dagger?" Janik pressed once more.

Cyrus shook his head. "Don't worry about that. Just bring it to me if you find it."

Janik nodded reluctantly. "So the other person that is searching for the dagger thought that Lady Caspen had it?"

Cyrus smiled wickedly and laughed. "That would be the logical conclusion."

"How can you be sure?"

"Because I was there. I saw the marks of a ghoul in Lady Caspen's study. There was likely another creature as well, as I can't imagine she would have been defeated by a single ghoul. Nevertheless, those are the only marks I saw in the room. Her desk was shattered, and books were strewn about. The rest of the house was undisturbed. They were looking for it."

"Maybe they were looking for something else," Janik said.

Cyrus shook his head. "There are scrying tools that help unravel the mysteries of the past." The old wizard smiled. "I won't bother you with the details, but I know she had it."

"Are you sure the others didn't find it?"

Cyrus shrugged. "Of that I am not certain, but I am optimistic. I know the man who is hunting it. Let's just say that if he had it, I would know by now." Cyrus turned and put the candle out with a flick of his finger. The room went dark again. "Search the girl's room. If it is there, bring it here. If it is not there, then keep an eye on her. Watch her carefully. I have a feeling that the others will come for her next. If they do, you had better keep her alive until I get back."

"Why not just take her and have her tell you where it is?" Janik asked.

"No, that would turn her against us. Your first priority is to make her an ally. When she is grown, we will need her strength on our side. We mustn't jeopardize that, not even for the dagger."

"You keep saying that, and yet you don't tell me what it is we need her for, or even why she is so special compared to the other hundred Apprentices of the Staff in Kuldiga Academy. Is the daughter of a vampire truly so remarkable?" Janik asked. His words were met by silence. "Cyrus?" Janik whispered. Still no answer. He moved to the far side of the room and lit the candle. He was alone.

CHAPTER FIVE

For about a month, the other apprentices ceased teasing Kyra. They weren't overly nice to her, but the rumors all but stopped and the mean pranks were abandoned. Still, she would have gladly had all of the bad treatment back, even doubled, if she could also have had her mother returned to her. She still hadn't been able to bring herself to read the letter that came on that horrible night. She placed it on top of her dresser in her dorm room, which she now shared with no one. She hardly spoke, and her studies suffered considerably. Feberik tried to cheer her up, but it didn't help much.

Now she was more alone than ever before. In the few days immediately after the news had come, other professors would sit with her at lunch and offer their condolences for her mother's sudden passing, but of late even they keep their distance.

As the time passed and Feberik continued to call upon Kyra both morning and night, the rumors began to flare up again. Another two weeks and the other apprentices fell right back into their old habits.

It was a particularly sunny Tuesday when everything came to a head.

Amelia, a tall, blonde apprentice walked by Kyra's desk and pretended to accidentally knock Kyra's book to the floor. The skinny blonde put a hand to her mouth and made a gasp of feigned horror.

"Oh dearest me, I'm so sorry, I didn't see you there."

"Oh I'm sorry, were you talking to me? I can't hear you with that frog in your throat," Kyra replied.

Amelia's eyes went wide and she dropped her books, clutching both hands at a bulge in her throat. She opened her mouth, presumably to scream, but instead a large toad slipped out with trails of opaque slime clinging from it to Amelia's lips. Amelia turned and fell to her knees, dry heaving.

"Miss Caspen," Lady Priscilla shouted. "We do not use our magic like that in here. Let me show you why." Lady Priscilla drew out her wand in a flash and banished the toad that Kyra had summoned. Next she turned to Kyra and glared at her. Kyra knew that it was common for instructors of magic to employ spells on the students as punishment, particularly if the students used magic to agitate each other, but Kyra was not about to back down.

"Let us see how you like it." Lady Priscilla narrowed her eyes on Kyra and it was obvious that Lady Priscilla was not going to chastise Amelia for her rude treatment of Kyra.

As far as Kyra was concerned, the instructor had thrown her lot in with those who teased her.

No more. No matter how many demerits it cost, Kyra was done silently bearing everyone else's rudeness and contempt. Kyra was not going to accept any more harassment. Kyra held up her left hand and cast a ward spell of reflection. No sooner had Lady Priscilla finished her spell than her own neck bulged out in three different places. When the sorceress opened her mouth, not one, not two, but three green frogs leapt out from her mouth to rest upon her desk. Lady Priscilla's watery eyes flashed red with anger. She glowered at Kyra as she raised her wand high over her head and prepared another spell. This time it was not to be frogs. A ball of sparks and fire gathered around Lady Priscilla's wand.

Kyra felt an enormous wave of power rise up within her. It wasn't just anger, she knew that much, but what it was she didn't know precisely. She leapt up to her feet and gathered both of her hands in front of her. She sent a powerful gust of air rushing toward Lady Priscilla. The tall woman was blasted into the wall behind her and fell to the floor. Her wand broke and her spell fizzled into smoke.

Not a single student spoke. Many of them glanced between Lady Priscilla and Kyra, but none of them uttered a single word. As Kyra met their gazes, each student jerked their head downwards to stare at their desk.

Kyra summoned one more spell. Not one to attack anybody with, but something to cover her escape. The thick fog appeared in the classroom around everyone's ankles. Several of the young girls, including Amelia, screamed and clambered on top of their desks. A couple of the boys did too. The fog filled the room and then Kyra left. The young sorceress bolted down the hallway, turning left at the first intersection and running straight for the southern exit.

She got outside as a class in procession with twenty-five or so students sat around a pair of male instructors, busily jotting notes in their field books about various mushrooms and herbs that were growing on the large stump in their midst.

One of the students looked up and the instructors rose to stop Kyra, but she was in no mood to slow down. She called the fog to her and disoriented the instructors as she ran by them out to the forest in the south. She must have run for thirty minutes, perhaps longer. She cried with each step, not because of what she had done to Lady Priscilla or Amelia; they had deserved it. No, she cried because she wanted to run to her mother, but she knew that was no longer possible.

There was no one left. Her father was of little use unless she wished to talk about books, and Feberik was so old he may as well have been her father. None of the instructors at the Academy could be trusted either. So she ran. She ran through the ferns in between oaks and pines and around blackberry briars. She ran through a shallow stream and then turned up to the north, climbing a gray hill that led into a small depression at the base of a larger mountain. She picked her way through the rocks and large boulders in the depression until she came to one that she could sit upon comfortably. She let herself cry till there were no more tears to give. When she finished, she stood on her feet and started to walk back. There wasn't anything else she could do.

There would be hell to pay for accosting an instructor, she knew that much. Still, Kuldiga Academy was likely the only place she could call home now. She gathered herself together, smoothing out the front of her black dress and clearing her throat. Kyra stood, but she only made it four steps before she started to question herself.

"Why should I go back?"

She already knew the answer of course. Her mother had gone to a great deal of trouble to ensure that she would be provided for. If she didn't graduate from the Academy and marry Feberik, then the land and the money would revert back to Feberik and Janik.

Still, she had enough magic that perhaps she could run somewhere else. Perhaps she could live in the forest. She knew it wouldn't be like anything she had ever known, but building a shelter and using her magic to find food was not such a daunting thought. Though most people might abhor the idea of living alone as a hermit, she was already alone, if she truly thought about it. Whether in a crowded room at the Academy, or sitting in her portion of her mother's study at home, there was no longer anybody who would appreciate her presence. She corrected herself, Feberik would appreciate her presence, but she did not want his. Perhaps she could find it within her power to befriend Janik, if only he weren't Feberik's brother.

She turned around and searched the depression until she found a wall of rock jutting up from the ground. It was smooth and concave on one side, with a fairly large overhang that provided for a natural shelter against the elements. With her magic, she could easily use the spare rocks around to build the walls out a bit more. As she studied one of the rocks, she noticed there was a small, gray lizard no longer than her middle finger standing on the granite, cocking his head up crookedly to look at her with one eye.

"Hello there," Kyra said. Unlike most of the girls at Kuldiga Academy who would fawn over horses or cats, Kyra had never felt any sort of bond with an animal before. Certainly she was not one to see a fluffy ball of fur and start to swoon. This lizard however, was different. The way its scales interlocked and slid seamlessly over each other as the animal moved intrigued her. Perhaps it wasn't the kind of animal most others would consider cute, but she found herself enjoying its company. She reached a hand down to scoop it up.

The lizard turned in an instant and darted down the opposite side of the rock. Kyra smiled and followed it, now tempted as much by the chase as she was by the lizard itself. She hopped over the boulder and watched as the little creature darted around the rocks and then leapt three feet to a lichen-covered boulder. It scurried up and over just before Kyra's hands dropped down on the stone. She growled at her failure, but didn't give up. She pushed off from the rock and continued to follow the little lizard until it finally disappeared down a hole in the ground amidst four larger rocks.

"Clever little bugger, aren't you?" Kyra said. She knelt down and pulled away the rocks, allowing herself to get closer to the hole in the ground. The first rock was slightly larger than her head, but it moved easily enough. The second was a great, flat stone. As she lifted it, her eyes went wide with surprise. There, next to the small hole in the ground, was a large egg.

Kyra cast a quick glance around herself. She didn't see any sign of other eggs nearby, nor could she see any hint of what might have laid this particular egg. She slid the large, flat rock off to the side and marveled at the large egg. It was a creamy color, with no markings other than the smears of dirt and mud around it and bits of black and white lizard excrement, presumably from the egg's neighbor that lived in the ground nearby.

She stretched out her right hand and placed her palm on the shell. She could feel a great warmth coming from the egg, as if a fire burned from within. Soon it became uncomfortable to leave her hand upon it and she had to pull back. Kyra stared at the shell for a long while, wondering what to make of it.

The little lizard emerged from its hole after many minutes and expanded its throat just before opening its mouth and hissing at Kyra. The young woman regarded the lizard curiously. Certainly the little creature had no relation with whatever was in the egg, but it almost appeared to be guarding it. She decided to test her feeling by slowly inching her hand closer to the egg. The little lizard jumped onto the egg and snapped its small, toothless mouth at Kyra's finger.

Kyra laughed and pulled back her hand quickly. "Well aren't you just full of surprises?" she asked. She moved her right hand toward the little lizard, keeping its focus on her index finger while she moved her left hand out in an arch behind the lizard. When she was certain she was close enough, she scooped up the lizard in her left palm, cradling it just behind the forelegs so it couldn't bite her.

The lizard responded by expanding the pouch of thorny skin below its lower jaw. The thorns looked much more ferocious than they were, especially when the sack of skin became purple and red in color, but the threat didn't work on Kyra.

"I mean you no harm," Kyra said. She waved her right hand in front of the lizard, casting a charm spell that her mother had taught her when she was younger. The lizard relaxed and the skin flap deflated and returned to its normal, tanish color. Kyra opened her palm and the little lizard curled up and went to sleep.

Kyra turned her attention back to the egg. It was more than half as big as she was. Just under three feet tall from base to tip if she had to guess, and at least as big around as a large man, perhaps even thicker. But what dropped it here? She set the little lizard back near its hole and then retreated off a safe distance to wait for whatever had laid the egg to come back. Given the size of the egg, she thought it best to not appear as a threat.

Her mind started to race. Could a dragon have laid the egg? No. That was preposterous. Dragons were extremely rare in these times. Ever since the great battle in Hamath Valley, there were no regular sightings of dragons. Those dragons that did remain were wicked, vile creatures with an insatiable thirst for blood. That said, no dragon had been seen north of Ten Forts in over a century and a half. Certainly none had been allowed to nest within the Middle Kingdom either.

So if it wasn't a dragon, what was it?

She waited for hours to answer her riddle, crouched behind a large rock and carefully glancing over her shoulder every so often to ensure nothing was sneaking up behind her.

Nothing came.

She sat there until the sun began to hang low in the sky. The only movement she saw was when the little gray lizard tracked her down and curled up on a rock in front of her. She tried to shew the creature away, but it wouldn't go. Thanks to her charm spell, it was more than content to stay by her side.

Kyra watched and waited, having fully forgotten about the events at Kuldiga Academy, until the sun dropped below the western horizon and the sky was set ablaze with pink, orange, and red hues. Only then did the little lizard get up and make its way back to its hole. It darted down, only to come up a moment later. It stood rigid, its head high in the air and its forelegs nearly straight on their claws as it cocked its head at Kyra and made a chirping sound. Three chirps and then it disappeared down again. A moment later it came back up, looked right at her, and chirped three more times. When Kyra didn't respond, the lizard became more animated.

It leapt from a rock to the egg and then out to the large, flat rock, chirping incessantly. Three chirps, a quick hop, then three more chirps and another jump. The lizard continued acting this way until finally Kyra rose to her feet and approached the egg. As she came closer, the small lizard jumped from the egg to the flat rock and back to the egg. It kept jumping and chirping, seeming almost panicked.

Kyra grabbed the flat rock and slid it back into place over the egg. No sooner had she concealed the egg than the lizard calmed down. It dropped into its hole and disappeared.

"Curious little guardian," she said with a smile.

A cold wind blew in from the north and chilled her to the bone. Goosebumps tightened her forearms and she rubbed her shoulders. The dark shadow of twilight swept over the hillside and reminded her of the events at Kuldiga Academy. Hesitantly, she drew in a breath and decided that she had better forget about discovering what kind of creature had hidden the egg here.

Before she left, she cast a spell around the egg to help it remain warm.

*****

Janik limped through the countryside. It had taken him the better part of the afternoon to shake off the other instructors that had insisted on coming with him to look for Kyra. If not for the charm spells that Cyrus had taught him, Janik would not have been able to convince his brother to head in the opposite direction. Now, however, he would find Kyra and have her all to himself. Despite her spell, he had seen in which direction she had fled and had managed to cast a tracking spell just before she had run out of range.

He couldn't so much see where she was as feel the direction that would lead him to her. It came as a mixture of vibration and sound that pulled at his mind. The closer he got, the stronger the sensation. He wound his way through the forest until he came to a large clearing. The last of the day's light fell upon the bending, golden grasses softly as a gentle layer of fog began to form over the ground.

Seeing Kyra emerge from the trees on the opposite side of the clearing, Janik couldn't help but see her for what she was. She looked less the girl, and ever more part demon as she walked into the mist in her full-length black dress. The dark hair and the strong expression on her face only accentuated the feeling in him upon finding her. He was much larger than her, and had many years of experience, and yet he couldn't help but feel as though he were stepping alone into a field with a great beast. Reflexively, his right arm went to his belt for his axe. As his fingers touched the cold steel, he shook the feeling from his body and pressed into the clearing.

She saw him when he waved and smiled.

"Come here, Kyra, I am alone. There are no angry instructors with me," he called to her. Even from across the clearing, he could see the smile brighten her face and lift her mood. "If we hurry, I might be able to put in a good word with the Headmaster," Janik added.

Kyra didn't run, but she did speed her pace until they met up.

"You heard then?" Kyra asked. Janik forced a smile.

"Everyone at the Academy has heard." He watched as Kyra turned slightly red in the face and sighed. He put a hand on her shoulder. "One does not throw an instructor into the wall without everyone knowing about it."

"She was going to throw a spell at me, I stopped her," Kyra said matter-of-factly.

"Lady Priscilla has gone home," Janik reported. Kyra's eyes went wide.

"I didn't mean to hurt her, I only wanted to stop her from attacking me."

Janik nodded. "Turns out, she was somewhat ill anyhow; the scuffle today exacerbated that fact. She should be alright in a few days, but I think it best you keep your magic under control from now on."

"Where is your brother?" Kyra asked.

Janik smiled. "Well, I thought it best if I found you first. I sent him in a different direction."

"You knew where I was?" Kyra asked. Her eyebrows scrunched in together and she cast a nervous glance over her shoulder.

"No," Janik replied truthfully, "but I saw which direction you ran. I was outside at the time." He smiled wide. "You should have seen the army of angry instructors all chasing after you a few minutes later. They were huffing and puffing every which way for an hour or so before they all calmed down. You do know that Amelia's father is one of the Academy's larger benefactors, do you not?"

"Money doesn't mean you can taunt others," she said simply with a shrug.

"Quite right," Janik nodded firmly, "Though I dare say there are some who would disagree. One thing you must understand is that like it or not, money rules the kingdom. Those who have it are given more opportunities than those who do not. They also receive more deference in times of indiscretion."

"Then by that reasoning, I should be able to purchase my way back into the Headmaster's good graces," Kyra said slyly.

Janik looked at her, shocked, his mouth hanging open slightly. He wasn't sure what to say. He hadn't expected a response like that from the young lady. Finally, he pressed his lips together and then turned around and began the long walk back to the Academy, with Kyra next to his side.

"I suppose that isn't a bad idea," Janik said after some time. "Perhaps we can pull it out of the dowry promised for your wedding. What do you say?"

Kyra shrugged, but remained silent.

Janik smiled slyly. He wasn't just trying to use her logic to solve her current dilemma, he was changing the subject to the marriage. The alliance that Cyrus required.

"I have something for you," Janik said. He pulled a silver amulet from his pocket and dangled it before her as they walked. "It belonged to my mother."

Kyra looked at it, and then glanced to Janik questioningly.

"My father had no daughters, thus I was given the amulet as I was the eldest. However, I think it should be given to a woman, don't you?"

Kyra remained silent.

Janik pressed on. "Seeing as you will be my sister in the future, I thought it would only be right that it go to you. I would look rather silly if I were to wear it myself."

Kyra smiled at that. She held out her palm and the two stopped walking so she could inspect it. The amulet was small, no larger than a peach pit, but it was finely crafted into the form of a perched hawk upon a branch. A single, small ruby was set into the eye.

"It is beautiful," she said.

"Here, let me put it on you." Janik unclasped the chain and placed it around her neck. As he secured it into place, Kyra let her hair down over the back of her neck and he moved around to inspect the amulet. "A perfect piece to accentuate your ability, as well as your beauty," Janik said. "The hawk is one of the noblest creatures. It may not be as large as an eagle, but it is every bit as brave and cunning."

"Is that what you think of me?" Kyra asked.

Janik nodded. "I think I will call you that, my little hawk."

Kyra smiled and patted the amulet. Then they began to walk again. Janik took some time before speaking again. Despite having the amulet imbued with the spell Cyrus gave him, there was something that made him apprehensive. He kept glancing down toward the necklace between limps, wondering if it were truly strong enough to work on the young lady. It was too bad that her mind was not as susceptible as his brother's was. No artifact was needed to charm Feberik. Just a powder that mixed into drink.

Even on the night Janik was finally able to get Feberik to agree to marry Kyra, all he had needed to do was mix a bit of powder into his large brother's drink. Sure, he had to keep giving him the powder every few weeks, but that was not so hard to accomplish.

Then again, if Kyra could be so easily manipulated, Cyrus likely wouldn't have any use for her.

They were nearly back at the trees before Janik finally broached the subject that was his mission. He took in a great breath and then sighed. Even with the amulet, he knew this conversation would require delicacy.

"Kyra, can I ask what it is about my brother and me that you don't like?"

For all of Janik's hesitation, Kyra didn't seem the least fazed by the question; almost as if she had expected it.

"It isn't you I don't like," Kyra said quickly. "It is your brother."

"Ah, so you would marry me then?" Janik said playfully.

Kyra offered a half-giggle and shook her head.

"You are nearly the same age as my father," Kyra replied.

"There have been worse arrangements made," Janik said with a grin.

Kyra stopped suddenly and turned to him. "I don't mean to cause offense," she said. "I know the Middle Kingdom has always operated this way. The women are betrothed to men, almost always men that are ten or twenty years older. The noblewomen then attend the Academy, and upon graduation they are married. That works fine for most of them…"

"But not for you," Janik finished for her.

Kyra shook her head. "I want to live my own life." She sighed and began walking again. Janik limped quickly to keep pace with her. "I am not even sure I want to be married, but if I did, I would want it to be a man of my choosing. I know you rescued my mother, and I am forever grateful for that, but I want freedom." Kyra stopped again and held the amulet up from her chest with her hand. "When the hawk flies, it does not need to ask permission to leave the nest. It spreads its wings and takes command of the skies. That is what I want."

"My brother is a fine man," Janik said softly. "He will treat you right. You will be as free as you wish."

Kyra shook her head. "That is like saying that I will have a pretty bed set up in a dungeon. You can dress it up as you like, but you are still trapped."

Janik frowned. The amulet didn't seem to have any effect on her. He tried again. He placed his right hand on her shoulder and pressed the amulet back into place until she finally let it hang freely, close to her heart.

"There are many who would give much to marry my brother. You should consider yourself lucky to be his future bride."

Anger flashed in her eyes. "Well I don't," she said flatly. She turned and stormed off.

Janik stood and watched her go for a few moments before apologizing sincerely enough that she let him catch up with her.

"I won't speak of it again," he offered. "I didn't want to upset you. Come, let us get back to the Headmaster and see what kind of arrangement we can come to."

The two of them returned to find Feberik and two other

instructors waiting at the western door for them.

"I'll handle this," Janik said. "Wait here a moment." Kyra stood and waited while Janik moved up to approach the others. Besides his brother there was Master Fenn, one of the sorcery instructors, and Lady Gerigan.

"Is she all right?" Feberik asked.

Janik nodded and patted the air with his good hand. "She is a bit ruffled, as you might imagine," Janik replied. "Physically, she is fine."

"What does she have to say for herself?" Master Fenn pressed.

Janik turned a hard eye on him. "I suspect that is for the Headmaster to hear, and not you."

"I will not be told my place by a janitor," Master Fenn said gruffly. He started down the granite steps but Feberik snatched out with one hand and gripped the front of the man's cloak.

"I shouldn't have to remind you of what Janik has done in the past. He is not a janitor because of his lack of ability," Feberik snarled.

"On the contrary," Master Fenn said in an even tone. "His physical handicap is precisely why he can't instruct. He is literally useless in terms of instructing pupils how best to fight with weapons. I suppose that is why they let you take his place when he was disfigured. The headmaster pitied him his deformation, and pitied you for your lack of promise in the field."

Feberik picked Fenn off the ground several inches and held him there.

"Would you like to see my abilities?"

Janik grinned. There were times indeed when Feberik's temper was amusing to watch.

"Go on, show me what you can do with your hands," Fenn said. "Though I dare say that a man of true abilities could win the fight without lifting a finger."

"Oh, stop it, both of you!" Lady Gerigan said. "Janik is right. The Headmaster shall be the one to decide her fate. There is no need for this useless display."

Master Fenn arched an eyebrow and turned a fierce eye on Feberik.

"There is nothing to worry about, Lady Gerigan. Feberik was

66

just beating his chest like a wild ape might in front of a mate to display strength and dominance. It's just a basic instinct, you might say." Fenn vanished into thin air only to reappear behind Lady Gerigan in the doorway. "Should I have been worried at any point, I would have reduced him to a writhing worm on the ground."

Feberik glared at the sorcerer.

"When I am headmaster of this place, you will be looking for a new job," Feberik promised.

"The day you are headmaster, is the day I will throw myself from the Verignian Cliffs," Fenn replied. "Fie the day they should ever put a brute swordsman in place as the headmaster here. This is first and foremost a school of thought and magic. We only allow the brutes in so we have fodder to put on the field before the real heroes." With that, Master Fenn turned and vanished into the hall.

"Honestly!" Lady Gerigan huffed. She flattened the front of her dress and shook her head in disgust. "I know sorcerers have large egos, but that one takes the cake."

"It's all right," Janik said. "I am used to it."

"You shouldn't be," Feberik said. "It isn't a man's position that denotes his worth, it's his character."

"Quite right," Lady Gerigan agreed. "Now let's get her up to the Headmaster." She gestured toward Kyra.

Janik held up a hand. "Actually, it is probably best if I take her myself," Janik said. Feberik was the first to protest, but Janik shook his head. "She needs a bit of space from you brother, as you might imagine. It was not in small part due to your betrothal that she finds herself in this precise predicament."

Feberik sighed and then walked away. Janik smiled on the inside, wishing he had always had such control over his brother. Lady Gerigan looked as though she would put up an argument, but she followed Feberik inside without another word.

After they left, Janik waved for Kyra to come to him.

"What was that about?" Kyra asked.

"Ah, you mean my brother and Master Fenn?" Janik smiled. "They were arguing the finer points of magic versus strength."

"Who won?" she pressed.

"As always," Janik began, "the one with the brains won out." He offered her a wink and she let it go at that. The two of them made their way up into the second level of the west wing. They found the Headmaster waiting in a small study.

Janik had Kyra wait outside the room and closed the door behind him.

Headmaster Herion sat in his favored high-backed chair. Some had said it was fashioned out of dragon teeth and scales, but Janik knew better. The frame was made of cherry wood, and the inlay was of ivory and colorful scales. As masterful and inspiring as it was, there was nothing from a dragon on that chair. The detailed carvings within the frame were crafted out of ivory tusks from the north. The scales came from the ridgebacked crocodile, a ferocious beast that had once plagued the inland waterways of the Middle Kingdom but was now found only in Verishtahng. Still, the carvings depicted Kuldiga Academy's different areas of instruction and was often referred to as "the throne" despite the fact that it, of course, did not relay any amount of power to the one sitting in it. Still, that didn't stop Headmaster Herion from treating it as through it were *the* throne of the Middle Kingdom.

If Feberik ever is headmaster, that chair would be the first thing to leave the Academy, Janik promised himself. Master Fenn would be a close second.

The Headmaster looked up from a thick book and peered through a pair of gold-rimmed glasses. Headmaster Herion was old, but not so aged that his face was covered in liverspots. There were a few deep creases around the mouth and on the forehead, but otherwise he still held the visage of youth and strength. His kind, blue eyes sparkled as he flashed a smile filled with impeccably white teeth. Unlike many of the other wizards, Herion was clean-shaven, and dressed in a normal looking tunic. If not for the chair, one might actually suspect him to be nothing more than an understudy, or perhaps a visiting scholar.

"What can I do for you?" Herion asked in his gravelly voice.

Janik limped in and sat on the opposite side of the table from the headmaster.

"I know you heard about Kyra Caspen," Janik began.

"Yes, yes, that was quite a bit of naughty mischief," Herion said with a nod of his head. "Though I must say it is not the first time something like this has happened."

Janik offered a knowing grin. Something similar had happened once or twice in the many years he had been involved with the academy.

"I wanted to ask whether there can be any leniency granted?"

"I see." Herion leaned back in his chair and folded his fingers together over the open book. "The problem is that this was not a private affair. An entire classroom of students watched as their instructor was flung into a wall, and frogs were leaping out of throats. No, no leniency can be granted here. The students must know that there is a consequence for all actions."

"Might I interject?" Janik asked.

Herion sighed and cocked his head to the side.

"I know who you are Janik," Herion began. "I was headmaster here when you and your brother came through as apprentices. Still, your heroic career notwithstanding, the other masters will see it as improper if I show you mercy just because Kyra is betrothed to your brother. They won't like it, not one bit."

"Then hear me on my merits alone," Janik pressed.

"They won't be satisfied with that either," Herion replied. "Think of the rumors that would spread if the Headmaster bends his ear to the janitor alone. No, there must be a punishment."

Janik was undaunted by the old man's words.

"Her mother has recently died," Janik said quickly. "Her father has all but abandoned her here. He writes much less than any other parent who has a student here. She is alone."

"I know of her personal problems, Janik. I was there to deliver the news of her mother's death myself, but that is no excuse!" Herion shouted in a raspy voice. "She threw Lady Priscilla into a wall!"

Janik smiled. "Yes, well, she should have blasted Lady Priscilla into oblivion, from what I have seen." Janik rose to his feet and slammed his good fist down on the table before Herion. "The other instructors spread rumors about Kyra, despite the fact that everyone here knows she has had no improper relations with my brother. It is not her fault that he works here. He checks in on her because she is alone. Furthermore, nothing would have happened today if Amelia hadn't been taunting Kyra to begin with. You don't see it because you are up here in your books all day, but I see it. I sweep the chow hall and clean the dorms. I have seen the apprentices throw food at her, or play tricks on her, and I have heard their nasty rumors. Given her talent, it is a wonder that Kyra hasn't set fire to the Academy."

Herion mouthed a couple of words, but no sound came from his lips. He pressed his hands into the pages in front of him and then gestured about as if to redirect Janik's attention. Janik just glowered into the old man's eyes.

"If that isn't enough, then name your price," Janik said. "I control the dowry promised to Kyra. She and I have discussed the possibility of making an arrangement that might persuade you to overlook her transgression."

Headmaster Herion slowly rose to his feet. "Janik, I am insulted that you would think this is a matter of money. I assure you, it is not." Herion paused and pursed his lips while sucking in his cheeks for a moment. Then he took in a breath and nodded. "However, should an amount of funds find its way to the Academy's coffers sufficient to cover the cost of hiring a substitute instructor who can fill in for Lady Priscilla, then I suppose we can come to an agreement easily enough."

"No expulsion," Janik said. "Give her demerits and let her work them off with me. As janitor, there are many tasks that I have to complete that should be viewed by others as a punishment."

"Agreed," Herion said. "She will spend weekday afternoons with you. Her service will go on until the Midwinter Festival. After that, her service will be finished."

Janik nodded. "How long will Lady Priscilla be absent?"

Herion's face turned grim and he looked to the floor. "Lady Priscilla is pregnant," he said somberly. "That stunt today nearly caused her to lose the child." Herion held up a hand and shook his head. "Our healers were able to save the child, but I think it appropriate she take an extended leave of absence. I think it best for everyone involved."

"I didn't know Lady Priscilla was married," Janik replied with as much sincere empathy as he could muster.

Herion nodded. "After her first husband died at Ten Forts, she was sent here as an instructor. She and Master Fenn became quite close. Master Fenn's first wife had died several years before during childbirth. The two of them married quietly and have only told me and a few others of their pregnancy. I expect you will keep this to yourself."

"Of course," Janik said.

"So we have our agreement. I would appreciate it if you would leave me to my work."

Janik nodded. "Thank you for your time," he said. Herion waved him out and went back to his book. Janik limped out of the room and found a very nervous Kyra pacing the hall. She looked up expectantly.

"Well, what did he say?"

Janik smiled warmly. "Good news," he said. "I managed to talk him into giving you janitor duty with me."

Kyra scrunched up her face. "What did you have to pay him?"

Janik shrugged. "The windows can get really dirty, and with only one good hand it is hard for me to make them sparkle. With your magic, on the other hand, we should be done in no time. Then, I suppose if you happen to finish your work early, you could have more time for your personal studies."

Kyra's face lit up and she froze in place as she clasped her hands in front of her. "So I can go to the library whenever I want?"

"Well, when you are done with each day's tasks," Janik said.

"But I can use magic?" Kyra pressed.

Janik nodded. "There is no law that says we can't use magic to make things clean. Seeing as how the other students have already gone home for the weekend, we can start on Monday. Go and clear your head for the weekend."

"Thank you!" Kyra jumped up and gave the man a hug. She was so sincere that he almost forgot himself. Then, as she ran away, he went back into his scheming again. Perhaps the amulet didn't work, but there were other ways to gain trust. With Kyra now working with him each afternoon, he could ply other, subtler techniques to gain her trust. More than that, Janik had the perfect candidate in mind to replace Lady Priscilla.

CHAPTER SIX

Kyra returned to the rocky hillside early the following morning. She crept up to the bowl-shaped depression where the egg had been when she left. She was careful to watch for any creature in the area. When she found nothing there, she felt both joy and sadness. Sad that the egg was abandoned, but glad that she would be able to examine it more fully without fear of being eaten by some unknown monster.

After ensuring there was no animal nearby, she made her way across the boulders.

She wasn't more than forty yards away when the little gray lizard came skittering around a rock and chirped at her. Kyra was surprised to see the charm spell was still holding strong on the creature. She had only meant to set a temporary charm, but it also made her happy to see the little animal. It followed her, chirping as it jumped from rock to rock until she got to the site where the egg stood. She gently slid the flat stone aside and rested it on some nearby rocks. Then she reached around and pulled a small satchel which hung from the belt at her waist and set it in her lap.

She pulled three books from the satchel and took in a deep breath of excitement. Being that it was the first day in the weekend, there would be no instructors looking for her. She could remain there all day long if she wished, which gave her the perfect opportunity to identify her find.

"Let's see what we have here, Guardian," she said to the little gray lizard on the rock beside her. It chirped and launched onto her lap. Kyra laughed and watched as the little lizard extended its body slowly toward the nearest book and then tested it with its tongue. A second later it leapt away onto another rock and stretched out to sun itself.

Kyra shook her head and opened the first of the books she had brought. It was a compendium on known reptiles throughout the Middle Kingdom. She flipped through the first few chapters, knowing that this far inland it could not possibly be a marine reptile from the sea. She started going through the list of various reptiles, discounting most of them by their size, as there were not many exceedingly large lizards in the Middle Kingdom. There were pages and pages on whiptails and racers and several different types of thorned lizards. She was nearly to the end of the book before she found something that appeared large enough.

"A cavedog," she said aloud as she read the name next to the expertly drawn image on the page. "These giant lizards are so large that dwarves ride them into battle." She stopped reading and looked at the egg. She tried to imagine something as large as the egg coming out of a cavedog. "No, that wouldn't work unless we were talking about some very big dwarves," she said. Kyra confirmed her doubts when she skipped down to the length of an adult cavedog. "Ranging from five to nine feet," she said in frustration. "Definitely not a cavedog."

She skipped through the pages and then sighed when she realized that the last several pages had gone back to talking about smaller, more rare lizards. She took heart though when one of the drawings looked a lot like Guardian, the little gray lizard that was still sunning itself nearby. She read through the description, glancing back to Guardian after each line. If she was right, then he was a juvenile mountain pagona. A gentle-natured lizard that had all but gone extinct since the decline of the dragon. Though the entry didn't mention why that was.

"Is that it then? Guardian is a little mountain pagona is he?" The gray lizard lifted its head and offered two chirps. Kyra smiled. "Too bad you can't tell me what is inside this egg over here."

Guardian jumped up and launched into Kyra's lap. It must have been coincidence, she knew, for it couldn't have been intentional, but Guardian landed on the book in such a way that his nose pointed to the word 'dragon.' He looked up at her and puffed his throat. He looked down, licked the page, and then jumped off to land on the egg.

Kyra shook her head. It couldn't be that easy. She flipped through the last few pages of the book. The entries on rare lizards had a few flying lizard species, all but extinct, a couple of mountain tegus and monitors, but nothing large enough to produce the egg in front of her. That is, until she turned to the final page and saw the very last entry.

Her fingers trembled as she moved her index finger down on the page. There were several drawings on the left hand side, each with a small human figure drawn next to it for scale. They ranged from creatures as little as a sparrow to some that appeared larger than a manor. The title at the top of the page read simply 'dragons' and the page on the right held only a short entry.

> *Dragons have been all but eradicated from the Middle Kingdom since the battle at Hamath Valley in 1130 of the Common Era. However, in the interest of compiling the most complete compendium on reptiles within the Middle Kingdom, we have included a brief reference to them.*
>
> *The term dragon denotes an entire family of species, each a very distinguishable and separate creature with its own several traits, abilities, and varied intelligences. There are entire chronicles dedicated to their study, the most complete set of which can be found in the library of Valtuu Temple. For our purposes, it is enough to know that they come from The Ancients, seven progenitors of the dragon kind, and that modern-day dragons inhabit most parts of Terramyr.*
>
> *Within the Middle Kingdom, they were once a fair and wondrous race of beings. The Ancients are credited with founding Drakei Glazei, the Middle Kingdom's capitol, as well as Roegudok Hall, the mountain that houses the dwarven kingdom. Due to events detailed in other histories, despite the efforts made in Hamath Valley, the dragons of the Middle Kingdom have turned evil and chaotic. Initially, lesser dragons and drakes began to prey upon mankind, and any other animate creature small enough to be swallowed or chewed. Gradually, even the great dragons became an enemy to all living.*
>
> *For the last several hundred years, they have been hunted nearly to extinction within the Middle Kingdom,*

and a fair number of dragon slayers have ventured beyond the Middle Kingdom as well to take the fight to the winged demons. It should be noted that this is to the great lament of those priests who still devoutly, albeit naively, follow the old traditions of pseudo dragon worship.

Should you ever come across a dragon's egg, you would recognize it by its enormous size. There is no other beast that could lay such a large egg. If this should happen, destroy the egg. Do not let the demon within see the light of day, for if you were ever to find yourself in a dragon's shadow, they would show you no mercy.

Kyra flipped the page, but there was no more information. She glanced at the egg and a wave of fear washed over her. The hairs on her neck stood on end and she looked up to the sky when the hillside was darkened by a large cloud. Then she looked back to the egg and the fear left her. She knew there was a dragon inside. Yet, despite what the book said, she felt no fear of the egg.

Who was to say that the hatchling would be as ruthless as the text presented it?

If Kyra was to listen to what others deemed appropriate, then she would accept her betrothal as her destiny. She smiled then, finding great parallels between herself and the egg. Not only were both of them full of potential danger, but they also both had society deciding their fates for them. She was doomed to marry and live the life of a noblewoman, while the hatchling was condemned to die. Both had been judged, and their worth had already been assessed, yet neither were understood.

"I will not destroy you," Kyra promised the egg.

The little guardian lizard chirped loudly and then dropped down into its hole.

Kyra looked at the other two books she had brought. One of them, a treatise on the care of large monitor lizards, was entirely useless, but the other made her smile. She opened the cover and rubbed her hand out over the first page. She had been working faithfully to translate the book since her mother had let her take it from her father's library. Now she intended to make a go of it without her notes and read it aloud to the egg, translating as she went.

"You will like this story," she told the egg. "It is about a mighty dragon who also faced great challenges. He wasn't hunted by humans, like you would be, but he had his own trials. The dragon in this story is named Gorliad, and he lived in a place far from here. This book comes from a set in my father's library. It is entitled *The Dragons of Kendualdern*. This volume is my favorite from the set. It's called *Ascension*."

Kyra cleared her throat and began to read aloud. She spent the remainder of the day reading to the egg and sitting next to it. Guardian, the little lizard, even came up from his hole to sit in her lap while she read, in between chasing grasshoppers that is. She read until the sun hung low in the sky, forgoing lunch altogether and losing herself in the book. Only when the first several blue stars of night poked through the sky did she prepare to leave for the night.

She cast the warming spell again, careful to hide the egg with rocks, and then returned to the academy.

When she arrived back at the academy, she spied Janik in the dining hall, taking his evening meal. He waved at her and motioned for her to join him.

She hesitated, just for an instant, as if something in the back of her mind was trying to pull her in another direction. She shrugged it off, reasoning that it was likely just her apprehension about Janik's brother holding her back. Kyra moved toward the table and a few moments later one of the cooks appeared with a serving tray, carrying a pitcher of water, a wooden goblet, and a brown clay bowl filled with tomato with a side of toast.

"Thank you," Kyra offered as the woman placed the items down in front of her.

The cook smiled and disappeared back into the kitchen.

"You were gone a long time today," Janik noted. "Off in the forest again?"

Kyra plunged her spoon into the soup and was quick to place the spoonful into her mouth. Luckily, it wasn't so hot that it burned her tongue. It did, however, waken her stomach to the realization that she had only eaten upon waking that day. Her stomach let out a terribly embarrassing growl and she hastily took a bite of toast.

"Hungry, I see," Janik probed. He offered a half-smile and

picked his own bowl up with his right hand and poured the soup into his mouth. Then he set it down and wiped the excess from the corners of his mouth. "There isn't anyone else around to see if you wish to eat without the proper manners," Janik said. "I do it all the time. If I always adhered to proper table etiquette, I would likely never finish." He raised his crooked left wrist and waggled it at his bowl. "I was left-handed before this happened. It's still hard to do things with my right hand."

"I am sorry," Kyra offered. She looked at his hand, bent over permanently at the wrist and all red and purple in color. Even now it looked painful, as though it had only occurred a few days before.

Janik smiled. "The pain is gone now," he said. "Mostly."

Kyra shot him a puzzled look.

Janik shrugged. "It aches after a day's work, or sometimes when it's cold, or even just at night."

"So it hurts almost all the time, then," Kyra surmised.

Janik paused and then he chuckled with a nod, "I suppose you are right." He slipped his right hand around his own goblet and pulled it up toward his mouth. "So what is in the forest?" he asked just before the drink touched his lips.

"I just like to be alone," Kyra mumbled with a blush. To cover the warmth she felt in her cheeks, she quickly took a drink of soup directly from the bowl as Janik had suggested.

"Can I see the books?" Janik asked as he set the goblet down and gestured with his chin toward the small satchel. He didn't wait for an answer. Kyra had already set the satchel beside her on the bench, so he had free access to it. She started to move, wanting to stop him, but then she thought that might make it appear even more suspicious, so she stopped.

Janik pulled them out and set them on the table. He mumbled aloud as he perused the titles.

"Research?" he asked.

Kyra nodded. That was close enough to the truth.

"So why the sudden interest in dragons?" Janik pressed.

Kyra's heart stopped. She hadn't expected him to be able to decipher the title from her father's library.

Janik smiled and slid the books back into the satchel and placed them next to her on the bench.

"Don't worry, your hobby is safe with me," he assured her. "I mean, it isn't like you found a dragon out hiding in the woods, right?" Janik laughed and reached for his drink.

Kyra laughed nervously and nodded, hoping that he wouldn't see the fear in her face. She flicked her eyes down to her soup and took the bowl in both hands again. She raised it up and drained it before setting it down.

"Atta girl," Janik said. "No reason for pomp between friends. Eat to your heart's content." He pointed a finger at her. "Though, the next time you go out for a day, try taking something with you. It is good to feed the mind, but you mustn't forget the body."

Kyra nodded. "I'll do that." She stretched her lips into a forced grin and then set the bowl down. She considered the remnants of the toast and the untouched water goblet in front of her and then pushed them to the side.

"I think I will go off to bed now," she said. She was far too uncomfortable with Janik's questions to remain there with him.

If Janik suspected anything, he didn't show it. He simply finished his drink and then nodded.

"Sleep well," he said. "Oh, and if you are going to stop by the library on the way to your room, there is an interesting section on dragons."

"Yes, the manuals written by the dragon slayers," Kyra said. "I was thinking about reading those."

Janik waved his right hand in front of his face and flashed a sour grimace.

"No, no, not those books. The dragon slayers are idiots. They only know how to kill a dragon. Their study of a dragon's anatomy is noteworthy, but it is always slanted toward understanding only how to kill them. There are far more interesting texts for those with a scholarly mind, like yourself."

Kyra paused. She wasn't aware of any other books on the subject. Had she been, she would have taken them already.

"Where are they?" she asked.

Janik smiled. "Go to the third floor, and wind your way to section seven, in the back. You will find shelves of books there on the subject. Everything from identifying their eggs to predicting dragon type and all the way down to the companion lizards that are usually found in the nests."

Kyra's eyes went wide and her breath caught in her throat.

"Companion lizards?" she asked.

"I think we call them 'beardies'," Janik replied with a nod, "or 'bearded dragons' though they are neither dragons nor bearded. They are curious little lizards that hang around the nests of dragons. They sound alarms with a hiss, or sometimes a chirp. It is very quiet, but loud enough for a mother dragon to hear. In return, they are allowed to live in the nest and enjoy the protection of a much larger beast. At least, that's what some people say. I never saw it myself."

"Have you seen a dragon nest then?" Kyra pressed.

Janik nodded. "A couple, actually," he said. "Before the accident with my arm and leg, I went on several excursions south of Ten Forts. Mostly we were contracted to fight the orcs that ventured too close to the walls, but we still stumbled into a couple of nests. Most of them were smaller drakes, mind you, but there was one that had laid three eggs. Each one of them were half as tall as me and they were thick as barrels."

"What did you do?" Kyra asked.

Janik shot her a puzzled look. "Why, we hacked them to pieces of course. Tracked and killed the mother too, though it cost several good men." Janik sighed and his eyes went distant, as if looking into the past. "For sure, that was a bloody day. I had never been so scared in all my life as I was that day." His eyes refocused in the present and turned to her. "If you ever see a dragon, you run. You don't stay still and you don't freeze up in fear. You run. You hear me, Kyra?"

The young lady was disgusted by the thought of men hacking into unhatched eggs and destroying the life inside. Still, she could see the fear clearly painted on his features as he recalled the encounter with the dragon. She nodded and then turned to find the library.

Soon she was sitting cross-legged on the floor in front of the shelf Janik had described for her. A pile of books was neatly stacked on her left that stretched from the floor to her shoulder. She took the first off the pile and began to absorb the information inside as her eyes scanned the pages.

Within minutes she felt her heart skip as she found an egg that looked exactly like the one in the rocks. The words next to the sketch described the same color and size. It even went so far as to describe nests of rock often used when food was scarce, because the mother could heat the rocks with her breath, and they would remain warm until her return as she hunted far away from the egg.

That's when it hit her. The egg was alone. It had its miniature companion of course, but the rocks had been cold when Kyra had arrived and found it. They were warm when she went back this morning, but not so much as when she had placed the warming spell. That surely must mean that no dragon had come back in the interim period to warm the egg. For a moment, she wondered if the egg was dead, left long ago and perhaps rotting.

No, that wasn't it. She had been out in her father's chicken pens enough times to know what a rotten egg smelled like. There was no stench from the dragon egg.

Besides that, the little companion was still alert and active nearby.

Kyra put her nose back into the book and flipped through the pages, looking for any mention of companion animals. It wasn't until she was half-way through the book that she finally found it. A small drawing of a juvenile pagona just above and to the right of a drawing of an adult. The description said that adults could reach roughly two feet in length from tip of the tail to the end of the snout. They were light, agile creatures that hunted bugs, mice, and also fed upon plants.

"There is no mention of these small creatures ever playing the part of nursery keeper on Kendualdern, but here on Terramyr, it is not an uncommon sight," she read aloud. Kyra smiled and thought of the book her mother had given her. Was Gorliad's story real? If it wasn't, then why would it be mentioned in texts that discussed facts about dragons?

Now that she was certain of what was hiding in the rocks, she was ready for sleep. She would have a long day tomorrow, trying to find the right way to ensure the egg's safety. She gathered the books and trudged off to bed, thinking all the while what it must have been like to live on Kendualdern, a world ruled by dragons, and not by men.

*****

"That was an interesting conversation," a voice called out

from nothingness.

Janik glanced around the dining hall before nodding. "What do you make of it?" Janik asked.

The spell concealing Cyrus disappeared and the old wizard sat in front of Janik. He reached out a hand and took up Kyra's untouched goblet, filling it with wine by merely snapping his fingers.

"Our young friend has found a dragon, dear Janik."

Janik's eyes went wide. "Surely you must be joking. A dragon would swallow her whole."

Cyrus shook his head. "I took notice of a she-dragon making her way to the south three days ago. She stopped off in the forest near where Kyra goes. I would wager my left leg that she found an egg." The wizard cast a frowning glance through the table toward Janik's leg. "No offense, of course."

Janik reflexively rubbed his crooked wrist over his left leg.

"Of course not," he said half-sincerely. He had often wondered why the wizard wouldn't restore him fully, but the question was moot. He knew the reason already. If Janik were whole, he would be a threat. As a cripple, even one given access to magic, he was easily controlled. It was his handicap, more than the oath, that bound him to Cyrus.

"So if there is an egg, we should destroy it," Janik said decisively.

Cyrus took a long draught of the wine and then savored it in his mouth before swallowing.

"I don't see why," he said finally. Cyrus set the goblet down and pointed to Janik's bowl. Janik pressed the clay bowl toward Cyrus. A moment later there was a roasted quail nestled among sautéed onions and boiled potatoes topped with chives.

"I should like to learn such spells," Janik said.

Cyrus sneered. "Cooking, even with magic, takes a delicate touch. It is not something easily done with a heavy hand."

Janik sighed and worked the top of the table with his thumbnail, digging into a crack as he stared away from the wizard.

"What do we do with the egg?" he inquired.

"Help her," Cyrus said. "It is obvious that the girl wants to see it hatch."

"Harboring a dragon is a grave offense," Janik reminded him.

Cyrus nodded and swallowed a half-chewed bite of quail.

"Do you see a better way to ingratiate yourself with her? The charm I gave you has no power over her, you said so yourself. Do this, and you just might gain her trust."

"What if the dragon turns on her?" Janik pressed.

Cyrus held up a finger. "Not *if*, but *when*." Cyrus took another bite and forced Janik to wait while he chewed it thoroughly and then washed it down with another swig of wine. "As soon as the dragon emerges from its shell, it will fall prey to Nagar's Blight. You have heard of this, yes?"

Janik shook his head.

Cyrus sighed and threw his hands up dismissively. "Of course not," he mumbled. "Swordsmen aren't much for reading, I suppose."

Janik exhaled impatiently and tore a piece of wood from the table with his thumbnail.

"Just get to the point."

Cyrus arched a brow, as if to remind Janik who held the power. The warrior-turned-janitor didn't back down. He stared back at Cyrus' blue eyes and waited for the answer.

"Nagar was a powerful wizard. He fought alongside Tu'luh the Red in Hamath Valley. The two of them devised a powerful magic that could capture the very heart and soul of any living creature."

Janik remembered the history now. "Ah, *that* Nagar," he said. "Yes, I know of that magic, but what does that have to do with the hatchling?"

"Allun Rha didn't destroy Nagar's spell, he only crippled it. After the battle in Hamath Valley, the priests of Valtuu Temple seized the magic written down in a book called Nagar's Secret. What they didn't know, and couldn't have foreseen, was that the book itself is a powerful artifact. Any dragon within the bounds of the Middle Kingdom is doomed by its power so long as the book remains in existence. It doesn't work instantaneously, mind you, it has to wear down the individual dragon's willpower. Sometimes that is a relatively quick affair, taking perhaps a few weeks, while other times it can take years. There is no way of knowing when it will conquer a dragon, but it is certain that as long as the book remains, all dragons within the Middle Kingdom will fall victim to its powers."

"I have been an instructor here, and I have been assigned to units of dragon slayers, why haven't I heard this part before?" Janik asked. "The only thing we hear from the Battle of Hamath Valley is that Allun Rha stopped the curse and broke its power. Even the priests at Valtuu Temple hold to that fact."

Cyrus held a finger in the air. "It is a containment issue. Imagine the panic that would flood the land if the common folk all knew that the battle that supposedly won them peace really only bought them a semblance of peace for a limited amount of time." The wizard shook his head. "It is better to appease the simple folk with stories of heroism and derring-do than to show them the full truth in all its ugly and dangerous horror."

"So if the dragon will ultimately fall, then why risk losing Kyra?"

Cyrus looked around the dining hall. He snapped his fingers and suddenly he and Janik were enveloped inside a purple haze encased by a swirling, black mist. "The answer must not be overheard by itching ears," Cyrus warned. "I have been working with a group of warlocks recently. As you know, I have been pursuing certain artifacts for personal reasons. They assure me that they can help, but first they ask me for payment."

"What do they want with the girl?" Janik asked as he quickly put it together.

Cyrus shrugged. "I am not entirely sure. All they have said is that she can become an extremely powerful ally if handled correctly."

"What if she isn't handled correctly?" Janik pressed.

"Then she could be a terrible foe," Cyrus said. "So, our job is to befriend her, help her see the power that resides in her and shape it to something that can be useful. However, failing that, I suppose the order of warlocks wouldn't be too heartbroken if this potential enemy were killed by a dragon."

"So the betrothal was not to please you, it was to please others?" Janik asked.

Cyrus arched a brow. "The betrothal pleases me. With it, I can purchase the information I need for my own cause."

"You still have never revealed what that cause is," Janik said.

Cyrus laughed, "Nor will I. There is no need for you to know.

You are alive, you have your health, and you have a decent job here at Kuldiga Academy. That ought to be enough to make you content."

Janik thought for a moment, replaying Cyrus' words in his head. "You said 'we' were to befriend her," he said. "Have you met her?"

Cyrus shook his head. "No, but I suppose you had already thought about requesting that I replace Lady Priscilla, yes? I will have plenty of time to work my charms on the girl."

"Charms won't work," Janik said. "She is too strong."

"Yes, I have seen that," Cyrus noted. "As I told you those many years ago, she is the daughter of a vampire. We always knew that charms would have only a minute chance of swaying her mind," Cyrus laughed and pointed a bony finger at Janik. "It isn't like she is some oversized dolt who can be controlled with a simple powder that you mix into a drink!"

Janik smiled half-heartedly. "Yes, well, without that powder, my brother was dead set against marrying her. I remember trying to persuade him before we met with Lord Caspen on Kyra's fifth birthday. For days he insisted that he wasn't going to marry at all, let alone a five-year old girl."

Cyrus cut in and smiled. "See what a bit of magic can accomplish? You mixed the powder in his drink and then what? He has been a tamed kitten ever since."

Janik shook his head. "I don't know that I would call him a kitten, but yes, he has been much more agreeable since then." Janik then changed the subject back to Kyra, "Will she begin to hunt people, like her vampire father? Maybe that is why the warlocks want her."

Cyrus shook his head. "She will not turn to lusting for blood. Apparently, the only way to pass vampirism in its full form is through bite. However, she will have powerful magic swirling inside her. It will work to our benefit, though, as it will help pull her to the types of magic we use."

Janik nodded. He looked into Cyrus' eyes suddenly. "I want my brother to be headmaster," he said.

Cyrus' eyes went wide and he cocked his head to the side. "I suppose that could be useful. If I were to put him there, then you could continue to influence him, and in turn influence Kuldiga

Academy."

"Well, will you do it?" Janik pressed.

Cyrus shut the man's mouth with a fierce glare. "I will consider it. That is all. For now, I want you to go and tell the headmaster that Cyrus is ready to fill in for Lady Priscilla. I will make my arrival known on Monday, before the classes start."

"That is easier said than done," Janik said. "Do I need to remind you that no one has seen you since that day fourteen years ago? They might find it a bit strange if you show up now."

Cyrus waved a hand dismissively. "Nonsense. Tell them that you helped me escape the lair, but that I traveled across the sea. Make something up, anything. Tell them I wanted to retire, or that I was hunting some demon. It doesn't matter what you say."

Janik sighed and shook his head. "They will ask how I knew where you were."

Cyrus nodded and folded his arms for a moment while he contemplated the point. Finally he smiled. "Tell them that I traveled to the Eastern Wilds. Say that I stayed in contact with you because you pulled me out after the lair caved in. When they ask what I was doing, tell them that I was studying the Tarthuns and exploring the abandoned roads of the Sand Elves. Then say that as a favor to you, because you had to pay for the substitute, I was willing to help out an old friend. Leave it at that."

Janik nodded and then found himself sitting alone in the dining hall again, with no magical orb around him or sign of the wizard. He dug another piece of wood out of the table before slapping the hard wood and standing to leave.

CHAPTER SEVEN

Monday morning Kyra woke early and hurried to dress before slipping out and to the library. She wanted to get in a bit more reading before anyone returned for their classes in a couple of hours. She buried herself in a book about the great dragon riders of the north countries, their wars and conquests and how they lived in harmony with the dragons.

She lost herself in thought, wondering what life would be like if she could fly on the back of this new dragon she had found and escape not only her betrothal, but from the entire Middle Kingdom. She could leave it all behind, if only she could protect the dragon long enough for it to mature.

She moved to the nearest window that overlooked the courtyard, staring up into the clouds above and smiling as she imagined her dragon swooping down from the heavens to carry her away from here. The wizards would be too scared to interfere, and her betrothed would be helpless in the face of a dragon. No one would dare tell her how she was to live her life again.

A commotion down on the ground caught her attention. A circle of young apprentices, third and fourth-years by the looks of them, were gathering around a single apprentice. At first it looked as though they were going to tease him, or perhaps push him around. Kyra had experienced enough of that to know how cruel the others could be. She prepared a simple spell to throw a few smaller fireballs as a distraction in case the one in the middle needed help.

Just then, the young man looked up, directly at her. His dark hair waved slightly in the wind, and he smiled confidently at her as he shook his head and drew a waster, a wooden long sword, from his belt.

"Are you ready then?" the boy shouted as he turned his attention to the circle around him.

Kyra held the spell, wondering whether the boy had lost his senses.

That was when she saw one of the instructors approach the circle. He was a large man, wearing a tan tunic and black trousers. Over his shoulder he held a leather bag filled with additional wasters.

"Alright, Kathair," the instructor called out, "I do hope you are half as skilled as you claim, otherwise this week is going to be cut short for you."

The students in the circle laughed and jeered.

The instructor swung the bag around, moving to each third and fourth-year in the circle and letting them draw a weapon. When the bag was empty, he motioned for them all to put on their helmets. It was only then that Kyra realized all of the young men were wearing the padded leather armor which Apprentices of the Sword used for sparring practice underneath their oversized tunics. The young man in the middle, however, wore neither helmet nor armor. The instructor dropped the empty bag and pushed his way into the circle.

"A knight must learn that his word is his bond. We are not the barbarians of the North who live by mead and boasting. Every word we speak, we must be able to fulfill."

"I meant what I said," the boy asserted clearly.

The others in the circle laughed.

Kyra shook her head as she counted roughly thirty apprentices. If this was going to be a fight, it was going to be very short. She almost turned away, but the young man's next words held her in place.

"I am Kathair Lepkin, born in the Northlands and raised by the elves of Tualdern, and I will beat each and every one of you."

The others in the circle grew angry, spitting on the ground and shouting at him. The instructor moved in and whispered something into Kathair's ear. The young boy pushed him away and held his waster at the ready.

"You are only a first-year, Kathair. Come now, have some sense," the instructor implored.

The boy shook his head and pointed his waster at one of the

others in the circle. "That boy insulted my mother, and for that I challenged him to a duel. It is only his cowardice that brings the others into this."

A tall, wide-shouldered boy stepped into the middle of the circle. "*You* said that I was unfit to hold a sword, and that even if I had all of my friends with me, you would teach me a lesson. So I brought them."

"Culliver is right," the instructor said. "You boasted, declaring a direct challenge. That might be something you could get away with in the Northlands, but pride is not a trait we foster here, and today you shall be humbled." The instructor walked to the edge of the circle. "The rules are simple, knock Kathair to the ground, or make him drop his waster, and do try to be gentle on him, lads."

Those in the circle sniggered and laughed.

Kathair twirled his sword and jerked his head to the side. Even from the window, Kyra heard the popping joints in the boy's neck.

"Are you ready?" the instructor asked.

Kathair bowed his head and held his sword out to the side. "After I have put you on your back, you will apologize for what you said."

The boy the instructor had identified as Culliver stepped in closer. "I ain't apologizing for nothing!"

Two boys rushed in from behind. Kathair jumped back through the air with the grace of a valley deer. His waster came down hard, connecting with the side of one of the boys' heads and dropping the apprentice to the ground. The second apprentice swung his waster, but Kathair sailed over it effortlessly before chopping down on the apprentice's right shoulder. The boy cried out and slumped to the right. Kathair landed on his feet and whirled around with a great swing, crashing into the apprentice's ribs and sending him flying a couple of yards away to land on the ground.

Three more rushed in, yelling and calling Kathair the 'son of a trout-sucker' and a few other insults that Kyra didn't quite understand. The wooden swords clacked and smacked, and within seconds two of the three were down on the ground, rolling slowly and moaning. The third took a straight thrust to the abdomen, followed by a kick to the groin and then a left handed punch that knocked him to his back.

None of them had scored a hit on Kathair.

Three more rushed in. Kathair charged them. A moment later he was in the air again, leaping over the apprentice in the middle and clearing him by a foot. Kathair sent his waster down as the dumbfounded apprentice looked up, catching him in the face and sending him crashing to the ground. The other two ended up hitting each other as they swung at Kathair. They each grunted and hobbled away, making easy targets for Kathair as he whirled first to the right, bowling the apprentice over by rushing into him and dropping his shoulder into the boy's chest, and then spinning to the other apprentice with a savage chop that shattered the apprentice's waster and swept the boy from his feet upon impact.

Two more stepped in, but this time they weren't rushing. They circled around Kathair in opposite directions, trying to divide his attention.

"What's the matter, Culliver, not man enough to do your own fighting, is that it?" Kathair taunted.

The apprentice behind Kathair moved in. Kathair instinctively threw his sword up over his back and stopped the incoming chop. The apprentice from the front rushed in. As the momentum from the rear attack caused his opponents waster to continue down to the earth, and the apprentice himself to collide with Kathair's back, Kathair seized him from behind with his left hand, gripping the back of the boy's neck and lifting himself up to stick his boot squarely into the oncoming apprentice's face. Then Kathair reversed directions, planting his feet on the ground and crunching with his torso to pull and flip the other apprentice over his back. The flailing boy smacked into the one who was still advancing and both hit the ground.

Kathair moved toward Culliver then, beckoning with his left hand for the taller boy to come forward.

A mob of apprentices rushed in to protect their friend. Kathair moved like a ghost. He dodged thrusts and chops, letting them sail into his opponents instead as he ducked and whirled around his foes. With each and every strike, Kathair either deflected a blow meant for him, or dropped an apprentice. Within seconds there were twelve more boys lying on the ground.

"I'm coming for you, Culliver," Kathair promised as he

pointed at the tall, wide-shouldered boy. Seven more apprentices rushed toward Kathair. Kyra stood there astonished, for not only was he winning, but Kathair didn't seem to slow or tire either. He ducked and spun under a heavy-handed chop, only to rise and pummel an apprentice with four savage blows to the chest. The next took a hit to the side of the head, sending him into a forced cart-wheel before he collapsed on the grass. The third blocked two of Kathair's strikes, but then over-corrected when Kathair feinted at his face and then reversed the strike to sweep the apprentice's legs out from under him. A fourth took a savage kick to the jaw followed by a driving thrust in the stomach that sent him to the ground in a heap. The fifth and sixth went down under the force of one swing when Kathair's sword drove their heads together. The seventh apprentice wisely threw his sword to the ground and held his hands up while taking a knee.

"I yield!" the boy shouted.

Kathair turned to regard Culliver. "You're next," Kathair said dryly.

"Kathair, that's enough!" the instructor called out. "That's enough!"

The boy turned to the window once more and saw Kyra watching him. This time she saw the rage and strength in his reddened face. He didn't smile at her. He just locked eyes with her and took a few quick breaths. Then he whirled around and threw his sword. The wooden training sword whirled end over end until the pommel smacked dead center into Culliver's nose. Culliver emitted a strange sound half-way between a gasp and a cry for help. Even from the window Kyra could see the strings of blood stretching out from the boy's face.

"Kathair!" the instructor shouted.

Kathair didn't stop. He ran toward Culliver and pounced upon him, driving his fist into the boy's head twice before grabbing him by the collar and shouting at him.

"Take the words back!" Kathair shouted.

The instructor was there in an instant, grappling Kathair and ripping him off of Culliver. That was a mistake. Kathair slipped his arms under the instructor's and then reached up to grip the instructor's forearms as he pulled himself up and over the instructor's shoulder. Kathair seized his instructor around the neck with his arms as he dropped to the ground behind the man, pulling the adult down and dropping them both to the ground.

Kyra watched wide-eyed from the window as Kathair walked away from the field. The instructor must have had the wind knocked out of him, for he rolled along on the ground gasping and clutching at his throat and chest. Kyra was almost certain she would never see the young boy again, for if she had needed to buy her way out of being expelled, she couldn't imagine there being enough gold in the world to excuse what this young apprentice had just done.

*****

After lunch when Kyra went to the class Lady Priscilla had been teaching last week, she was surprised to see a tall, thin man with a long, gray beard sitting behind the desk. None of the other students were present in the class. It was just the two of them.

The old man narrowed his blue eyes on Kyra and studied her from head to toe without saying a word. He didn't smile, but he wasn't frowning or grimacing either. His expression was one of contemplation, as if he was trying to discern what kind of person she was. After a moment he motioned to the desk immediately opposite his and gestured for her to sit. Kyra went to the desk she was offered and set her book down on top, not breaking eye contact with the new instructor.

She couldn't place it, but there was something familiar about the way this man looked, as if she had met him before. She tried to think of any place she might have seen him, but her mind couldn't clearly recall any memory with him in it.

"My name is Cyrus, and I will be filling in for Lady Priscilla."

The name sounded familiar as well. Where had she heard that name before?

"Are you ready to begin?" Cyrus asked.

Kyra looked around the room and then back to the teacher.

"What of the other students?"

"The headmaster thought it best if perhaps I were to take over your instruction. The other students have been reassigned to other instructors."

Kyra leaned back in her chair and folded her arms.

"So I'm not allowed to have classmates. Am I so dangerous?"

Cyrus nodded his head. "It is not a permanent arrangement, but it is settled this way for the next several months. Lady Priscilla was pregnant, did you know that?"

Kyra's mouth opened in horror. She quickly glanced to the floor, too ashamed to look at the man anymore.

"That is what I thought," Cyrus noted. The old man rose from his chair, walked around the desk and came to sit in a student's chair next to Kyra. "That is one of the reasons I am to be your instructor. You see, neither the headmaster nor I assumed you had any knowledge of Lady Priscilla's condition, but in the future we would like you to maintain control over your abilities. You should know that Lady Priscilla is fine and it is expected that her child will be born in due time without any harm from the incident last week."

Kyra nodded thankfully. "I had no idea."

Cyrus offered a gentle smile and patted her on the back.

"So tell me Kyra, where did Lady Priscilla leave off in her last lesson that you attempted?"

Kyra reached down into her bag and pulled a brown leather journal out. She opened the first several pages, flipping through roughly a third of the book before finally coming to the page she was looking for.

"In class we were practicing lesser wards."

Cyrus chuckled to himself, reached over with his long, bony fingers and flipped Kyra's journal closed. Kyra startled and looked up to her new instructor with a questioning look.

"I think we both know you are a little beyond wards," Cyrus said with a big grin. "The other reason I was chosen as your instructor is because I am simply the best wizard. Any fool can teach from a book, you shall learn from my experience, which I gained from the real world outside of stone walls. You have talent, Kyra, real talent. There is no use in holding you back to the lowest common denominator in the class. You should be allowed to progress freely, at your own pace."

Cyrus rose to his feet and snapped his fingers. A flash of red and black smoke puffed in the air in front of Kyra and there hovered before her a leathery winged imp. The creature was only nine inches tall, but it looked menacing nevertheless. It had a long, wispy tail, hooked talons on its feet, and sharp, long claws on its hands. Though they were minute, a set of sharp, fearsome fangs protruded out from its mouth and looked as though they could do quite some damage despite their diminutive size.

"Today you learn defense against a real opponent," Cyrus said. He pointed to the creature he had summoned. The imp watched Cyrus' finger and let out a sharp growl. Cyrus then pointed to Kyra and the winged creature dove in for an attack.

Kyra ducked to her left, allowing the winged creature to sail past her. She jumped up to her feet and created a shield between her and the summoned creature. The imp snarled and dispelled the shield with a wave of its left hand. A moment later a large ball of lightning flew from the imp's right hand directly for Kyra. Kyra raised a ward at the last moment and the magical ball of electricity splattered against it, hissing and popping as streaks of silver lightning shot out to the sides. Kyra answered the small imp with a single fireball that she summoned. The fire blasted the creature down from the air and it flopped onto a student's desk several yards away.

The imp pushed up to its feet as tendrils of silver smoke gently rose from its leathery skin. It snarled ferociously and sent another barrage of attacks. Undaunted, Kyra sidestepped the spells while simultaneously casting wards to absorb their magic. Seeing that the fire had no effect on the creature, she moved for the opposite element. She summoned a sphere of water just over the imp's head and then dropped the deluge upon him. The imp collapsed under the weight of the water, coming up choking and sputtering after the spell had passed. It leapt into the air again, ready to launch another spell. Kyra, growing tired of the creature's resistance to magic, picked up her journal, ran three paces to close the distance between them and swatted the small creature from the air with as much strength as she could summon. The imp's wing and left leg snapped upon impact and the creature was hurled against the wall. A streak of blood was left upon the wall as the creature fell to the floor, barely twitching anymore and certainly no longer a threat.

"That is not an approach I have seen before," Cyrus said. "I would have preferred your solution to be a magical one. After all, this is a sorcery class. If all you want to do is bash things together and watch them break, you could join the Apprentices of the Sword and spend your days among the dull brutes that lumber over the land and hoard all the glory for themselves."

"The creature you summoned was immune to my spells," Kyra said. "I think there is something to be said for handling the situation with speed, even if the solution is not the most elegant."

Cyrus smiled to himself and nodded briefly before returning to his desk. "I will admit, the ability to think on one's feet is a virtue lacking among many apprentices and masters alike. So, for that I commend you. However, let me show you the proper way to dispense with an imp, or even a dozen of them."

Cyrus muttered a few words not quite loud enough for Kyra to hear and then there appeared a box of yellow, transparent energy around the old wizard and his desk. A moment later a group of imps was summoned as well. Without delay the creatures began attacking, swarming around the wizard ferociously and diving in with magic and with their vicious teeth and claws. Cyrus quickly created a shell of energy around himself and deflected the imps, then he cast a great spell that rendered each of them immobile in an instant.

Like Kyra had done, Cyrus brought forth large spheres of water. They sloshed and splashed as they hovered in the air waiting for the wizard's command. He sent each one at a separate imp, but he did not let the sphere break. Instead, each sphere of water swallowed their respective imp and then turned to a solid ball of ice. As soon as each creature was encased in its frozen jail, Cyrus sent them all crashing to the floor. Frozen hunks of ice shattered across the stone floor, tearing the creatures apart and killing all of them.

The box of energy dissipated with a wave of his hand and then Cyrus cleared all of the mess from the room with a snap of his fingers.

"I don't suppose Lady Priscilla has ever showed you something like that."

Kyra shook her head. Cyrus winked and then moved to sit back at his desk.

"I'm not an instructor," Cyrus said. "I am a wizard, but I do not answer to the title of Master. You may call me Cyrus. As long as you are my student, we will learn real magic. That means I expect you to spend most of your free time in the library or otherwise studying the applications that I will show you. You may practice magic, but only under my supervision, or far away from the school. I will not have you threatening the other students here or intimidating anyone, are we clear?"

Kyra nodded with a smile. This is exactly the kind of instruction she had hoped for.

"One more thing," Cyrus added. His blue eyes locked with hers and his smile faded. He jabbed a finger toward her, shaking it gently for emphasis. "You will undoubtedly have questions. There are some questions that the instructors and administrators at Kuldiga Academy do not understand, nor do they wish to. Bring those questions to me. I promise to answer your questions truthfully and honestly, and in return I expect you to follow my advice."

"I will, sir," Kyra promised.

Cyrus wagged his finger from side to side. "You will call me Cyrus, not Sir." He then pointed to her bag intently. "Do you have any questions regarding your reading material?"

Kyra's heart skipped. Had Cyrus seen the books about dragons in her bag? Perhaps while she was fighting with the imp, the old wizard had seen one of the titles. No, these books were situated in the middle of her normal text books, there was no way he could have seen them. How could he have? Still, judging by the expression on his face, she had to wonder.

Cyrus smiled again, but this time it did not comfort her. Instead it looked almost as if he were teasing her - touting his discovery and flaunting it in front of her to watch her squirm. If he did know the truth, he did not press the matter any further. He quickly turned his eyes to a book on his own desk then motioned toward the door.

"In the library you will find a small book on imps. You know where the section dealing with familiars is located in the library, yes?"

"I know that section."

"Then go and get the book. It has additional information about the creatures that is useful in deciding how to deal with the pests. Take it and go into the forest where you can study it in peace. As you learn more about the creatures, go ahead and practice the spells that you would like to use tomorrow. Try to cast your spells on rocks or dead logs. Don't use trees or animals, understand?"

Kyra nodded her head.

"Good. Tomorrow morning when we meet again I will expect you to know three methods of effectively dealing with imps."

"As you say," Kyra said. The old wizard stop talking and poured himself into his book. Kyra rose from her desk, gathered her things, and went straight for the library.

*****

After having retrieved the necessary book from the Library, Kyra had quickly returned to her room and changed from her school clothes into something more appropriate for a day in the outdoors. On her way out to the woods, Kyra was careful to ensure that nobody was watching her. The book that Cyrus had instructed her to read was not very thick and would not detract from her time with the egg. She smiled as she thought about the additional free time she would have as compared to her original schedule before Cyrus had arrived. If every day was like this, she would be able to spend hours in the woods every day. She was so lost in her thoughts contemplating her new schedule, she failed to notice the young man in front of her until he called out to stop her from running into him.

"Hello," the boy called out.

Kyra looked up to see the young boy she had watched from the library window earlier that morning. He was about her age and perhaps an inch or two taller than her with wide shoulders and lean muscular arms.

"Hello," Kyra replied.

He smiled at her and pointed to the bag full of books.

"What are you reading?" He asked.

Wanting to end the conversation quickly, Kyra offered a short answer.

"These are just books for my studies."

The boy looked at the bag, cocking his head to the side, judging its thickness.

"It seems to be a much heavier load than the average first year

I see wandering the halls." He smiled again and offered his hand. "I am Kathair Lepkin." When Kyra didn't respond by shaking his offered hand, the young apprentice bowed graciously with a flourish of his hands out to the side.

"Yes, I know. I heard your name this morning when you were in the courtyard," Kyra said.

His smile faded and his skin blushed just a touch at the checks.

"That wasn't what it looked like," he said.

"I'm sure it isn't any of my business," Kyra said. She started to move around him, but the boy held out a hand and stopped her. She bristled at first, preparing to knock him on his rump with a spell if he didn't mind his manners, but she soon saw he had no ill intent. His eyes looked to hers longingly, as if pleading to be heard.

"Do you know what it is like to be teased?" he asked. "Some of the third-year and fourth-year apprentices tried to run me out of this Academy because of my heritage."

Kyra softened at this, empathizing with his situation.

"Who are your parents?"

Kathair shook his head and shrugged.

"It is not so much my parents' names as it is the fact that they are not nobles, nor even from the Middle Kingdom. They are from the Northlands, where I was born." Kathair stopped and dug his toe in the dirt, finally uprooting and kicking a small rock away before continuing. "In any case, they both died a long time ago and I was raised by the elves in Tualdern."

"And you thought it was appropriate to bash all of their heads in with a wooden sword? How does that make everyone else like you?"

The boy smiled and folded his arms over his chest.

"Am I being judged by the apprentice who threw her instructor into a wall?" He pointed back to her bag of books and then nodded his head. "I can see you have a lot to do, perhaps we will see each other again later on." Kathair walked by her, but Kyra turned and followed him with her eyes.

"Weren't you expelled?" she asked.

He turned around and shook his head. "I wouldn't exactly call the elves family. I didn't really belong in their society either. However, they can be very persuasive. They were able to come to an agreement with the headmaster."

"If you only just fought this morning, how could the headmaster meet with any elf from Tualdern? That's the other side of the Middle Kingdom."

"You are studying to become a sorceress, and yet you question whether magical methods exist for communicating over long distances? Perhaps now I understand why you have so many books to read."

Kyra bristled. She turned her back on him and walked away.

He called after her, "Perhaps I will see you in the library sometime."

Kyra didn't respond. Her feet continued walking, stretching the distance between the two of them until she was certain he could no longer see her. Still, she made sure to take a much longer, wandering route to her egg just in case.

When she finally arrived at the rocky area where the egg was hidden, she saw Guardian sunning himself on a large boulder. The pagona lizard began chirping happily upon her arrival. She quickly went to the rock covering the egg and removed it. Immediately, she placed another warmings on the egg and the surrounding rocks. She set the palm of her left hand against the outer shell, testing the temperature. Something magical happened then. Even through the shell Kyra felt a swirling movement, or at least she thought she did. After the sensation passed she left her hand there for several minutes hoping to feel it again, but she did not.

Kyra set her bag down and followed Guardian as he jumped from rock to rock catching crickets. They spent half an hour doing this, with her following and observing his every move. When the little lizard had finally had his fill, he returned to the egg. Kyra took the long way around and spied a raspberry bush. She reached in to pick some, but scraped the back of her left hand on an exceptionally sharp thorn. She recoiled back and called out in pain.

Guardian was there in an instant, chirping and hissing.

"It's alright," Kyra told him. "I just cut myself on a thorn." She cleaned the wound on the back of her shirt and then led Guardian back to where her bag was.

She took up her books and began to read. First, she read a compilation of folk tales, and then she finally pulled out the book Cyrus had assigned to her and read it. Perhaps it wasn't the best text to read to a developing egg, but she had an assignment to do and she didn't want to read silently. Even if the hatchling inside could not hear her voice or understand it, the act of reading to the egg helped her feel closer to it. It was as if she finally had a pair of friends who would listen without judging, and who genuinely enjoyed her company. As before, she read until dusk, not bothering to gather her things together until the very last moment that would allow her just enough light to return to the Academy before dark.

She placed the last book into her bag, bade farewell to Guardian, and then augmented the warming spell upon the egg. She slid the large, flat rock back into place and turned to leave, but something caught her attention. There was a shift in the air near the tree line. She couldn't quite see the movement. The hairs on the back of her neck stood straight and goosebumps formed along her forearms. Something was there.

Kyra secured her bag over her shoulder and prepared a couple of spells in case she saw the prowler. She aimed her head toward the ground while watching through her peripheral vision for the intruder. At first, she thought perhaps that boy had managed to find her in the forest, but she dismissed that notion very quickly when she heard a strange hissing sound.

A moment later some of the rocks cracked together as something large emerged from the tree line, speeding toward the egg. Kyra turned around to face the danger. She saw not an animal or bird, but a strange creature half running, half floating over the rocks toward the egg. It appeared as though the creature was made of a thick mist. Kyra could not see any legs as the beast continued to come closer to the egg. It was as if its bottom half was made of a tangible cloud that shifted and moved the rocks in its path as it flowed toward its prey. A pair of long arms wrapped in a silvery coating stretched out from the creature, reaching to grab the egg behind Kyra.

Kyra didn't waste any time. As she had done with the imp, she decided the best way to fight was to attack with everything that she had. She sent a pair of fireballs. They passed harmlessly through the creature. Its silvery essence opening around the flaming orbs and then closing behind them. Next Kyra sent water, then ice, and finally lightning. Nothing slowed the creature down. Out of desperation she ran back to protect the egg. A few yards away from the egg, the creature stopped and shrieked so loudly in its deafening, shrill voice that Kyra fell to her knees, grabbing her ears. She looked up to see Guardian jumping up from a boulder and snapping its jaws at the ethereal creature. The little lizard jumped through the being time and time again. Somehow Guardian was able to hold the creature in place, but the little lizard's attacks caused no harm.

One of the arms took on a more focused appearance then, with long, bony fingers stretching out from a strong, thick hand. As Guardian leapt at the creature one more time, the bony hand snatched the little lizard up and brought it toward a hideous face which was slowly becoming discernable. Bumps emerged from the silvery mist until at last Kyra could see a short snout filled with jagged teeth. The creature bit Guardian in half and discarded the tail and hind legs carelessly upon the nearby boulders. A pair of yellow, sick eyes glared at Kyra from within the misty face. It started to advance once more.

Kyra, enraged that her little friend had been destroyed, poured her entire soul into her next attack. She held out her left hand and sent a massive shockwave through the air. A great clap of thunder shook the ground and the rocks around her as the blast ripped through the silvery creature. For a moment it seemed as though the thing might be ripped apart for good, but it was not to last, for the creature's essence began to regroup steadily. A pair of legs, long and lean with knobbly knees, grew out from the bottom half of the mist and it started to walk toward her.

Kyra didn't stop. She summoned a vortex around the creature, swirling it around and around, creating a vicious trap so that the creature could not escape. Next she used her powers to summon a great sphere of fire and dropped the flames into the swirling vortex, and then cast the misty creature away. The roaring tornado of fire shattered against a nearby wall of rock. Kyra called down a single bolt of white lightning, blasting the ethereal creature into pieces.

This time she did not let the monster regroup. She threw several more psionic blasts and further broke the several pieces and scattered them, preventing them from coming back together.

The monster hissed and screeched again, but disappeared into the twilight sky.

Kyra crawled over to Guardian's bottom half and placed a hand on either side of the torn body and cried. Within moments, overcome with grief from the loss of her friend and fatigue brought on by the large expenditure of magic, Kyra slid down to lean upon the rock and passed out.

Many hours later when the night had covered the land in darkness, and a cold wind blew in from the south, Kyra felt a pair of hands slide under her. One wrapped around her back, sliding one of her own arms over a pair of shoulders, while another hooked under her knees. She felt the sudden jerk, and then the rocks fell away from below her. Despite the disturbance, Kyra still could not fully regain consciousness. Her body still demanded rest from the overexertion earlier that evening.

Her head bobbed up and down and her feet dangled loosely, bouncing in sync with her head. Finally she felt her cheek fall against a warm, firm chest. She noticed a large tree pass by in front of her, but she was not fully aware that she was being carried away. A voice said something to her, but she could not understand the words.

After a while, her ears finally distinguished the sounds of footsteps below with their sturdy, dull thumps falling in rhythm with her bouncing feet. A twig snapped below and suddenly she twisted out as the person carrying her turned to move sideways beyond a large, thorny bush that just managed to scratch Kyra's left ankle with one of its barbs. Perhaps she had rested enough to wake, or more likely the sudden scratch from the thorn forced her body to come to its senses, but whatever the reason, she finally woke and realized where she was.

She could see the lights of Kuldiga Academy breaking through the wall of trees. Only a few more minutes and she would be out of the forest. She looked up to see who was carrying her, expecting Feberik or perhaps even Cyrus. The face was covered in shadow, but as soon as her rescuer realized she was awake he spoke to her.

"Don't worry, I won't tell anyone," promised the voice of a young man.

It wasn't either Feberik or Cyrus. It was Kathair Lepkin, the boy who had trounced thirty apprentices and an instructor in Kuldiga Academy's courtyard. Suddenly a panic came over Kyra as she remembered the creature that hunted the egg.

"Let me go!" Kyra wrenched herself free and dropped to her feet.

"Be careful," he said. "You're still weak."

Kyra moved to walk beyond him, but stumbled and started to fall. Kathair caught her and propped her up.

"Let me go," Kyra demanded.

"You need to rest."

"You don't understand, I have to go back!" Kyra pushed away from him and lifted her hand to summon an orb of light to help her see. The spell failed. Barely more light than that of a fleeting spark ignited in the air over her hand before popping and fizzing into darkness. She started to fall again, but Kathair was right there to steady her.

"Please, everything is all right, but I must get you to your room before anyone sees you."

Kyra started to cry. She was so tired that tears would not form and her eyes burned. "You don't understand, I have to go back."

Kathair gently guided her down to the ground so that the two of them knelt face-to-face.

"You need not worry. I moved it, it's safe."

Kyra looked up in her mouth fell open. "You moved *what?*"

Kathair placed a hand on each shoulder to steady her. "I found a good place to hide the egg. Nothing will find it again. Tomorrow, after you have rested, I can take you back to it."

Kyra formed a weak fist and thumped him on the chest. "No! You can't move it, it will not have enough warmth for the night. I had a spell on it."

"Trust me, it's safe. I don't have any magic, but I know how to make a fire. After I hid the egg I heated several rocks. When each one began to glow and hold heat, I formed a nest out of them. The rocks will hold the heat through the night. Then, tomorrow you can put your spell on it again after you have rested." He pushed her back from him and fiddled with something at his waist. She couldn't see what he was doing because of the darkness, but his hands worked with something for several seconds before a small satchel was placed in her lap.

"I didn't know what else to do, so I used some large leaves to wrap the body of your small lizard pet." A short silence ensued as the words trailed off into the night. "I thought you might want to bury it."

Kyra nodded and took the satchel in her hands.

"Come on, let's go before someone finds us here." The two of them got up to leave. Kathair wrapped an arm around Kyra and helped her walk the rest of the way back to Kuldiga Academy and then to her room.

Neither of them noticed Feberik Orres watching them from an upper story window.

CHAPTER EIGHT

The next day Kathair took Kyra to a deep cavern a short distance from the rocky area where the egg had been discovered. He again promised not to disclose the egg's existence to anyone. Kyra returned as often as her studies and her duties with Janik would let her, but Kathair was often kept away by some intensive training program. Apparently, he was too dangerous to allow to mix with the other apprentices, the same as she was. She had even heard that a few of the sword Masters would take Kathair out of the Academy for several days at a time for field studies.

Kyra continued to read books to the egg and set spells to protect and warm it. She excelled in her studies with Cyrus, outpacing even his expectations for her development. Even still, she kept the ethereal creature a secret from Cyrus, preferring to dive into the subject through books rather than discuss the issue with anyone and risk the secret of the egg being uncovered. The days turned into weeks, and the weeks into months. The autumn leaves fell, leaving the trees bare and stick like, except for the evergreens which stood staunch and stoic in their place as winter set in and covered the land in a blanket of white snow.

Soon, the mid-winter festival was upon them. All of the apprentices hustled about, decorating their halls and dorms and offering gifts to one another. The winter solstice was never a holiday that Kyra understood. She had heard that it was a celebration of hope; a sign that longer days would soon be coming and things would turn for the better again, spawning new life and renewal throughout the Middle Kingdom. Still, it seemed an awkward time for such celebrations. By definition, the winter solstice was the shortest day of the year. It was always cold, and the night was quick to end any sunlight that dared to reach into the wintry land. This particular mid-winter festival seemed colder than most, for it was the first without her mother.

Kyra's mother had never been a fan of the festival either. There had always seemed to be something on her mind. Lady Zana often spent additional time creating wards and staring out the window to the south, as if she had expected something to come out from the darkness. Of course, whenever Kyra had asked her mother about it, Lady Zana smiled gently and would say that there was nothing to worry about, but that she was only waiting for the dark to be over.

Kyra's father, on the other hand, was very fond of midwinter festival. He often recited the history of its origin, and lauded those who had created the holiday. He always insisted on re-enacting the traditional rite of placing an apple wood log in the fire while the family drank spiced cider and sang the traditional songs. His gifts were usually something that he would like more than a thoughtful present for the receiver, but it was one of the few times he seemed genuinely happy to be around people more than his books.

Even that had been taken away from her this year. Her father was not coming to get her. Instead, while all of the other apprentices prepared to go home for a three week holiday, Kyra received a letter from her father telling her that she would be staying in her dorm.

She glanced down at the unopened letter sitting on the library table in front of her. She reached out and turned the envelope over in her hand, studying her family seal embossed in the wax that held the envelope closed. She had thought to open it when she first received it in the morning the day before, but the more she looked at the envelope the less she wanted to know its contents. She knew her father well enough to guess what it would say. There would be a short report about the weather since her absence, followed by an accounting of the chickens and other livestock animals, and ended briefly with a list of books that had been acquired after her departure from the house. Perhaps there would be a small portion where he would question where some of his books had gone, as they had been secretly tucked into Kyra's belongings by her mother before she went to Kuldiga academy, but that would likely be the only departure from the otherwise drab and stale letter. The signature at the bottom most appropriately would be signed in a businesslike manner, the same as her father would write to any other acquaintance with whom he had to deal personally.

Knowing that, what reason was there for her to open the envelope? At least this way, with the seal still intact, there was a part of her that could pretend that things were different. Somewhere inside her mind, she could allow for the possibility that her father had written a loving, tender letter expressing how sorry he was that he could not come and get her and how much he missed her and her mother.

If she were to break the seal, she would dispel that fantasy.

She pushed the letter away from her on the desk, rose to her feet, and went to the window. She looked down into the courtyard and saw a mass of apprentices circled around a large bonfire. The various Masters observed the apprentices to ensure order, and some even doled out mugs of cider while the group broke into song. Many of the students had already gone home the day before, but others waited to be picked up tonight. It was common enough for those who lived farther away to be among the last to leave.

The door to the library closed, sending a low echo throughout the hall. Kyra turned expectantly, looking as far as she could see before a bookcase obstructed her view of the library's entrance. She could hear the pit pat of feet walking toward her. For a moment she worried that it might be Feberik, but she dismissed that thought as she listened to the light footsteps. His boots always fell heavy upon the floor. She also knew that it was not Janik, for his left leg would drag due to his terrible limp, and she did not hear any sign of that. She thought perhaps it was Cyrus, but doubted that because the steps were a little faster than his usual pace. She turned and went toward the edge of the row of to discover who her visitor was.

She smiled when she saw the dark-haired, blue-eyed young man that had helped her save herself and her egg.

"Not going back for the festival holidays?" Kyra asked.

"No, the elf who raised me is in the Eastern Wilds, fighting Tarthuns. There is little reason for me to go back now."

"I would like to see the city of the elves. Tualdern has long been a place I have wanted to visit and experience," Kyra said.

Kathair smiled. "Then in that case, perhaps someday I will go back, as long as you go with me."

Kyra blushed a bit and nodded her head, agreeing to the innocent, fanciful date. Kathair spotted the letter on the table and pointed to it.

"From your family?"

Kyra shrugged. "It's from my father."

"Aren't you going to open it?"

Kyra shook her head. "The headmaster has already informed me that he received a letter from my father saying that I was to stay here for the mid-winter holiday. I suppose it is his way of keeping me closer to Master Orres, and of protecting his investment."

Kathair frowned toward the table. He scooped the envelope up in his hand and turned it over a few times.

"Don't worry, I won't open it either," he said. "I never get any letters. I thought it would be fun just to hold one for a minute." He offered her a sly wink and set the letter back on the table. "How is your friend doing?"

Kyra smiled wide. It was good to have someone she could share her secret with. She moved toward the table and sat down. "I guess he's doing well," she said. "Hard to tell, really, since I can't see inside the shell."

"Does your book say when he should hatch?"

Kyra shook her head. "Best I can figure, it will hatch sometime in the spring. The books mentioned not only the type of dragon, but also that the abundance of magic in an area can affect when the egg matures and hatches. I have tried to find other books that discuss this very subject, but haven't had much luck yet."

"Have you asked Cyrus?" Kathair pressed.

"I did ask him about the magic abundance in the Middle Kingdom," Kyra said. "He didn't really give me a straight answer. Instead he launched into a lecture about how magic is passed from parent to child."

Kathair waved a hand in the air.

"Everyone knows that. If he is going to give you such a basic lesson on magic he should have started with what a shadowfiend is and how they create deals with the demons in order to get magic because their parents never had magic to pass to them."

"He did," Kyra said dryly with a roll of her eyes. "I was stuck there for nearly an hour listening to the origins of the first shadowfiends. It was interesting for the first few minutes, but by the time twenty minutes had passed I was already gone. I just kept nodding my head and he just kept talking."

The young Apprentice of the Sword tapped a finger on the letter beside him. His face went from one of mirth to a more somber expression. He glanced up toward the window as if to think of something else to say before breaking some sort of bad news, but in the end he shook his head and looked back to Kyra.

Sensing his apprehension, she broached the subject for him.

"What is it?"

"You know that the headmaster has sent me on field expeditions over the last several weeks, don't you?" Kathair asked.

Kyra nodded her head and waited for the young man to finish.

"I have been training with different groups of dragon slayers," he said suddenly.

Kyra shook her head. "That is impossible! Nobody works with dragon slayers until after their graduation. Even then most of them have to go through additional training at Ten Forts before they can be permitted to work with the dragon slayers."

Kathair nodded. He picked the envelope up again and fiddled with it, staring at it instead of looking to Kyra as he continued.

"Well, I have. I'm the only first-year apprentice in the history of Kuldiga Academy to work in the field, let alone with the dragon slayers. Anyway, I don't bring this up to boast. There is something you need to know. I wanted to warn you about it."

"About what?"

Kathair thumped the letter onto the table and sighed.

"There is a group of them coming tomorrow morning. You have to move the egg."

Kyra's heart sank. A wave of fear came over her, but it was quickly replaced by a hot, boiling anger that rose within her chest.

"Did you tell them?"

He shook his head quickly and looked into her eyes.

"No, no, nothing like that. It's only that they will take me with them. It is part of my training, to take me to diverse areas looking for signs of dragons. They intend to go into the forest. It isn't because of the egg, but rather because many years ago there were several dragons that lived nearby. I guess this was during a time when the dragons were still mostly good. I heard that the dragons were able to lend their teachings to some of the apprentices here. In any case, there are some different nests in the forest that are centuries old, as well as sites with bones, and they want me to look at those."

"I haven't seen anything like that," Kyra replied.

"The first place where the egg was, I think that is one of the nests they are talking about. In the old times there would have been scores of eggs there. All of the rocks and boulders have been carved out of the mountain and brought to that spot to create a nest that they could continually keep warm. I don't know that the dragon slayers will want to go into the cave where the egg is now, but it is so close to the nest, I would hate to risk it. You will have to move it tonight."

"Come with me, we can move it now," Kyra said.

"I can't. In fact, I should probably leave," Kathair replied.

"But why?"

Kathair glanced toward the doorway and sighed. "Your fiancé was quick to give me a warning upon my return this time. He made it extremely clear that he saw us coming out of the woods several weeks ago, and that he is partially responsible for some of my fieldwork. Though I am sure my escapade in the courtyard with the other apprentices had just as much to do with it as anything else, we should still be careful."

"But we haven't done anything," Kyra protested. "Am I not allowed to have friends now?"

Kathair smiled and his eyes twinkled at her. "I am now, and will always be your friend. Even after you marry that brutish oaf, I will still be around. I don't fear anything he could do. Honestly, out of the three of us, if I were to fear anyone, it would be you." Kathair offered a playful smile.

Kyra returned the smile. She knew of course that he was referring to the night he had helped her escape the forest. Afterward he had told her that he had seen the last half of the battle. He swore that he was charging in to help finish the strange monster, but had stopped when she had brought out a tornado made of fire. She looked at him then, locking eyes briefly with him, and her face reddened.

"I should go," she said. "The egg is going to be difficult to move on my own."

Kathair nodded briefly. "I should go too. I am sure Master Orres will come looking for you soon. I will go to my dorm. Perhaps that would draw his attention toward me."

"Thank you."

He smiled wide and then slid off the table. He went a few paces and then turned back and pointed to the letter. "You really should open it. You never know what kind of opportunity there is if you never try to peek inside." The expression on his face made her wonder if he was only talking about the letter. She watched the young man walk away and thought about what it might be like to travel with him to Tualdern. Maybe they were only friends now, but perhaps there could be other possibilities for them.

"What kind of a name is Feberik, anyway?" Kathair called out over his shoulder before he slipped out and closed the library door.

Kyra laughed softly, biting her lower lip as she stared at the closed door for a moment.

Then she looked down at the letter. Kathair was right. She might as well open it and see what was inside.

Perhaps she would open it tomorrow. For now, she had a dragon egg to save.

CHAPTER NINE

Kathair arrived at his room safely, though he had seen a few individuals trying to be inconspicuous as they followed him through the halls until he entered his room. No doubt they were instructed to do exactly that by Feberik Orres. He didn't let it bother him though. Truth be told, Master Orres was right to do so. Even that first time when Kathair had seen her standing in the library window overlooking the courtyard he couldn't help but feel a connection with her. That was to say nothing of her beauty. Her hair was the color of night. It looked soft and welcoming as it fell around her face and rested upon her shoulders. He smiled even now thinking about her, which was unusual for Kathair.

Unlike many of the other apprentices, who spent much of their mealtime or other pastimes talking about their supposed conquests with their female counterparts, Kathair Lepkin was not easily impressed by human beauty. After all, he had been raised in Tualdern, the oldest continually inhabited city, and the only city of elves within the Middle Kingdom. He had been surrounded by a race whose beauty surpasses that of all others. Yet it was Kyra that captured his heart.

He knew that was why he was protecting her. If any other apprentice he knew was harboring a dragon egg, he would likely inform the headmaster immediately, or destroy the egg himself. Even now he was considering doing just that. After spending time with the dragon slayers, he had come to understand the true danger within the egg. He had even promised himself that if the dragon ever turned on Kyra, he would be there to kill it.

Kathair had laughed at himself then, and still did when he thought about it.

Kyra would not need his protection from a baby dragon, she

would likely evaporate it with some spell the way she had destroyed the monster that had attacked her previously at the nest.

He admired, and respected, Kyra's talents, but there was more to it than that. There was something about her, something beyond her power and abilities. Maybe it was her confidence, or perhaps it was the desperation he could sense in her to find freedom. Whatever it was, there was definitely a bond that he felt was growing between them. For the sake of that bond, he would not disclose anything about the egg to anyone.

His thoughts drifted away from Kyra and the dragon as the songs became more boisterous outside his window. His room was a small area, barely more than a closet really. The window was narrow and short, but it allowed him a vantage point from which to look out over the courtyard. He moved to it and looked down. Many of the students had already left, and the bonfire was beginning to die down. Kathair watched the others sing for a few moments before turning back toward his bed and removing his shirt. He slung it lazily over the foot of his bed. Next he ripped off his boots, stuffed his socks inside, and then slid them underneath his bed. Last came his trousers. He tossed them over his shirt and then reached under the blanket to retrieve his twill pajama pants. There was also a shirt that went with them, but he didn't like it. He liked to sleep with his legs warm, and his chest and feet out from under the blanket. Just before jumping into bed, he walked back to the window and cracked it open a bit to let the cool, wintry air in. He took a deep breath of the crisp night air and smiled, then slipped into his bed.

He was quick to fall asleep, with thoughts of what life might be like if he and Kyra were able to go to visit Tualdern together. His mind raced forward through time, imagining that perhaps they would even team up and go on grand adventures. He would be the legendary swordsman, and she would be a widely revered sorceress, making them the perfect team to track down any monster in the Middle Kingdom. He knew the fantasies could never be. Master Orres was far too jealous and controlling. Still, Kathair didn't let those thoughts interfere with the planning and dreaming playing out in his mind as his body drifted into sleep. What would be the point of such a realistic fantasy? Dreams were to be exciting, not sad.

Several hours later, as the last embers from the bonfire rose into the air outside his window, Kathair's door opened. They were so silent that Kathair didn't wake. They stalked in noiselessly as if they were nothing more than ghosts. The door closed as quietly as it had opened. They gathered around him, and then upon the agreed signal, it started.

Kathair woke with a start as several pairs of hands seized his ankles, knees, wrists, shoulders, head, and mouth. He moved to fight against it, but then a massive, solid force struck him in the stomach. Whatever hit him slid off his chest, and then another one came just as soon as the first was out of the way. The second one drove deep into his solar plexus, forcing the breath from his lungs. His body convulsed as his limbs struggled for freedom and his lungs fought for breath. He tried to scream, but somebody fit a large wad of gunnysack into his mouth. All the while the beating continued. Slam–thunk-wham! Soon he had no energy left to fight with. He lay still, silently sobbing and gagging on the gunnysack.

Someone moved in close to the side of his face. He could feel their hot, onion filled breath on his cheek as they whispered.

"Everyone needs a gift for mid-winter festival," the person said. Next came a barrage of clenched fists. They pummeled Kathair's torso, legs, and face. He was still conscious when they left, but he was nowhere near alert enough to uncover who, or even how many, had attacked him.

There was no way for him to know how much time passed after the last attacker had left and the door had closed, to the time when he finally managed to sit upright in his bed. He could breathe, so he was fairly certain none of his ribs were broken, but he felt as though he had been chewed up by a dragon and spit out and left to rot. Slowly, using his hands for support on the bed, he inched his way toward the door. He never got far. Two paces after he stood from the bed, he collapsed on the floor as his body succumbed to his injuries and his consciousness faded away.

The morning light streaming in through the narrow window did not wake him. The two dragon slayers who had been sent to his room to look for him could not wake him either. They picked him up and put him back on his bed, but there was nothing they could do to rouse him. One stayed with him, and the other left to find the headmaster.

Unfortunately, with all of the remaining students gone for the holiday, there was no one left to question by the time the dragon slayer located Headmaster Herion.

*****

It was another two days before Kyra heard about what had happened to her friend. She didn't need to investigate possible motives for such an attack. Kathair had already told her about Feberik Orres. Angry and hurt, she stormed her way through the halls. She wasn't exactly sure what she was going to say or do, but she was not going to let this stand.

She found him in the hallway, carrying a small vase with three yellow flowers in it, as if he had nothing to hide.

"Ah, I was just coming to see you," Orres said with a smile. His big hands stretched out to offer the vase of flowers to her.

Kyra pointed at them and a bolt of fire leapt out from her finger to destroy the blue and white vase. Water exploded all over Orres' face, and shards of pottery clashed and clanked across the stone floor. "Did you think I would not find out?"

Orres' smile disappeared and was replaced by a foul grimace. "What do you think you are doing?"

Kyra stormed up, closing the remaining distance between them and slapped him across the face. Her small hand left a red mark across Orres' left cheek. "He is my friend. He did not deserve what you did to him."

"Who?" Orres asked. "If you mean the boy raised by elves, you should know that I was not there. He has done enough to make his own enemies here, and you of all people should know that."

Kyra stabbed a finger in the large man's thick, meaty chest. "If you want to survive a night with me after the wedding, then you will ensure that nothing like this ever happens to him again."

The large man smiled and chuckled. "I do not fear you, nor do I have any reason to interfere with the boy."

"He told me it was you who tried to send him away."

Orres held his wet hands up defensively and patted the air. "I am one of the instructors. It is my duty to watch over all Apprentices of the Sword. I was one of many who voted to send him away. I did this as much for his protection as for his development. He is the most talented Apprentice of the Sword to ever come through this Academy, and I wasn't about to see that talent wasted and squandered on squabbling third and fourth year apprentices who would seek to beat him at every opportunity they get. The other night's event should only show that my choice of voting to send him out was the correct one. But I had no part in what happened. I did warn him of our betrothal, and told him that it was improper to go gallivanting about in the woods with you alone. I told him if I saw such behavior again he would receive more demerits than he could ever work off in his lifetime. I am a jealous man, but I am not a brigand. I would not have a boy beaten."

The large man took two steps back away from her and then put his hands down at his sides. Then Master Orres bent down to collect the flowers and shards of pottery near him.

Kyra watched him from under her furrowed brow. Still, as much as she wanted to reach out and kick him as she watched him clean up the mess, the sincerity in the man's tone struck Kyra. She wasn't sure if he was telling the truth, but if he was lying, he was exceptionally good at it.

After he was done picking up the larger pieces, Orres rose to his feet and looked at her with kind eyes.

"I shouldn't tell you this, but the headmaster is investigating one of the instructors here. There has been a history of abuse from this particular instructor." Orres glanced down the hall and then back over his shoulder before continuing. "It is my belief, as well as the belief of many others, that this individual is responsible for agitating many of the other apprentices against your friend. The headmaster has sent for three priests from Valtuu Temple. The dragon slayers that were going to take your friend out for training have now gone to fetch the priests and bring them back. It will take some time, but they will find the truth. If the instructor was involved, he will face criminal charges. Suspected apprentices will also have interviews with the priests. If they are found guilty, they will be expelled dishonorably from Kuldiga Academy, with no option of returning."

"Why wait for the priests?"

"These are not priests in a religious sense," he said. "They have the ability to discern when people are lying. They have some magical gift that allows them to see into a being's energy, or soul, or something to that effect." Orres looked around for a place to discard the shards of pottery he held in his hand.

"How can they do that?" Kyra asked as she folded her arms. She wanted to believe him, but she was still not softening her tone.

Orres shrugged, glancing down at the awkward pile of rubbish in his hands. "I don't understand it that much, but the headmaster swears that this will be the best way to ensure all those responsible are punished. In the meantime, anyone who is guilty is encouraged to confess early. If it would help you, I would be happy to have a separate interview with the priests. You could be there and watch them so that you know that I had nothing to do with this. I know it is hard for you to accept me, but the last thing I would do is hurt an innocent person. I only fight to protect others."

Kyra nodded and turned away frustrated. Her pace quickened until she found that she was sprinting through the halls and out into the snowy field. Soon she was running through the forest, out and around the mountains to find the new place where she had placed the egg after Kathair's warning. She needed some time alone to clear her head. When she finally arrived at the secret location she dropped to her knees.

The egg was gone.

CHAPTER TEN

Kyra looked all around. She was in a valley several miles to the south of the forest where she had first seen the egg. It had taken her a long time to move it here, and she needed the assistance of magic to get it done without damaging the egg or cooling it too much. Now it was gone, and there was no way to know what had taken it. It was no animal, she knew that much. She had placed it in a large depression beneath a fallen oak tree. She had made sure to encase it with spells and wards that would keep animals away from it.

She searched frantically, but it was nowhere to be seen. After a while she gave up the search and sat upon the fallen oak log in disbelief. That was when she heard the music. It was a sweet melody of high-pitched notes flowing upon the wind like a gentle butterfly. She looked around, but saw nobody there. She moved into the growth of evergreen trees, sliding between the closest branches and boughs to discover something in the middle of the trees she had never seen before.

A strange creature sat upon a rock playing a set of pipes. Its hands were like those of a human's, with nimble fingers working the panpipes quickly and accurately. The creature wore no shirt, for it was covered in thick, shiny black fur. It had pointy ears that flicked to each side as she approached. It looked up at her with golden eyes under a brow crowned with two thick, curled horns. It sat with one leg crossed over the other, its hoof dangling over the edge of the rock.

Kyra had found a satyr.

The satyr made a sound that seemed a mix of a grunt and a bleat. Then it spoke. "I have been expecting you," the creature said.

"Who are you?" Kyra asked.

The satyr slipped his panpipes into a small satchel at his left hip, then stood from the rock. He held out his right hand and a large, gnarled staff appeared in it.

"That is why I wanted to see you," the satyr said. "Most humans would ask *what* I am, but you asked *who* I am. You are a rare person indeed, just as I thought." The satyr bowed graciously, flourishing his left hand out to the side and holding onto his staff with his right. When he rose upright he introduced himself. "I am Njar Somoricliar!"

"And what do you want with me?" Kyra asked.

The satyr positioned his staff in front of him and grasped it with both hands so as to lean upon it slightly. His golden eyes locked with Kyra's eyes as he spoke.

"I wish to inquire why you are harboring a dragon egg. Surely you must know how dangerous a dragon is."

"You are not from Kuldiga Academy, so who are you to ask me what my intentions are?" Kyra replied.

"I am the chief of a small clan of satyrs. I seek balance, as do my brothers and sisters. A dragon is a very dangerous creature, and if given the chance, it may disrupt the balance in the world."

"Can't every creature disrupt balance?" Kyra asked

Njar raised his hand and grunted. "Not in the way that a dragon might, for I am not talking about petty violence, or a simple nuisance. The danger that a dragon possesses is far-reaching, and possibly immeasurable in scope. You may not know this, but a dragon is a creature not originally from this world."

"I have read much on the subject," Kyra rebutted. "The dragons may technically be categorized as creatures not of this world, but the seven ancients were given permission to promulgate the dragon kind on Terramyr when the world was first formed by Icadion and the Old Gods."

"Interesting," Njar said. "And from where does your love of knowledge come from?" The satyr swept his arm around as if to indicate others around them, despite the fact that they were alone in the glade. "It is rare to meet a human, let alone a youngling, who can tell me the true origin of the dragons." She was about to answer, but the satyr smiled and its golden eyes twinkled as he continued on for her. "I'm sorry, I should have explained. That was a rhetorical question. I know who you are, and I know from whence you came. I have seen you in visions granted to me by the Pools of Fate. In truth, I also understand why you keep the egg."

Kyra shook her head. She couldn't believe that he would know why she was keeping the egg.

"You know?"

The satyr nodded, and his smile widened.

"I understand, though I believe your motivation to be misguided. That is why I have come. I am here to show you what a dragon will become in this land. I warn you now that it will not be easy to watch and learn the things that I have to show you, but it is necessary. If I am to protect the balance, then you must understand."

"Where's the egg?" Kyra pressed.

Njar turned to the rock he had been sitting upon and tapped it twice with his staff. In an instant a ring of golden light enveloped the rock and turned it into a translucent object, revealing that the egg was safely kept within the boulder.

"Get it out of there! It needs warmth."

The satyr held up his hand and Kyra felt a strong force hold her in place. "I cannot allow the egg to hatch. If you will trust me, I will show you why. As a sign of good faith, I promise that the egg will be safe here until I have shown you all that I have to show you." The satyr tapped the boulder again and the same light went in reverse over its surface, returning it to its original state and hiding the egg inside.

"Let me go," Kyra said as she struggled against the satyr's magic.

"If I let you go, will you come with me to see what I have to show you?" Njar asked.

Kyra studied the strange creature's golden eyes, searching for any sign of what his true intentions might be. Before she could answer, the force holding her in place faded away and she was again free to move. The satyr walked three paces away from the boulder and tapped the ground with his staff. The very air seemed to split apart as blinding white light ripped a hole through the fabric of time and space itself. Njar waived his left hand out and the rift grew to form a golden-rimmed portal. Through it, Kyra could see a small village surrounded by green grasses, beautiful trees, and myriad wildflowers growing freely throughout the village.

"Come with me," Njar said. "Not many humans are ever invited to Viverandon. However, I will take you there and show you the Pools of Fate so that you might understand the danger you are playing with." When Kyra didn't move, the satyr glanced to the rock then back to her. "I should explain. There is no magic you possess that can free the egg. If you do not come with me, there is no hope that you can ever save it."

"And if I do go with you," Kyra started, "what guarantee do I have that you will free the egg?"

The satyr studied her for a moment. It was hard for her to read the expression on his face. It was human enough, but there was a small snout, and the nose was more animal-like than human. Still, she found herself locking onto his eyes trying to search for any sign of hope in those golden orbs.

"I am not one to lie," the satyr said. "I genuinely doubt there is any possibility you could convince me to release the egg. My gesture is solely to help you understand why this must be."

"Why not destroy the egg and then leave before I could find you?" Kyra asked.

"Because, Kyra. I know you."

Kyra blanched, she had not told him her name and she was quite certain she had never seen him at any point before in her life. If her mother had known him, she certainly would have mentioned it before. This creature was using magic to uncover things about her that she had not shared.

"You have grown fond of this dragon, but your affection is misguided and will only result in your sorrow. This egg does not contain the magnificent creature you read about in the Chronicles of the Dragons of Kendualdern. The creature in this egg will either be born a monster, or he will die piece by piece until nothing remains of his soul and he is overcome by a terrible bloodlust like a rabid dog, or more appropriately, like a crazed demon."

Kyra shook her head. "I don't believe you."

The satyr nodded his head. "I knew you would not, and that is why I offer you the chance to come with me. If you worry for your safety, you need not. The daughter of Lady Zana Caspen has no enemies in the home of the satyr clan. If you need further enticement, I also have a library that contains a book you may be interested in. Beyond that, perhaps I can tell you about your future

120

husband."

"That has already been decided," Kyra said dismissively.

"No," the satyr said with a chuckle. "I do not speak of the man your father arranged for you to marry. I mean to tell you of the man you *will* marry."

Kyra watched as the satyr disappeared through the portal. It didn't take her long before she followed him. When she stepped through, there was a warm breeze that seemed to pull her into the satyr's village. As the portal closed behind her, she looked around and saw that they were on the edge of the village. Njar motioned for her to follow him. She was confused at first as they walked away from the village, but as a large pool of water came into view, she understood where they were going.

Njar instructed her to sit on a large stump near the bank of the green pool. He moved toward the water and touched it with the bottom of his staff. Ripples radiated out from that point, disrupting the smooth surface. A silvery fog began to rise from the water as if the staff had heated the entire pool to the evaporation point.

An image began to form in the mist. Great wings stretched out over the pool connected to a thick, muscular back supporting a long, serpentine neck that held up a massive, horned head.

"Do not fear this," the satyr instructed. "This is one of the ways in which I can peer into the threads of fate."

"So this is the future?" Kyra asked.

The satyr shook his head. "No. I am going to show you the past. This is a friend of mine, or at least she was before she died. What do you know of Nagar's Blight?"

"I heard that it was a powerful spell once used to try and control man and beast within the Middle Kingdom," Kyra answered. "It led to the battle of Hamath Valley. There was a great war between man and dragon with legions of each on either side of the battle. A great wizard was able to counter Nagar's Blight and the evil dragons and men were destroyed."

"Not quite," Njar said. "In reality, the curse lives on and it corrupts every dragon that lives within the Middle Kingdom. Some the curse corrupts sooner, and others are stronger and can resist its power for many years, but eventually they all succumb to it. Perhaps it would be easier for you to watch."

Kyra sat quietly as the dragon form in the mist in front of her flew through the air and landed in a town of humans and seemed to be living among them. Out of the mist formed houses and people and shops. Kyra watched intently as the dragon spent day after day, even months with the humans. She watched as the dragon used its power to help the people in the village, finding lost animals for shepherds and protecting flocks from predators. One time the dragon even repelled a group of marauders that came to the town. Kyra was about to ask what the point of all this was, but then she noticed a change in the dragon.

A dark tendril reached out through the sky, stretched into the dragon's heart, and then coiled around it. The dragon became sick and angry, occasionally snapping and flaring its fire at those around it. Knowing that it was sick, the dragon flew away and left the humans alone. It went into the mountains and deposited a single egg in a nest of rocks in a small depression upon a hill nestled between two mountains. Kyra then realized that the egg she had found had been laid by this dragon that she was watching now.

The dragon tried to stay with the egg, but its illness addled its mind and turned it feral. The beast flew back to the south and laid waste to the town that it had once lived in. Every building was burnt to the ground, and every living soul, both human and animal, was killed. The dragon then continued south into the borderlands, killing orc and human alike as it continued its way along its bloody path.

The next scene showed several groups of dragon slayers attacking the crazed beast. She fought well, killing three of the dragon slayers before her wing was damaged so that she could no longer fly. The dragon slayers overwhelmed her, and continued to hack her down bit by bit until she succumbed to her wounds and died.

Njar waved his hand and the mist dissipated, sinking back into the green pool. "If there were any in the Middle Kingdom who wish to see the egg you found thrive, it would be me. However, I know the truth of the curse. Liloriel was one of the strongest dragons to ever live in the Middle Kingdom. She was the last to succumb to the curse. She lived long before the battle at Hamath Valley, and fought alongside Allun Rha, the great human wizard you spoke of. As other dragons with lesser willpower succumbed to Nagar's Blight, she helped to bring down each and every maddened dragon. Sadly this included her mate, Pendriad. He was not shown in this, because it was not necessary." The satyr went to wipe a tear from his left eye and sniffled as he looked down to the ground. "Pendriad hatched here in Viverandon some two thousand years ago. He taught my great-grandfather how to use the Pools of Fate. Afterward he taught my grandfather, my father, and then me.

"I pleaded with him not to leave. There is a special grove here that filters the curse out. He would not heed my warning. He said it was better for him to live on the mainland, at the southern border of the Middle Kingdom. He took his mate, and they had one final egg. Shortly thereafter, Pendriad succumbed to the curse and went mad. It was Liloriel and I who killed him. I trust you will forgive me if I do not show you that part of my life in the Pools of Fate. I hope it will suffice to show you what I have already shown."

"But how can I be sure what you show me is not a trick?" Kyra asked.

Njar sighed deeply and shook his head. "If you wish to see, then I will show you, but I will not watch it with you." The satyr walked toward her and gently placed his palm upon her forehead.

Instantly she was snatched from the plane of the living to some sort of astral realm. It was dark all about her and she saw nothing but blackness. Suddenly a light formed around her and she found herself in the satyr's village, but not in the current time. She watched as the male dragon the satyr had spoken of hatched in the village. His arrival was marked with a great celebration and feasting that lasted for days.

She watched the dragon grow and wizen as years, decades, centuries, and finally eons passed. She felt the bond between Pendriad and the satyrs of the village. Next she watched the battle at Hamath Valley. Dragons and men whirled about her as blood and fire flowed over the ground. It was a brief glimpse at the horrendous slaughter, as if she was living the entire episode in only a matter of moments, but she could still feel emphatic cheers of victory when Nagar fell and found herself caught up among a throng of warriors, and saw as they did how Tu'luh the Red, a great and terrible dragon, was destroyed.

That feeling of joy and excitement was ripped from her when the first of the good dragons fell victim to the curse. The realization that Nagar's Blight lived on swept through the land like a disease. Many dragons fled, flying to the north, never to be seen again. Lesser dragons fell to the curse rapidly, as if some horrible plague spread through the dragon kind. Greater dragons helped the soldiers of men put down the crazed, demented beasts. A few wizards gave the mad dragons a new name to separate them from their wiser kin. They called them nightwings. Kyra watched in horror as dragons fell victim to the curse by the dozens. Some nightwings escaped far to the south, but most were killed by the greater dragons.

Then, as the stronger dragons began to fall victim to the curse as well, the armies of men formed a corps of specialized fighters, the dragon slayers. These men were exceptional fighters, and they wore ridged and spiked armor made of Telarian steel, a black metal strong enough to survive the dragon's flame. The battles were fierce and the dragons were hunted nearly to extinction.

Kyra cried as she watched the dragon folk destroyed at the hands of men. The final two dragons were Pendriad and Liloriel. She watched, hoping that somehow their fates would change. She watched as the pair of dragons tried to outrun the curse. They moved from city to city, always going farther to the south. Finally the male succumbed to the horrible magic. Liloriel defended the village from her mate. As Njar had said, he was there too, along with many other satyr warriors. Several of them were killed by the demented male dragon, but in the end, Njar and Liloriel killed Pendriad. Afterward, Liloriel moved as far south as she could without being discovered by the dragon slayer camps near Ten Forts.

Kyra had already watched the rest in the pools of fate, but she relived the experience now with more detail and a more intimate understanding. When the female dragon, in her desperate, half-crazed state laid the egg in the nest, Kyra did not feel threatened by the new dragon. Instead, she felt only more sure that she was doing the right thing advocating for the egg. She moved forward in the astral plane and stretched out her hand toward the female dragon.

"I will protect him," Kyra said.

Liloriel turned and looked right at Kyra. The dragon stretched forth her neck so that her snout just grazed Kyra's fingertips. Kyra's breath caught in her throat. She had moved and spoken as a result of the strong connection she felt with the egg, but she had not expected that she could actually interact with the vision in any way. As the dragon touched her, Kyra felt a surge of power run through her. The female dragon turned her head so that her right eye stared directly into Kyra's face.

"Save us," the dragon pleaded. Then she flew off. Kyra expected to finish the history, but instead she found herself standing in the rocky nest where the egg lay. She watched the sun rise and set over the rocky nest. After a while the small lizard that she had named Guardian came out from its tunnel and began its watch over the egg. She smiled at seeing him again. His little, agile body leaping over the rocks as he hunted crickets.

A sadness came over her then as she realized that she would not see Guardian again, for she had buried him after that peculiar creature had attacked the egg.

Kyra felt herself pulled backward, almost as if she was falling over a precipice. Within an instant she was standing before the satyr again and all around her was as it had been before Njar had given her the vision.

"How did you do that?" the satyr asked.

"How did I do what?" Kyra replied.

The satyr shook his head, rubbing the space between his horns with his left hand and scratching his right ear with the tip of his staff.

"You reached through the vision and talked with Liloriel. You even touched her. How did you do that?"

"I'm not sure. Am I not supposed to be able to do that?"

Njar reached out with his left hand and grabbed her shoulder.

"Of course not! You reached through a vision and changed the past. She never saw anyone after she laid the egg. And I have never seen you interact with her before. What you just did is impossible." Njar released her and turned to the Pools of Fate. "I need some time to figure this out."

Kyra stepped beside him. "Let me keep the egg."

The satyr looked at her and shook his head emphatically. "Out of the question."

Kyra stepped in front of the creature and folded her arms across her chest.

"If I have changed the past, then we can change the future.

This egg is the offspring of the two dragons that were the strongest against the curse. She asked me to save them. That is exactly what I am going to do."

"How do you propose to do that?"

Kyra shook her head. "There must be a way. If there was no way, then how could I have reached into the past?"

Njar nodded and opened a portal. This time he was not nice nor well-mannered about it. He grabbed Kyra's hand and pulled her through as the two of them rushed back to the egg. She protested, asking what he intended to do, but he did not answer her. He tapped the rock several times with his staff and the boulder encasing the egg hovered above the ground, spinning slowly and humming in a low tone. The satyr then turned and opened another portal. This one opened to a view of land covered in snow with a grove of white trees all around.

The satyr directed the boulder through the portal. Not two seconds after the boulder had passed through, he pulled Kyra through with him as well. Kyra's stomach flipped and lurched. Njar was quick to steady her and hold her upright.

"This is not far from where we just were," the satyr said. "I used a portal in order to save time and ensure the safety of the egg."

Kyra looked up at him hopefully and smiled, "Is this the grove you spoke of?"

Njar shook his head. "No, that grove has died, the last of its trees was uprooted and it rotted on the ground."

Kyra wanted to ask what had happened, but the satyr's tone prevented her from feeling comfortable enough to do so.

Njar quickly spun around and shook his staff at the trees around them.

"This one is similar though," he said.

"You will let him live?" Kyra asked.

Njar shrugged. "I am willing to wait until I have more answers," he replied. He directed the boulder to the center of the grove and placed it securely between the trees. He whirled his staff in the air and caused a great warmth to come from the ground below the boulder. The great rock melted away as if it were nothing more than ice, leaving the egg open to the air and vulnerable.

"We have to hide it better than this," Kyra said. "There are dragon slayers nearby, and any predator could see the egg out in the open."

The satyr shook his head and pointed to the trees. "This is not an ordinary grove of aspen trees. These are the oldest trees in all of the world. You see, each one is actually a clone of the other. It is not really that you see a grove of many trees, but rather you see many versions of the same tree. As such it has the collective wisdom of the entire world, and it is the purest of all places any mortal can get to with the exception of the hallowed ground that houses the sacred seed. This grove can filter energy in the air and delay the curse's effect on the egg. I will agree to let the egg live a while longer while I search for answers, so long as you agree to let the egg remain here where I can watch it."

Kyra nodded. She was so happy, she jumped forward and gave the large satyr a hug, pulling his furry chest in toward her face and squeezing his torso tightly.

CHAPTER ELEVEN

Njar told Kyra how to create a magic portal from her dorm directly to the glade of aspens where the dragon egg was hidden. This afforded her much more time with the egg, as she no longer needed to travel by foot. At first, the young apprentice sorceress had taken it as a sign that the satyr trusted her, but as time went along she realized that the portal also served the satyr, for it prevented Kyra from knowing exactly where the egg was hidden since she had never traveled there by foot, nor had she seen a map marking its location, nor would Njar describe in more detail where it was. After seeing the vision he had shown her, she could understand his trepidation and wariness, so she did not let it bother her. Instead, she chose to be happy with the fact that the egg was still alive and she was allowed to come and read to it whenever she wished.

Often, when she did come to visit, the satyr was already there. Sometimes he was sitting nearby, and other times he was more actively checking the egg, ensuring the ground was warm, and sometimes gauging the purity of the glade itself. He said it had something to do with making sure the energies were in balance, whatever that meant. She was happy for his presence, because Kathair had been sent away to train more with the dragon slayers.

As the days turned to weeks, the satyr would come not only to check the egg, but also to listen to Kyra as she read the stories. On occasion the two of them also discussed magic, though the satyr was hesitant to show her any additional spells beyond the portal. He was kind and friendly, but there was always a barrier between them. There was an ever-present scrutiny in his eyes whenever he was around, as if he had not yet made up his mind about the egg, or even Kyra herself.

The weeks rolled by and slowly the snow began to melt. Small green buds appeared on the aspen trees, unfurling into fresh, vibrant leaves. Flowers began to push forth from the soil and stretch their leaves and petals toward the sun. The air began to warm and the night skies cleared of any clouds harboring snow. Thanks to the portal, Kyra was able to stay beyond sundown, and she did so nearly every night.

Then, on a sunny afternoon when Kyra had finished her study session with Cyrus early, she arrived to find the satyr standing next to the egg flanked by several other satyrs. Unlike him, none of them had staffs. Instead, they were each dressed with leather armor and armed with spears and axes.

"What are you doing?" Kyra asked.

Njar smiled at her and held a hand up to settle her nerves. "It is only a precaution. The dragon will hatch today. When he emerges from his shell, I will be better able to judge his strength and energy. The warriors are here only in case the dragon has already been turned. If he is unharmed by the curse, they will return home to my village without a word."

Kyra heard everything that he said, but her mind grasped only upon the fact that the dragon would hatch today. She dropped her books and ran to the egg, placing her hands upon the smooth shell and checking it for any sign of cracks. "When will he come?"

As if in answer to her question, a sudden thump slammed into the egg directly below her palm. Kyra jumped, pulling her hand back for a moment and laughing. Her eyes sparkled as she looked to Njar. He smiled, but his expression failed to hide his serious doubts. Kyra looked back to the egg and placed her hand upon it again.

"Well, come on out then," Kyra coaxed. "I have waited a long time to meet you."

Another jolt, and the entire egg quaked as cracks tore through the top end of the egg and ripped through several inches of shell. Next, there was a bright glow coming from within the egg. The satyr reached out and gently pulled Kyra back just a couple of steps. She looked to him questioningly, but he pointed to the egg. A blast of fire tore its way through the cracks, the flames hissing and crackling as they stretched out several feet into the air.

"Be careful not to get too close until he is out," Njar warned.

"A hatchling will use everything it has to escape its shell. Until it can see you, it will have no regard for your safety, for it is unaware of your presence."

Kyra shook her head. "I will be fine." She pushed him away and move back to the egg.

"Be careful not to help him," the satyr said. "Struggling against the egg helps prepare his body for the world. Should you help him break his capsule, it is possible that his muscles will not develop."

Kyra nodded. She had figured as much already, for she had once had large butterflies at her home. She had nursed them from Caterpillar to butterfly, and had received much the same warning from her mother when it came time for them to burst out from their cocoons. She placed her hand against the other side of the egg and called out again to her dragon. "Hit it over here."

A moment later a great force struck the inside of the shell just under where her hand was. So strong was the assault that a piece of shell roughly the size of a saucer plate popped out and fell to the ground. Kyra held her breath and positioned herself to look into the hole.

At first she could see only large, brown scales. They shifted, and then an eye slightly smaller than a hen's egg looked up at her from inside. The pupil was large, round, and dark, and it was surrounded by a golden yellow iris that had small green flakes in it. The eye twitched up and down as it looked at Kyra. She smiled and the two stared at each other for quite some time. Then the eye disappeared, and the egg shook terribly. Cracks appeared in various places as the egg fell to its side. A pair of long, sharp claws emerged from the hole that had been pecked out and then ripped another hunk of the egg off. Half a minute more of struggling and the egg shattered apart, falling to the ground all around the dragon. Great leathery wings with a span longer than the height of a man stretched out to either side of the dragon. It lifted its head into the air and roared triumphantly.

The satyr chief was quick to examine the dragon. He was not intrusive about it, for he was able simply to assess the creature's energies from a distance. After a moment he nodded and all the other warriors disappeared through a portal back to the village.

"He is yours to name," the satyr said. "You are the closest

thing he has to a mother, and I want no part of naming him."

Kyra looked at the satyr and understood without asking that the reason he wanted no part in naming the dragon was because he still assumed that one day the curse would overtake it. If he were to give it a name, it would be harder to label the dragon as a monster and kill it if that day were to come.

Kyra walked toward the dragon and his head twitched back suddenly to look at her. She stopped, half wondering if the dragon would attack her. After all, she had no experience with such creatures. It was one thing to read about them in a book, but it was quite another to see one in person. From the snout to the tip of his tail he was just over six feet long, more than big enough to do serious damage if it wanted to. The dragon cocked his head to the side again and their eyes met and locked for several moments. The slight apprehension she felt melted away and again she was confident that the dragon would receive her kindly.

"Do you know who I am?" Kyra asked.

The dragon made a strange sound, something like a purr, but much, much louder, and then it came to her and stuck its head under her hand using his neck to make her pet him along the back of his head. She was surprised to see that he was not scaly as she had thought when she had first seen him. There were lines that appeared to be in the shape of scales, but his skin was leathery and smooth.

"A hatchling will form its scales in the first few weeks of its life," the satyr said, as if he understood what she was thinking.

Kyra smiled wide as she reached down to pet the creature with both of her hands.

"I have a name for him." She gently slipped her hand under the dragon's lower jaw and tilted its head so that she could look into its eyes once more. "I will call you Leatherback." The dragon let out a small puff of blue flame and then he circled around Kyra and dropped to the ground to rest.

Njar moved in close and spoke softly to her, "He will need food. If you are sure you want to undertake this, then it will be up to you."

Kyra looked at the satyr and drew her eyebrows together. "I don't even know where I am, how can I find enough food for a dragon?"

Njar smiled and nodded knowingly. "Perhaps I can help for the first night. You may enjoy his company for now, but I would warn against forming a deep bond with him."

"But you said his energy was clear."

The satyr nodded again and sighed. "For now," he clarified. "But there is no way for me to know how long that will last. His parents were already established adults before the curse came into the land. Even if he possesses their strength, he is not mature."

"Then help me keep him safe. We only need to protect him until he is able to fly. Then we will fly northward together. He will escape his curse, and I will escape mine."

The satyr chief began to shake his head, but his expression softened when he locked eyes with Kyra and he gave in. His shoulders slumped and he looked to the ground and nodded slowly. "I will do what I can, for I still do not understand how it is you could reach into the past. Perhaps there is a chance." He leaned in close to her ear and whispered, "But if he turns, we will have no choice but to destroy him. You must remember that."

*****

The next morning, before her studies began, Kyra used the portal to come back and visit Leatherback. She couldn't wait until after classes had finished for the day. She found the young dragon curled up next to an aspen tree. It lifted its narrow head as she approached and turned to the side so its golden eye could focus on her. It was unlike any other animal she had ever encountered before. There were no expressions on its face, like perhaps with a dog, to show that it was happy at her approach. It neither wagged its tail nor rose to its feet. Still, she felt calm and excited at the same time as she moved toward it and stretched out her hand to pet its head.

Leatherback closed his eyes as her hand stroked over the top of his head and down the first part of the back of his neck. Her fingers traced the lines in his skin that denoted where the scales would eventually form. Today she noticed that there were several small bumps along the top ridge of the dragon's forehead. From the many books she had read, she knew that these would turn into horns of different sizes.

Leatherback tilted his head back, exposing his throat to Kyra. She stroked it gently and then turned to sit next to the large creature. The young dragon made a sound somewhat like a large cat purring and then it snaked its neck around to lay its head in her lap.

"I brought a book," Kyra said, reaching into her bag to pull out the book that she had read several times over the last few months. "This is one of my favorites. I read it to you a long time ago, while you were still in the egg, but I think we should read it again now that you are hatched. Plus, I am much better at reading it fluently now." Kyra flashed an open page at Leatherback, as though he would understand that the writing was in a language foreign to Kyra.

"It's about a dragon like you. He didn't have a curse over him, like the satyr says you do, but there were others who tried to discount his abilities and prevent him from becoming all that he could be. They wanted to choose a lesser life for him, like many would do for you."

Leatherback lifted its head to sniff the pages, his nostrils flaring with each breath. He laid his head down and closed his eyes as Kyra began to read.

"You will like this book, I promise." She read the first two chapters of the book with the dragon laying his head in her lap and listening intently. She knew that she should go back to class, but she figured Cyrus could do without her for one day. After she finished the first two chapters, she closed the book and asked Leatherback if he was hungry.

The dragon snapped his eyes open and pulled his head back, cocking it slightly to the side to look at her better. She asked again if he was hungry, but Leatherback just sat there motionless.

"It will be some time before he can speak," Njar's voice called out from beyond the trees.

Kyra turned, straining her eyes to find the satyr.

"I didn't know you were here," she said.

The black furred satyr stepped into the grove and smiled as he leaned upon his staff.

"I never left. After you returned yesterday, I stayed to watch your little friend." Njar swept his right hand out, gesturing toward the trees. "The aspens here seem to do a fine job of cleansing the energy. As of now there is no sign of the taint in the young hatchling, and I will work on finding ways to strengthen the grove to keep it that way as long as possible."

Kyra smiled and reached her arm out to embrace Leatherback's neck.

"That is wonderful," she said softly.

The satyr moved in closer to her. Leatherback stood on all fours and moved between Kyra and the satyr. He didn't growl, but he stood firm with his eyes intently studying the satyr.

"He has bonded with you," Njar said. "He is already showing signs of protective behavior."

Kyra smiled proudly. "He is a gentle soul. Don't hurt me and he won't hurt you," she said with a wide smile.

Njar sniffled and wrinkled his nose as he looked down at the dragon. Then he looked back up to Kyra.

"There is something else I wanted to discuss with you."

Kyra leaned forward and used her hands to help push up to her feet. She looked down and realized that Leatherback, even though it had only been one night, had already grown several inches taller than he had been yesterday. Now his back was level with her waist.

"Do dragons normally grow this fast?"

Njar shook his head. "Since he will be more susceptible to the curse the longer he is immature, I have added magic to the grove that will help him grow and mature at a much faster rate than normal. Hopefully this will strengthen him against the curse and give him as good of a chance to fight it as possible. There won't be any adverse effects, but if we are wrong and he does fall victim to the curse, then it will make it harder to put him down."

"Stop saying that," Kyra demanded. "He isn't going to turn on anyone."

The satyr nodded, but she could tell from his expression that he was unconvinced. "The other thing I wish to discuss has to do with you."

"What about me?" Kyra looked at him and drew in her brows.

"You have changed something," Njar said. He sighed and looked to the ground before continuing. "Before I took you to the Pools of Fate, I was able to see much about your destiny. I couldn't see everything, mind you, but I could see some of the larger events in your life. For instance, I knew you would find the egg, and I knew you would fight for his survival. Up until yesterday, I knew that if I showed you the fate that awaited him, you would allow me to do what needed to be done. In none of my previous visions had I ever suspected or seen any hint that any other outcome could be achieved so long as you saw the visions at the Pools of Fate. However, after you altered the past by reaching out to this dragon's mother through the vision, all of that changed. While the dragon slept last night, I tried to revisit my visions about you. Kyra, I could see nothing. It was as if when you reached back into the past, you destroyed your future; like you simply do not exist in the grand design of fate anymore."

"I have never believed in fate," Kyra said.

The satyr held up a hand and nodded his head impatiently.

"I don't mean fate in the sense that everybody has a prescribed destiny that they must fulfill. Instead, I see fate as a grand design; a series of events that logically and predictably affect each other. Usually when I have visions, I can see what people will choose to do based upon certain knowledge. Sometimes, my visions show me forks in the path of destiny. Such was the case with you. There was a fork, where if I intervened I could save much suffering and protect the balance by killing the dragon. The other path from that fork would lead to destruction and sorrow were I not to interfere. So you can see, there was a choice for me to make, and not one prescribed way. This is how fate works for all of us. The problem is that now I can no longer see any path that lies before you."

"Most people cannot see the future," Kyra replied. "I suppose I will have to make my own."

The satyr went silent and frowned. His eyes alternated between watching her and studying the dragon. She could tell there was something on his mind, but whatever it was, he wasn't sharing it. The silence soon became unbearable and Kyra broke it with a different idea altogether.

"Leatherback is hungry, how do I feed a dragon?"

The satyr pointed to the book in her hands.

"All this time studying dragons, and you have no idea how to feed one yet?" Njar asked with a wry smile.

"I don't exactly have an army of servants who can hunt elk

and deer at will and then pile them up in front of him," she snipped.

Njar laughed softly and pointed to the far side of the glade.

"Take him hunting."

"But you said only inside this grove is he safe from the curse. If I take him out, will he be in danger?"

"Undoubtedly. However, no deer or other game animal is going to wander into this grove smelling of dragon as it does. You will have to take him out to hunt. I will follow you, and watch over the dragon."

Kyra nodded grimly. She knew that the satyr chief did not mean 'watch over' so much as 'watch out' for what he may do. She understood the very real possibility that the strange wizard would kill the dragon if he were to see any change in his energy.

"What if I hunt for him, and then use the portal to carry food back, will that work?" Kyra asked.

"The dragon must learn to hunt for himself, unless you plan on gathering enough food for it even after it is fully grown and requires several tons of food every day. Are you able to do that?"

Kyra shook her head. She knew that she could not. She looked once more at Leatherback and his calm, trusting eyes. She thought about the promise she had made to Leatherback's mother and then swept her eyes across the crowns of the aspen trees as they shuddered and whispered in the light breeze.

"If the aspens help to cleanse and protect him, would it help if I carried one with us?" she asked Njar, stepping toward a sapling which stood a few feet taller than herself and placing her hand on it.

The satyr stroked his beard thoughtfully as he glanced up and down the tree, then over to Leatherback, and back to Kyra.

"It may be a worthwhile ward to carry. I do not know that it will have any significant influence against Nagar's Blight, but a sorceress could find many worse places to take her first staff from – that is, as long as the aspenwood agrees." Njar raised his own staff into the air and circled the glade once. For a moment the aspens stood quiet, and then suddenly, with no noticeable increase in the wind, all the aspens began to sway together, their leaves pattering against each other like a melodic voice whispering to her. Njar turned to her with a smile.

"It seems the aspenwood agrees," he said, gesturing to the sapling she had chosen.

Kyra stooped to the base of the young tree and shot a bright bolt of lightning from her hand, severing the thin trunk in one blast. She tested the weight briefly, then showed it to Leatherback. He sniffed it once and purred. Then, with her hand on his head, she and the dragon left the glade and the satyr followed silently a short distance behind them.

Kyra tried to think of how to show Leatherback what it was they were trying to do, but she needn't have worried. A large, white snow squirrel ran across the ground in front of them. Leatherback caught sight of it and leapt through the air with such blinding speed and ferocity that Kyra stumbled back out of the way. So fast was the strike, that Kyra almost missed the impact when Leatherback used his tongue to pull the snow squirrel into his mouth. Two chomps and then a quick swallow and the snow squirrel was gone. Leatherback opened his mouth and looked eagerly from side to side. From that point, Kyra followed Leatherback as he used the scents upon the ground to track game. They spent the rest of the morning pursuing snow hares and other winter creatures.

Leatherback must have eaten twenty small animals before he finally slowed his pace. Every time he took each animal whole, chewing only a couple of times before swallowing it. Kyra would have gone and watched Leatherback all day, but the satyr chief came up to her with a worried look on his face. Kyra prepared for the worst news, wondering how she could convince the satyr not to kill her friend.

"You need to leave," Njar said quickly. "I will take the dragon back to the grove. He is fine, but there is something that pursues you."

"Something?" Kyra looked around them and then back to the satyr chief. "What is it?"

Njar shook his head. "It is something evil. Go, now!" Njar opened the portal for her and taking the aspen sapling from her hand, motioned for her to go. At the same time he opened a second portal that led back to the grove. He looked to Leatherback and pointed for the dragon to go inside.

"Are you going to hurt him?" Kyra asked.

Njar shook his head emphatically. "The dragon is fine, but I must protect you now. Go! You can come back later tonight."

Kyra looked to Leatherback and pointed toward the portal that led to the grove. The dragon leapt through the open portal. As soon as he was safe on the other side, Kyra went through hers and found herself back in her room. She turned around to look through the portal, catching only a glimpse of Njar as he jumped through the other portal to the grove. Both portals shut and she was left alone to wonder what it was that had spooked the satyr chief.

She wasn't left alone for long, as a knock rapped on her door loudly.

"Kyra, you had better be extremely ill, for I do not take lightly to being stood up for hours on end."

Kyra's eyes shot open wide, and goosebumps rippled across her forearms. Cyrus wasn't exactly the most warm and tender person to begin with, and now that she had to face him while he was angered, she was rethinking how she had decided to spend her morning.

The door opened and the thin wizard walked in, shaking a bony finger right at her face. "Just what is it you have been doing?"

Kyra opened her mouth to speak, but Cyrus waved a hand and cut her off.

"You had a report due today, did you forget?" Cyrus asked. "You were supposed to choose a creature, and present to me as much vital information about them as possible. Don't you remember? I gave you this assignment shortly after I introduced you to the imp."

Kyra had to think fast. She had forgotten about the assignment until now, though at this moment she recalled precisely when it had been given to her. It was three days after she had battled the first imp. Cyrus had wanted her to expand her repertoire of knowledge so they could broaden her defensive skills.

She did the only thing she could think to do. She pulled the now well-worn book out of her satchel and held it out toward Cyrus.

"I have been reading about dragons," she said.

The expression on Cyrus' face changed instantly from one of anger to a wide smile and incredulous eyes as he began laughing at her.

"You are a talented apprentice, but I believe a dragon is a bit far out of your reach. Or is it that you are hoping to be assigned to a unit of dragon slayers, so that you can see your young friend again?"

How could he know about Kathair? She stared at him blankly. Cyrus moved in close and took the book from her.

"I wasn't reading this to join the dragon slayers," Kyra said.

"I'm not concerned with your fantasies," Cyrus said pointedly. "Your wedding is a matter strictly for your father and your fiancé to decide. I am concerned only with your level of focus and that has been wanting significantly of late. You have great potential. One day you may be more powerful than me, though I dare say that day is quite some time from now. All the same, it is a possibility, but it will be farther off still if you cannot focus on your studies."

"But I have been reading about dragons," she insisted. In the moment she was so focused on getting out of trouble that she forgot to consider where this conversation might take her if she was not careful.

"Why?"

"Why?" Kyra echoed. Suddenly she realized her mistake. The old wizard's piercing eyes were staring directly into her soul and interrogating her silently, searching for the truth behind her motivation to read about dragons.

"Why the fascination with dragons?" Cyrus pressed.

Kyra thought quickly, and came to an answer that she was sure would pacify the old wizard.

"My mother gave me the book, it is from my father's library. It is one of the last books that she gave me."

Upon hearing those words, Cyrus changed from being a cold callous wizard to being a human being. He offered the book back to her.

"I understand what it is to lose family," he said sincerely. "Take the rest of the afternoon off. Take tomorrow as well. You've had some hard times of late, and I can respect that. When your head is clear, you will find me in the classroom." Cyrus turned without another word and started for the door.

The mention of her mother only served to dredge up all of her feelings that she had been bottling up inside since the news of her death had come.

"Thank you," she called out to the old wizard.

Cyrus turned around and offered a sincere smile.

"Of course." He turned back for the door but Kyra stopped him.

"The letter the headmaster gave me when my mother died, I read it."

Cyrus paused and glanced over his shoulder at her, waiting for her to finish what she wanted to say.

Kyra stumbled through the next bit of information.

"The letter said that my mother was murdered."

Cyrus nodded. "Yes child, she was," he said softly.

Kyra felt a lump rise in her throat, but she pressed on anyway.

"Did they ever find out who it was that did it?"

Cyrus sighed heavily and looked to the floor for a moment as he shook his head. He turned back and looked at her with those strong, fearsome eyes of his.

"My dear child, it was not a *who*, but rather a *what*."

Kyra balked and took a step back. Suddenly she drew a connection between what the satyr had warned her away from just a few minutes earlier, and her mother's death. She had seen some sort of strange creatures before leaving her home and coming to Kuldiga Academy. One of them had even chased her, and her mother had fought it. Was it possible that her family was being pursued by creatures unknown?

Her mouth fell open as she recalled the ethereal creature that had attacked the egg and killed Guardian. All this time she had thought it was going for the egg, but now she wondered. The possibility seemed too likely to be shaken. It had been after her.

Cyrus closed the distance between them in an instant and grabbed her by the shoulders.

"What have you seen?" Cyrus asked insistently.

Kyra wasn't sure whether to trust him. If she told him about the ghoul near the dragon's nest, then Leatherback would be in danger. Still, perhaps she could tell him of the creature she had seen around Caspen Manor. Maybe that would be enough for him to help her unravel this mystery.

"They look somewhat like ghosts, don't they?" Cyrus asked, too impatient for her to answer.

Kyra nodded slowly.

Cyrus pushed her away and shook his head.

"I had intended to wait for a day when you were in a better frame of mind," Cyrus began, "but I should tell you, the reason I have brought imps and other such creatures into your training regimen is because I believe you are in danger. Given what you have already seen, and the recent events with your mother, then perhaps now is the appropriate time to tell you. I was with Janik when we rescued your mother from the vampire. However, ever since that day, there have been dark forces chasing after your family."

That was it! Now she knew where she recognized Cyrus from. He was the wizard in the painting in her father's study. He was the other hero that had rescued her mother. All sorts of thoughts and questions flooded into her mind, but Cyrus grabbed her by the shoulders again and was quick to bring her back to the conversation at hand.

"Did you hear me Kyra? I am telling you that there are dark forces pursuing your family."

"You knew my mother was in danger?" Kyra asked as she contemplated the wizard's words.

"No, I did not." Cyrus shook his head. "I believe these creatures are after a specific artifact, a dagger with three rubies in its hilt to be precise. It is a powerful relic, and can be put to devastating use if it falls into the wrong hands. I had believed this dagger to be lost after we rescued your mother from the vampire's lair. However, it seems I had been mistaken. I now believe that your mother had this dagger all along, and that is what they seek."

"I never saw such a dagger," Kyra said quickly. "Why would she take it?"

Cyrus pouted out his lower lip and tugged gently on his beard with his left hand.

"Come sit down. I will tell you what I know, and then you and I will decide how to deal with the forces that are stalking you."

"No." Kyra looked into the old wizard's eyes and folded her arms over her chest. "I want you to teach me how to kill them. Then I will track every last one of them down, and destroy them for what they did to my mother."

Cyrus looked at her for a moment, before finally nodding his agreement. "Until you are ready, you must stay within the walls of

Kuldiga Academy. I do not think anyone will venture here, for there are far too many masters of sorcery that could defend you. When you are ready, I will help you vanquish this enemy."

"Do you know where we can find it?" Kyra asked.

"I have only some clues, but nothing certain yet. I am confident we can figure it out together."

CHAPTER TWELVE

Cyrus stepped through the portal, his skin adjusting quickly to the cold, humid air in the cave. He conjured a small orb of blue light that hovered over his left shoulder to light his way. Moss and algae grew along the inside of the wet rocks that formed the walls of the cave. His feet splashed in the shallow water as it trickled along the floor. He followed the cave around the bend to the left, holding his robes up just a touch so that they would not get soaked from the floor.

He hated coming here. To Cyrus, it showed weakness to ask for help. More than that, he knew the man that he was about to visit was only interested in what Cyrus could do for him. The deals were always cut in the warlock's favor it seemed. Perhaps that was karmic justice for the way Cyrus treated others. The old wizard laughed the notion away. There was no justice of any kind except that created by those with the power to enforce it.

Around the bend the cave opened up into a large chamber. The inside was barren except for a long table made of stone in the center of the room. A pair of iron candle holders flanked either end of the table, standing roughly four feet tall and holding seven candles each. The candles were lit, and burned with a blue fire that, despite the magnitude of the chamber, managed to chase away every shadow.

Cyrus walked to the table and sat down. On the far side of the chamber was a single door made of black stone. It was plain, without decoration or knob. Unknowing adventurers would try to open the door, but that would only result in their death. Cyrus knew better, having been invited here several times before. He sat at the table and gave three slaps on the slab of stone with the palm of his right hand. For a while nothing happened. The chamber remained silent and the door did not move. Then, after a few minutes, the door began to glow, changing from black to blue and then finally disappearing altogether. A man dressed in long black robes walked toward Cyrus.

As the man came closer, Cyrus was able to see the purple trim on the sleeves of the black robes. A long hood hung loosely over the man's face, covering his features. Locks of silver hair poked out from the hood like small snakes. A medallion hung around his neck in the shape of a gleaming triangle of gold enclosing the image of an open eye. A staff of wood appeared in the man's left hand as he closed the remaining distance to the table.

"I do not suppose you have come to tell me that Kyra has pledged her service and loyalty?"

Cyrus shook his head. "As I said before, the girl is headstrong. She is not only extremely talented, but she is wickedly smart, and not easy to convince. Since her mother's murder, she has grown ever more wary and watchful of everyone around her. It will be some time before I can gain her trust."

"The Order of the All-seeing Eye is not concerned with time. Whether it takes three weeks or ten years is irrelevant. The mission must be accomplished. Kyra must join our cause."

Cyrus sat up straight and looked at the warlock, trying to peer through the darkness cast by the man's hood. Even with his magic orb of light, the shadow seemed all but impenetrable, allowing only for faint images and shadows, but nothing distinct to be seen.

"Tell me why the girl is so important to you."

The warlock cackled and leaned heavily upon his staff as he swung his right leg over the seat and then eased himself down. Then he set the staff on the table between them and laced his fingers together as he leaned over to speak with Cyrus.

"A dog does not question its master when it is sent to fetch the fowl."

"You know I am more than a dog," Cyrus said.

The warlock laughed again. "Unless you were to swear fealty to the Order of the All-seeing Eye, there is nothing more for us to discuss. What we want with the girl is our business. You came to us those many years ago to locate items that you were searching for. We agreed upon a price for the information you sought."

"There is another who seeks the dagger," Cyrus said. "Why

didn't you warn me of him?"

"To see the future is like trying to drink from a geyser. No sooner do you stick your face in it, than it shoots much more than you could ever handle straight at you, and just like a geyser it is roiling with danger. We have devised tools to help peer into the future and limit these dangers to ourselves, but there is still room for improvement."

Cyrus shook his head. "Perhaps I would be better off on my own," he said.

The warlock shot his right hand across the table with the speed of lightning and seized Cyrus by the throat, pulling him in close. "You have come in to our circle. You may not leave unless we say you can. Whatever you view as our shortcomings, let me remind you that it was you who came to us for help. No one else could give you the information you sought."

Cyrus calmly reached up and grabbed the warlock's hand, prying it free from his neck and pushing it back as he sat down again.

"You may have me outnumbered, but if you attack me again I will burn you from the inside out. Your brothers may finish me off, but I guarantee I will drag you down to Hammenfein with me."

There was a moment of silence. Neither of them spoke nor blinked for the space of several minutes. Then, the warlock laughed again and tapped a finger on the table.

"I like you," the warlock said. "If you would join our order, not only would you have the information you seek, but you could have so much more."

"Why does that matter to you?" Cyrus asked.

The warlock held up both his hands palms up and shrugged his shoulders.

"It is wise to surround yourself with strong, capable men. Especially when times of war are soon at hand."

"I'm not interested in war, or politics," Cyrus said. "My interest is purely personal."

The warlock held a finger in the air.

"I know what it is you seek. The others know as well. The journey ahead of you will not be an easy one. If you were to join with us, we could add additional power to your cause."

"At what cost?" Cyrus asked.

The warlock slapped the table and drew his hand back slowly.

"I can see now is not the time for negotiating. Perhaps later. Let me offer you a gesture of goodwill, and you can think on the offer to join us for a future conversation."

"What are you suggesting?"

"The man that seeks the dagger you are hunting is a dangerous one. I won't lie, it will serve our order to remove him, as much if not more so than it will serve you. As agreed upon before, you may of course keep the dagger when and if you find it. The man who searches for it is a necromancer. His name is Severin. Have you heard of him?"

Cyrus tapped the table nervously and sighed heavily.

"I know him." The short answer was terse and dripping with anger, something that the warlock did not miss.

"An old friend of yours then?"

Cyrus shook his head slowly. "I made a deal with him many years ago. He reneged on his part of the deal and left my rump swinging in the wind. I had my suspicions that he might be involved; I was hoping that I was incorrect."

The warlock reached down under the table and pulled up a small, silver ring a moment later.

"If you know Severin, then you know he will not to be an easy foe to conquer. You will need the girl, and you will need her dragon. If any of the other masters were to catch wind of what you are doing..."

Cyrus nodded his head when the warlock's words trailed off into nothing.

"The girl will be easy to convince on this one. I can see the hunger for revenge in her eyes. As for keeping the secret, she will be good at that as well. So far she has managed to hide her dragon from all at the Academy. I'm sure if I offer her the chance to avenge her mother, she will keep quiet about it rather than lose the opportunity."

The warlock nodded and rose to his feet. He set the ring down on the table in front of Cyrus and pointed to it.

"In order to hunt the necromancer, you will have to teach the girl how to recognize magical presences. As she has vampire blood within her veins, it is an ability she already possesses. You need only unlock it. The danger in doing so, of course, is that as she hones her skill, she will recognize the dark magic within you. Wear this ring and it will help dull her senses to what you are."

Cyrus took the ring and examined it. It was a simple silver band with a small emerald set into it. He slipped it over his right ring finger and then rose from the table to leave.

"One more thing, Cyrus," the warlock said. "If for some reason she were to decide to disclose anything about hunting Severin, you will have to find a way to silence her."

Cyrus nodded knowingly. "If she were to double-cross me, then I will expose her dragon. That simple threat ought to be enough to seal her mouth. Still, I am confident enough she will be more than eager to avenge her mother. She will keep the secret."

*****

With her time off from class, Kyra spent every waking minute with the dragon. When she had returned to the aspenwood after the mysterious near-encounter with whatever force had spooked Njar, the satyr had been waiting with a wonderful surprise. The aspen sapling she had chosen had been transformed into a beautiful staff with a carved dragon's head set into the top. Njar had delivered it and the sapling's small stump to Viverandon where satyr craftsmen had worked a marvelous transformation in the few hours she had been gone.

In the days and weeks that followed, Kyra took her staff every time she and Leatherback went hunting for his meals following her sessions with Cyrus, and left it with him in the evenings. Despite the doubt Njar had expressed about the power it would have in warding off Nagar's Blight, Kyra couldn't help feeling that she was in possession of a vital protection as she carried the aspenwood staff beyond the bounds of the glade.

As they hunted and played, Njar was there each time too, though he gave them much more freedom than he had the first day. He still followed them of course, but not as closely, and his countenance became much softer than it had been right after Leatherback had hatched. Kyra had asked Njar if he had ever discovered what had been following them the other day, but the satyr would only cryptically answer that all was handled.

Kyra and Leatherback walked along the stream searching for

rabbits or squirrels. When they came to a deep eddy in the stream, Leatherback moved over to the water and thrust his head deep into the liquid, splashing water all about. He came up with a rather large trout nearly the length of Kyra's forearm. He tossed it up in the air and then swallowed it down his gullet. Kyra laughed and moved to pet Leatherback. The brown scales had already formed along his entire body now. Whatever the satyr was doing to accelerate the dragon's growth, it was magnificently quick. Leatherback was now almost the same height as a small horse. The top of his back just a few inches below Kyra's shoulder line. The horns along his forehead were beginning to grow out as well. There were several straight horns that protruded out slightly backward over his neck, and there were two horns that curled out from the sides of his head like sharp hooks.

As with his physical appearance, Leatherback was maturing in other ways also. He could now produce a blue flame and sustain it for a few seconds. Mostly he shot balls of fire into the air to impress Kyra. Leatherback's eyes seemed to sparkle when Kyra laughed and clapped after each fireball. They spent as much time interacting with each other as they did hunting for food. Upon returning to the glade, Kyra pulled her book out and began to read to Leatherback again.

Njar sat near the edge of the glade, resting his back upon a large aspen as he listened to the story as well. As with the other days previous, Kyra read two chapters before closing the book and putting it away. Leatherback had curled beside her for the reading, and now slid his large head into her lap again, careful not to poke her with his horns. Kyra leaned down and kissed the top of Leatherback's head as she pet his neck.

"You are a good listener, Leatherback."

Leatherback turned his head to her and she could have sworn that he was smiling at her. His eyes burned into hers as though he had something to tell, but no words were spoken between them. After a while Kyra rose up and went to return to the Academy. She looked up at the darkening sky and saw the first star in the night sky.

Leatherback looked up as well and roared when he saw the star.

Kyra looked back at the Dragon smiled.

"Do you know the story of how the stars came about?" Kyra asked.

Leatherback looked at her intently as if to say he did not and was waiting for the story.

Kyra dismissed the idea of creating the portal and went back to Leatherback, sitting beside him and curling up next to him. Leatherback in turn curled his tail and neck around her and stretched his right wing over her back to keep her warm in the cool evening.

"My mother used to tell me a story when I was little. She said there was an ancient story of how the stars came to be. If you like, I could tell that story to you."

Leatherback growled in a high pitch, something she had learned to take as an affirmative answer to a question.

"Very well. Many years ago, before recorded history, the world enjoyed a time when there was no night. The sun gave its warm light to the world during the day, and when the sun went to sleep, the world was bathed in beautiful shades of pink, orange, red, and even purple, like a grand sunset which lasted until the sun awoke.

"During this magical era, in a village that time has since long forgotten, there lived a young boy named Aiden. Aiden loved to play. He would run around the village chasing other little boys. He also loved to climb trees and big rocks. He would climb up high and then jump off, pretending to fly through the air like a Dragon.

"Aiden was a smart, curious boy who loved adventure. He often explored the area around the village, carrying his wooden sword that his father had made for him. One day, while Aiden was exploring in the grassy meadow near the village, he found a Skyte."

Kyra looked down at Leatherback and set a hand upon the back of his neck.

"You know what a Skyte is, right? It's a kind of small Dragon, like you, but small enough to fit in the palm of a human's hand."

Leatherback purred and nuzzled its head against her.

Kyra smiled and then continued, "As I was saying, Aiden found a Skyte basking in the sun. Most boys would have been afraid, but not Aiden. He was brave. He walked right up to the Skyte and roared at it, holding his sword high over his head.

"Most Skytes would have flown away, but not this one. The

fearless little Dragon reared back onto its hind legs, puffed smoke through its nose and beat his small wings furiously. The two of them looked like great warrior's about to do battle, with Aiden standing over the Skyte growling and the little Dragon puffing smoke and hissing fire.

"Aiden shouted at the Skyte, 'protect yourself,' and then swung his sword over the Skyte's head. The Skyte launched into the air and blew a ring of smoke into Aiden's face. Aiden coughed and dropped his sword on the ground, stumbling backward a few steps, sputtering and hacking at the thick smoke. Aiden flailed his arms and fell to the ground.

"The Skyte was confused, for it had not meant to hurt the little boy. It had only blown the smoke to play with him. The Skyte flew down and landed on the boy's chest. Aiden was still and quiet. The Skyte crawled up slowly toward Aiden's face and sniffed.

"Suddenly, Aiden sprang up and caught the Skyte by rolling over, entrapping the little Dragon on its back. Aiden pinched the dragon's mouth shut and playfully tickled it saying, 'I got you,' and laughed. The two of them became fast friends. Aiden took the Skyte home, and with the help of his parents made a small bed for it in a basket. They hunted and played together every day from then on, becoming inseparable friends. Now, usually, Skytes and children don't become friends. Most little boys during this time would never accept a Dragon in their home, but Aiden was different. He had a heart big enough to share his home with all. Aiden named the Skyte Boba.

"Some of the adults in the village tried to make Aiden take Boba back to the wild. Aiden always refused, telling them that every boy should be so lucky as to have a dragon for a friend, for there were many things that dragons can do that boys cannot.

"Boba was happy too, for he had never had a friend as nice as Aiden, to give him a bed and food. Boba felt lucky to have Aiden as his friend and wished every day could last forever so they could always play together.

"However, things never remain the same. One evening, after a particularly long day of playing, the sun went down, and a dark shadow of night fell upon the land for the first time. It was a darkness unlike anything that had ever been known before. It was hard to see anything at all. Worst of all, when morning came, the sun did not rise in the sky, and the world stayed dark.

"It was too dark for Aiden and Boba to play. It was too dark for them to climb. It was too dark for them to do anything. They sat in the house, sad that they could not play anymore. Then Aiden had an idea. He thought, 'maybe if somebody could fly high enough in the sky, they could find the sun and bring it back.'

"Boba liked the idea, but he cautioned Aiden that they would have to find somebody very, very strong to fly so high that they could find the sun."

Leatherback suddenly rose his head and looked at her, interrupting the story.

"You will be able to speak soon," Njar called out from across the Glade.

Leatherback glanced at the black furred satyr and then looked back to Kyra with questioning eyes. He opened his mouth, but no words came out. Instead, only a series of gurgling sounds escaped his mouth. Kyra laughed and patted him on the head.

"Don't worry, Leatherback, you will speak soon enough. Shall I continue?" Kyra asked.

Leatherback again offered his high-pitched growl and then nestled his head firmly in her lap and began to purr softly. Kyra settled in again and looked up at the sky as she continued the story.

"Aiden and Boba set out to find somebody strong enough to fly and find the sun. First they found a Robin and told him of their plan. They asked him to fly to the sun. The Robin flew high into the sky, but soon returned. He was too weak and slow to fly high enough to find the sun.

"Aiden and Boba continued on to find a faster bird. When they found a sparrow, they asked him if he could fly high to see the sun, and the sparrow promised he would try his best. He launched into the air, flying quickly up, up, looping and swooping through the sky, but it soon returned, exhausted from its flight. The sparrow said that he was not smart enough to find his way in the darkness, and therefore could not fly above the night to find the sun.

"Aiden and Boba set out to find a bird that was both fast and smart and they soon found in owl. They asked him to fly above the night to find the sun so that the light would return to the world. The owl scoffed and laughed at them, asking who would want the light, for owls love to fly in the dark of night.

"Seeing that the owl was smart, but not wise, they set out again to find a different bird. Soon they found a great raven. The raven agreed to try. He spread his large, black wings and soared off into the darkness. Up and up he flew, but soon his wings were too tired and he returned back to the ground, exhausted. He was just not strong enough to fly above the night and find the sun.

"So Aiden and Boba set off to find a bird that was fast, smart, and strong enough to fly above the night and find the sun. Soon they found a great eagle. The mighty eagle spread its wings and gloriously declared that it would end the night. The eagle launched into the air, his wings beating the air so fiercely that Aiden and Boba had to shield their faces from the breeze the eagle's wings created. The eagle flew high into the night and disappeared for a long time. Aiden and Boba were sure that the Eagle would finally find the sun and bring back the light, but a little while later the Eagle returned, exhausted from his flight. He told them that he had flown to the top of the night, but could not get through it to find the sun.

"Aiden and Boba began to lose hope. It seemed now that the world was doomed to continue on in the eternal shadow of night. They returned home, tired from the long journey. The next morning Aiden did not wake up. His mother and father tried to wake him, but his eyes would not open. Boba even blew fire and roared, and tried to tickle Aiden's stomach, but Aiden still slept.

"Boba flew out from the hut quickly to find the medicine man. He brought him back, and the medicine man checked Aiden thoroughly. The medicine man said Aiden had fallen under the spell of night. The only cure would be to find the sun and bring it back.

"Boba cried for the first time in his life. There was no one strong enough to find the sun. He could not bear the thought of his friend never waking up to play with him again. Boba left the hut and looked up to the sky. The darkness was so daunting, but he knew that Aiden needed a friend now more than ever. Boba wiggled his tail, flexed his legs as he stretched his wings, and steeled his nerves. He wasn't just any friend, Boba was a Dragon! Boba jumped into the air and beat his wings, flying up and up, leaving the village far below. The higher he flew, the more tired his wings became, but Boba did not stop. He pushed higher until finally he reached the black blanket that covered the world.

"It was not at all like Boba had expected. He thought that the night was a large, black cloud that he could fly through, but it wasn't. Instead, there was a thick ceiling. Boba clawed at it and blew fire until he managed to rip a small hole in the blackness. White light poured through and blinded Bob. The light was so intense that he had to return to the village and rest. When Boba landed, the medicine man was there to give him water and food to help him recover his energy. The medicine man then pointed to the sky and showed Boba that the light was bright enough to reach them, but it was not enough to wake Aiden.

"Boba decided that perhaps he would not be able to find the sun, but maybe if he made more small lights in the sky, Aiden would wake. Off he launched back into the sky, flying toward the ceiling of night. He furiously tore a second hole in the night, and again a bright, white light burst through. Boba worked endlessly tearing holes, then flying back down to see if Aiden had woken. But no matter how many lights appeared in the sky, Aiden would not wake up. The new lights just weren't bright enough. Boba resolved to tear a hole in the night big enough for him to crawl through and find the sun. Up and up he flew until he again reached the ceiling of darkness and clawed at it ferociously and blasted it with fire. His muscles ached and his wings could barely move, but he did not stop. He knew he had to help his friend. At last he burrowed through and wiggled out above the night.

"The light was so glorious, Boba almost forgot what he had come for. Almost.

"He flew on until he found the sun. He passed over the jet wall of night until he came to a crystaline land, and eventually found the sun resting upon a great cloud of gold. Boba told the sun what had happened to Aiden and asked him to come back. Boba could barely speak he was so tired, and his wings only faintly beat. The Skyte fell and landed on the thick, golden cloud. His weary body sank into the mist partly, floating just enough that he did not fall through. He lifted his head to the sun and tried to repeat his request, but his words would not come. He then looked back to the covering of night, but he was too tired to even crawl back to the hole and return to the village.

"When the sun saw that the little dragon had spent all of his strength, he scooped up the little Skyte in his warm, golden hands. The sun said the little boy was lucky to have such a friend, and was so touched by Boba's sacrifice that he decided to chase away the night. His warm, bright light once again swept through the world. Then, the sun created the moon where Boba had clawed through the night to find him, and set Boba down on the silvery surface. Boba was far too weak to return to the village, so he closed his eyes and slept on the moon. The sun then came down to the village to wake Aiden. When Aiden awoke, his family and all the other villagers were so happy they started dancing and singing. None of them even noticed that Boba had not returned. Just as the sun was about to leave, Aiden asked where Boba was.

"The sun told Aiden that Boba had spent all of his strength and could not come down. The sun reached out to hug Aiden close, and whispered so that only the boy could hear. He told him that he had created a new home for Boba where he could fly forever and play all the time. The sun said that now the Skyte was a Moon Dragon. The sun said that in honor of Boba's sacrifice for Aiden, each time he would go down to sleep, the blanket of night would come back to cover the world. But this time Aiden would see the many holes Boba had ripped in the blanket of night to bring the light back to his friend. The sun told Aiden that these small holes would be called stars. He then said the biggest light of all is the moon, and that if he were to look closely, Aiden would see Boba curled up, looking down upon him as he gave light to the whole world during the night. Aiden smiled when he heard that Boba the Moon Dragon would rule the night until the sun came back each morning to rule the day. Never again would the world be cast into total darkness.

"The sun returned back into its place and left Aiden in his village. From that day on, the world has been blessed to have the sun shining during the day, and the light of the moon and stars during the night. Even now, if the moon is full, you can still see Boba watching over us, making our world a little brighter."

Kyra reached down and gently raised Leatherback's head so that she could look into his eyes. She smiled warmly as she could feel his body tensing in anticipation.

"Don't worry Leatherback," Kyra said. "If you ever look up

and can't see the Moon Dragon, do not fear, for he has not abandoned us. My mother said that those nights are magical. She said that whenever the moon is dark and missing from the sky, it's a special night when Boba can return to play with Aiden. Somewhere they are still climbing, exploring, and having as much fun as two best friends can."

Leatherback purred loudly and nuzzled its snout gently against Kyra's nose. She laughed and then rose to her feet as she patted the dragon good night. She waved to the satyr chief who smiled and waved back at her, and then disappeared through the portal back to her room at the Academy.

CHAPTER THIRTEEN

After the short break Cyrus had given her, he began a new program of instruction, one that involved using all of her sense to try and detect magical energy. This proved to be more challenging for Kyra than the previous regimen. In lessons that involved battle, Cyrus was fairly straightforward in his training. He would present a challenge or an obstacle and ask her to defeat it. Usually he would present the monster first and the information about its weaknesses after, and Kyra excelled in these tasks. They had long ago moved on from imps and had tackled scamps, giant spiders, and small wyverns. But the hours spent honing her ability to sense magic left her feeling agitated.

Her mental focus was consumed by two things: caring for Leatherback, and thoughts of finding her mother's murderer. For her it was nearly impossible to clear those things from her mind for a task that did not produce immediate, devastating results like the creature battles. Cyrus constantly chided her for not clearing her mind properly, and often asked what she could possibly be day dreaming about, but Kyra kept her mouth shut.

This day started like any other. Kyra met Cyrus in the classroom and immediately she was set to her warm-up spells. She ran through several different wards, ranging from minor shields that would block a specific area of the body, all the way up to large, transparent shells that would encase her entire being and protect her for several minutes while allowing her the ability to continue to cast other spells.

After that, Cyrus closed the door and put a magical lock on it, as he always did. He conjured several orbs and set them hovering in the air in the classroom.

"Close your eyes, and fire when I tell you."

Kyra did as she was told, this time using her ears to sense where the magical objects were. The orbs spun around her. She waited for the signal, summoning a series of lightning bolt spells in her hands that crackled and popped as she held her palms facing each other to concentrate the energy. When Cyrus gave the signal, she opened her eyes and sent all three bolts of lightning simultaneously. One went to the front of the classroom, striking its target and destroying the ball. The other two arced around her, one striking up near the ceiling and destroying a ball there while the third and final bolt went low between the desks to destroy the remaining ball.

It was the first time she had successfully located all three orbs, and Cyrus complimented her, but Kyra was tired of this exercise. She wanted to go after the creature that had killed her mother, and so far she was no closer to that than she had been before she talked with Cyrus about this very thing. Her patience was running low. More than that, she had a dragon that now stood twenty feet tall and was nearly thirty-five feet long, thanks to the satyr chief's magic accelerating his growth. While Kyra wasted her time repeating the same old training exercises that she did every day, Leatherback was learning to fly.

He wasn't very good at it yet, but he could manage to glide twice his body length, which Njar said was quite a feat for his extremely young age. Kyra knew the satyr was right, for all the dragons she had read about took years before they could learn to fly. The satyr had explained that since the Middle Kingdom was located extremely close to the heart of the world, the place where the sacred seed was hidden from which sprang all life upon Terramyr, he was able to focus the magic in such a way that the dragon would grow over the next couple of years to full maturity rather than over decades.

If only she knew where this mysterious creature that had attacked her mother was hiding. With the dragon on her side, surely she was more than ready to face it now.

Something stung her backside and she wheeled around to look at Cyrus. The old wizard had an arched eyebrow and pointed to the floor at her feet.

"You are losing focus again," he said. "Take care of the imp."

Another imp. Kyra rolled her eyes and hardly had to muster

any effort whatsoever to conjure a ball of ice from nothing to encase the imp. To make her point she called down a flurry of lightning bolts that destroyed the sphere of ice and obliterated the creature within.

"I am ready for more," she said.

Cyrus nodded and snapped his fingers. Kyra heard a rushing sound as wind picked up within the room, sweeping the desks off to the sides. A black fog rolled in and the floor dropped out from beneath her. She fell into a black abyss that swallowed her whole. The air was hot and humid, causing her to sweat almost immediately. When she finally felt a solid surface beneath her feet again she was nowhere near the classroom she had started in.

"Very well," Cyrus called from the darkness. "Let's conjure forth something a little more ambitious."

There was something in Cyrus' voice that unnerved Kyra. She wasn't sure what it was, but she definitely felt uncomfortable. The darkness swirled around her, unyielding in its attack on her senses. The fog was so thick that it not only hampered her vision but it dampened her hearing as well. Something moved in the shadows, breathing heavily and walking with labored, lumbering steps that shook the ground every time its massive foot fell. Something made a scraping sound off to her left, as if a large, iron ball of spikes was being dragged across stone.

This time she did not wait for a signal from the old wizard. She put up her large ward that encased her entire body. Next she summoned forth four orbs of light and put them in orbit over her head. The rays of white and yellow light managed to penetrate the darkness for a few feet around her, but they did not defeat the shadows. Something shimmered in the distance, just beyond the reach of her magical light. It flashed a few times and then was gone, disappearing further into the black fog. Kyra called forth a wind to sweep away the fog, but all it did was stir it up. Black vapors swirled around her as one of her magical lights was swallowed and overtaken by the darkness.

A terrible screech sounded from behind her. It was like claws on glass, high in pitch, yet shrill; holding the promise of something sharp and ferocious. She turned around and directed a column of fire ten yards in front of her. Again she saw a quick flash, a shimmer in the darkness. Could it be scales? Was she to fight a dragon? Surely many people come to Kuldiga Academy to learn how to fight dragons, but she doubted that Cyrus had the power to summon one, especially given what Njar had told her about the curse.

No, the indistinct shimmer must have been something else. Eyes perhaps. That certainly made more sense. Any number of creatures have eyes that shine similar to what she had just seen. Something tapped stone behind her. She whirled around again but this time she had no time to create a spell. A large beast standing upright on massive hind legs lunged toward her. Luckily, Kyra's ward held and the beast was deflected by her protective shell. The creature reeled backward and screamed loudly, revealing a mouth filled with fangs the size of her fingers. Its face could almost pass for that of a large human, except that it was covered with fur.

The beast stepped in close and tested her shell with a finger. Kyra studied the monster, noting that it was nearly humanoid in shape, somewhat like a great ape. It stood roughly nine feet tall, with arms and legs as thick as tree trunks. Each hand had two fingers and a thumb tipped with sharp, curved claws. The torso was extremely blocky and covered with a dark gray fur, but as solid as if the animal had been made out of boulders. There were no ears that she could see upon the creature's head, but it had three eyes that watched her every move.

Just then the creature rotated slightly as his body jerked to the side and something slammed into the shell down and toward her left. Kyra just barely caught a glimpse of the massive tail as its spikes clashed against her protective shell and then scraped back across the stone. Nothing she had ever heard or read about fit the description of what she saw in front of her. Her shell held against the tail's assault, but the vibration she felt from the strike was enough to get her refocused on the fight at hand.

The beast cocked its arm back as a human might before launching a punch, then brought it forward with tremendous force, striking with its fist against the shell. Kyra jumped back as a small fracture appeared in the translucent shell, leaking a golden light through the crack. She knew if she did not think of something, she was going to fail this exercise.

Kyra summoned forth a spear made of ice and magically hurled it at the beast. With unnatural speed, the monster turned aside and allowed the spear to sail past. It then turned back and growled with a voice so loud that it shook the shell around Kyra and made her chest vibrate from within. As she watched thin lines of spittle drip from the beast's fangs, she felt the urge to scream and cower in fear.

The young sorceress did not let it stop her. She gathered her courage and summoned forth another column of fire, just under the monster's feet. The flames rose up and singed the creature's hair, but the spell did little to deter the creature. The monster leapt up out of the flames and landed on the shell that protected Kyra. As the ward started to crack, she heard many popping sounds and saw that little tendrils of energy were shooting off in every direction as the magic began to unravel. Tiny fissures tore through the shell, informing Kyra that she had only moments left before the beast could get her.

She knew that if she wanted to find her mother's killer, she could not admit defeat to Cyrus now. If she asked him for help, there was no telling how long it would be before she was able to avenge her mother's murder.

The sorceress in training acted on impulse rather than wisdom, trusting instincts to know what to do. She darted out to the right, purposefully destroying the already fractured ward spell to create a directional blast at the same time. The explosion was near deafening, and the flash of light that came from the giant bolt of lightning she called forth out of the ground blinded and deafened her momentarily. She heard the beast howl as it was thrown to the side. She could hear the howling grow distant as the creature's body was flung upward from where the shell had been. A few seconds later there was a large crash as the monster landed several yards away from her.

Assuming that she only had a second or two before the beast regained its senses, she turned and ran toward where it had landed. Her three remaining orbs of light hovered over her, following her as she sprinted through the darkness. The creature roared again, somewhat incoherently, but strong enough that Kyra took the threat seriously.

With a flick of her left wrist she cast the three orbs of light at the creature. They slammed into his face and pummeled it. The gargantuan beast swatted at its own face, clawing and ripping at the orbs of light, trying to get them off. The distraction was exactly what Kyra was hoping for. She called forth several large spears of ice over the beast's body and dropped them down. Two of them missed, but three others struck their target. One drove through the beast's left thigh and the other two pierced its torso. Kyra jumped into the air and called forth a ball of lightning between her hands. She came down on the beast's chest, driving the ball of lightning into its face before tucking into a roll and escaping just before the beast swatted at her with its claws. The beast writhed and howled on the ground in pain, but Kyra was not done yet.

Remembering how she had defeated the ghoul at the dragon's nest, she called forth a tornado and dropped it down on the beast. The wind swirled furiously, sucking in the black vapors from the area around her. Next she brought a column of fire down from the sky into the center of the tornado. The beast spun slowly, sliding across the stone and grasping with its claws to try and regain control. When the column of fire drove through the monster, the fight was over. The beast let out one final howl and then collapsed inward on itself as the tornado pulled it in and crushed its now lifeless body.

In the distance, Kyra could hear slow clapping. A moment later she found herself back in the classroom, standing in the middle of the floor with Cyrus near the door of the room. The old wizard was smiling ever so slightly and continuing to clap. Kyra breathed heavily and moved to lean upon a nearby desk to catch her breath.

"I have never seen someone so young defeat the Baukin before. In fact, I would wager most of the recent graduates from Kuldiga Academy could not defeat such a creature."

Kyra, still breathing heavily from the exertion, nodded her appreciation of the compliment. She did not collapse as she had after the fight with the creature at the dragon's nest, but she could feel that she had used much of her energy in the fight. Still, she wanted to show strength to the wizard. She was tired of training, she wanted the real fight. Surely if she was half as good as he said she was, then she should be ready. She pressed off from the desk and forced her burning lungs to make do with shorter, even-paced breaths.

"So when do we leave?" Kyra asked.

Cyrus stopped clapping and looked at her, confused.

"Leave?" He shook his head and folded his arms. "We aren't going anywhere."

Kyra's face flushed and she could feel the anger rising within her.

"Surely the thing that killed my mother was not more powerful than this thing," she said.

Cyrus pointed at her and shook his head in disbelief.

"You think your mother would fall to this? This is not the same being that broke into your home and killed her. This creature didn't even have any magical powers. It had a natural resistance to magic, and an inordinate amount of strength, but this was no demon. It is going to take months of training before you are ready."

Kyra wanted to argue. No, she wanted to fight. Perhaps the old man was playing it safe because he was scared. There was a part of the young apprentice that wanted to test her strength against the wizard and see who came out on top. Luckily, the rational part of her brain took over as she remembered her mother's words. Kyra chose quiet acquiescence and the appearance of submission. She forced the anger out and nodded her head. She would continue with this day's lesson, that way Cyrus would have no reason to watch her or restrict her activities. Then, when she was free for the day, she would take Leatherback and see if they could hunt down clues of their own.

After the apprentice had calmed down, Cyrus motioned to the books on the far shelf near the desk.

"Go and pull the book entitled *Masters of Shadow* and use the index to find the section on what is called a shade. The rest of today will be spent studying that creature. You are not ready to fight it yet, but I believe that is what broke into your mother's home."

Kyra turned, hiding her smile as she walked away from the wizard toward the bookshelf. Her mother had been right, the appearance of submission would give her the opportunity she needed to make her own choices. She hungrily pulled the book down from the shelf and took it to the nearest desk. She flipped through the pages until she found the section she had been instructed to read. Glancing at where the section began and ended, she noted that there were nearly one hundred pages about this creature. She flipped through from the back of the section toward the front to get an idea of what she would be reading. She stopped when she saw a page with a subtitle that read 'Companions' and had a very strange picture sketched next to it. It wasn't exactly the same, but then again she wasn't sure that any pencil rendering could provide an accurate depiction of the creature it purported to show. There on the page before her she saw the ethereal creature she had fought in the dragon's nest. Now she was more certain than ever that it had not come for the egg; it had come for her. It was called a Bibkin Wraith and was said to be a servant of the creature known as a Shade.

"Read it from the beginning," Cyrus chastised as he moved toward his desk. "You can't just start a subject in the middle."

Kyra nodded and flipped the pages to the beginning of the section, not wanting to give the old wizard any reason to question her curiosity about the strange wraith.

CHAPTER FOURTEEN

In the late afternoon when she had finished her reading assignments that Cyrus had given her, Kyra snuck back to the classroom to take the book about shades. She slipped it into her satchel between the other books that she normally took to read to Leatherback. She wasn't quite sure how she was going to deal with Njar just yet. If Cyrus wasn't of the opinion that Kyra was ready for the shade, then Njar would be three times more defensive about the idea. Kyra wasn't sure how she would escape the satyr's scrutiny, but she knew she would think of something.

She closed the satchel and opened the portal. She could see the satyr chief sitting near Leatherback on the ground, playing his panpipes. She moved through the portal, arriving just a few feet away from Leatherback.

The dragon rose to stand, towering over her now as he stood nearly twenty feet at the shoulder. His horns had grown tremendously, and had she not known him from the time he had hatched, she might have mistaken him for a fearsome beast. But she knew better.

The dragon lowered its head down toward her and allowed her to pet him between the eyes. It softly nuzzled its snout against her body and then dropped back down to the ground with a *tha-WUMP!* The entire glade shook and the aspen trees vibrated as the massive creature flopped onto the ground. Kyra nearly lost her balance, but was able to reach out and steady herself on one of Leatherback's horns.

The satyr chief rose to his feet and moved around Leatherback's large head to hand Kyra her staff.

"He has received the magic well," the satyr said. "He is roughly a third of the size he will be when he is fully mature."

Kyra looked at Leatherback in astonishment. If he was only a third as big as he would be eventually, then he would be nearly one hundred and forty feet long. He would tower over the trees in the glade and be a veritable moving fortress of teeth and fire. Now, for the first time, she understood Njar's apprehension. Any creature of that size could destroy entire settlements and be nearly unstoppable. Of course, Kyra knew from her books how large dragons could become, but it was another thing entirely to see his sheer size in person and try to picture him three times larger than what she saw in front of her. As it was now, he could swallow her in one bite if he wanted to, just as he used to do to the squirrels they had hunted together.

Leatherback must have sensed her wonderment, for he cocked his head so that his eye could look at her more directly, and he smiled at her with his slightly parted lips and kind eyes. As Kyra looked upon him she knew that he would never hurt her, or anyone else. She patted his head again and then turned to speak with Njar.

"I will need to stop accelerating his growth for a short while," the satyr said.

"I thought you said it was better for him if he grew as fast as possible?"

The satyr chief nodded his head and shrugged sheepishly.

"The truth is I'm tired. To sustain that kind of magic, even here in this grove of sacred aspens, a tremendous effort is required. For now I need to scale back my efforts. I can of course continue to augment the grove to ensure that the curse does not come within this area, but it will be a few weeks before I can return to helping him grow faster. Still, as it is, I believe he has made tremendous progress. He shows no sign of the taint, and he is able to hunt with you for extended periods of time outside the grove. Truly it is a wonder."

Kyra had a question she wanted to ask, but she did not want the satyr to catch any hint of why she was asking it. She had to be careful to hide her excitement. She took a couple of slow breaths to calm her nerves and slow her beating pulse, leaning her staff against one of Leatherback's large horns and using both palms to rub a spot between his eyes that he particularly liked. Then she turned to Njar and smiled.

"You will stay here with him, right?" Phrasing it this way, rather than asking if he was leaving out right, seemed the safer approach.

The satyr shook his head. "I will stay until nightfall. After you leave, I'll return to my village. It's just for one night. He will be safe here in the grove until I return in the morning." He smiled reassuringly and patted her on the shoulder. "He has already hunted today. I guess he couldn't wait to sate his hunger, so I rode him and we found three elk. It likely won't hold him for very long, but he'll probably last through the night on that."

Kyra's mouth fell open and she grabbed the satyr's hand in hers and nearly jumped with excitement.

"You rode him?" The satyr opened his mouth to speak, but Kyra did not give him the chance to answer. "He flew? I mean, he actually flew and you could ride him?"

Gesturing toward Leatherback Njar suggested, "How about you go and see for yourself." The satyr smiled and gently pushed her toward Leatherback.

Kyra turned around to see Leatherback was smiling and purring softly.

"When were you going to tell me you could fly?"

Leatherback emitted that soft, high-pitched squeak that Kyra had once categorized as a growl. He still couldn't talk, but she could tell he was excited to share this with her.

"If you sit on his neck just behind his horns, you can hold them for support," Njar advised.

Kyra didn't need to be told twice. Snatching up her staff, she ran over and jumped onto Leatherback's neck. After sliding the staff between a few of the top horns which grew like a crown at the back of his head, she reached up and grabbed the two horns closest to her, and a moment later, the large dragon leapt into the air, climbing high into the sky above the grove.

Kyra looked down and watched the world fall away from her. The satyr shrank to the size of a bottle and then the grove became the size of a rock. A few moments later he disappeared entirely as Leatherback took her high into the clouds where the air was thin and cold. She laughed and smiled, screaming his name and shouting for joy. Leatherback stretched his great wings, soaring through the air, obviously every bit as delighted as she was given his loud and reverberating purr. The two of them circled around in the sky above the clouds. The thick blanket of clouds that shrouded them from the ground below silenced any fears of being discovered. How far they flew, she had no way of knowing. All she knew was that she was having the time of her life. She looked off to the north and saw the far horizon there. She wondered how far Leatherback could fly now.

Was he capable of taking her to the northern lands, escaping both his curse and her prearranged fate?

For a moment she seriously considered instructing him to do just that, but her mother's memory was forefront in her mind and overrode even her desire for freedom. First, she would hunt the shade. Once it was dead, they would fly north.

For the moment she pushed the thoughts of revenge out of her mind, and went back to enjoying the cold breeze enveloping her and the exhilarating sensation of gliding through the clouds. She and Leatherback flew for a long time before the dragon finally glided gently back down to the glade and set her on the grass. He roared triumphantly and blew a great column of blue fire into the air while she and the satyr both clapped for him and his achievement.

"I should note," the satyr began, "that it is normally years before a dragon can learn to fly." Kyra nodded her head silently as tears of happiness for her friend fell down her face. "I would say his achievement has earned him a double portion of reading today, wouldn't you?"

Kyra smiled wide and pulled the book out of her satchel. "I believe it does. With the double portion of reading today, that is four chapters. That means we will finish this book today and know what has become of our dear dragon friend, Gorliad. Shall we get to it then?"

Leatherback let out a high-pitched screech and curled into a ball on the ground. Kyra stepped over the edge of his tail and nestled into his body as he craned his head around and set it next to her on the ground, for it was now far too large to ever lay on her lap again.

"All right, let us see what has become of our friend Gorliad," she said as she opened the book. They spent the rest of the afternoon reading together in the grove. Kyra managed to finish reading the book just a few minutes after the sun dipped below the western horizon and the first stars appeared in the sky. As she closed the book, Kyra turned and leaned down next to Leatherback's right ear and whispered into it, then she rose to her feet and opened the portal back to Kuldiga Academy.

Njar motioned for her to wait for a moment. "What did you say to him?"

Kyra looked up to the sky and pointed to where the moon should be. "I was just reminding him that on moonless nights both Aiden and Boba play together." She felt bad for lying to the satyr, but she knew she had to if she was to have any chance of coming back tonight without him knowing.

"That was a good story too," Njar said. "Not as good as this book that we just finished today, but good nonetheless. I think the story of the Moon-Dragon has a lot of parallels with you and your dragon. I don't want to jinx anything, but I do believe we have a real chance of getting him out of here before the curse can take him. You are a good friend to him." Kyra saw just the hint of a tear before the satyr turned away and opened his own portal. "I will see you tomorrow," he said, calling out over his shoulder as he walked away. Kyra nodded and walked through her own portal back to her room.

Kyra wasted no time gathering the last of the things that she figured she needed in order to hunt the shade. She slipped into leather trousers, somewhat similar to what the Apprentices of the Sword wore during their training. They were padded along the front with little studs of metal that both held the padding in place and provided a little extra protection from attacks as they had larger, flat pieces of iron just under the fabric to help absorb the shock of battle. Now that she knew Leatherback was capable of flying, she had to find some measure of rope so she could fashion a bridle, or at least something that she could use as reins to hold on in the night. She grabbed a large backpack and took it to the center of the room.

She wove a spell that her mother had taught her as a little girl, shrinking the outside of the bag so that it was no larger than the size of a coin purse, while still magically holding the same amount of volume within the bag. This way she could hang it from her waist while still in Kuldiga Academy, and no one would be the wiser. Moving toward her wardrobe, she grabbed a long set of blue robes and slipped into them, concealing her armored pants. As a final touch, she took her belt with the concealed pocket for her lockpick set out of one of her trunks and secured it around her waist. She paused in front of her mirror, running her hand across the leather for a moment as she remembered that last evening with her mother when they had argued about whether she would be allowed to bring this belt at all. She smiled painfully for a moment as she remembered how her mother had finally relented at the last moment before the trunks had been taken away, advising her to only ever break into the kitchen, as it would be the easiest misdeed to explain away since she was such a slightly built girl to begin with.

With all of her gear prepared, the young apprentice stole into the hallway, checking for any sign of activity. When she was certain the coast was clear, she made her way down the long, straight hall and turned left at the first intersection. She passed two stairways and then went up the third, heading toward the training room where the Apprentices of the Sword often sparred. She went to the door and gave a gentle twist on the knob. It was locked.

Kyra bent down and removed her lock pick set from the small pouch in the back of her waist band. She glanced up and down the hall, straining her eyes and ears to ensure no one was nearby. Then she went to work. She slid the pins in, studying the bumps and ridges as she inserted her tools. She moved them effortlessly, as she had done countless times before while breaking into her father's study.

Unlike many other things Kyra was able to do, lockpicking was not a skill that her mother had taught her. This was one she had learned all on her own, and she was good at it. The tumblers inside the lock clicked into place in less than a minute, allowing the door to open and giving her access to the equipment inside. She moved quickly, knowing that it would be easier to change in her room than risk being caught in the training chamber. She hustled and grabbed what she needed, stuffing it into her bag.

She grabbed a long shirt made of feather mail, a hybrid metal of extremely light weight that was often used during training practices for Apprentices of the Sword. It was nowhere near as strong as mithril, but it was the strongest armor she could find in Kuldiga Academy. More than that, it was by far the lightest. Next she moved and grabbed a padded tunic that looked much like the padded leather pants she was wearing. She stuffed it into her bag and then looked around for rope. She was unable to find any rope, so she left the room in a hurry, careful to lock the door behind her so that no one would suspect anything was missing.

The young apprentice knew where she might find some rope, though she had hoped not to have to go there as it might delay her for quite some time, for Janik was likely still awake. He often worked late into the night before retiring to his own bedchamber, and his office is where the rope was kept.

Kyra wandered through the halls, ducking behind a set of armor on display when she saw two masters walking together across the hall at an intersection in front of her. She held her breath and ducked low behind the metal, watching around from the back to see whether the masters spotted her. Luckily they were too busy talking to even glance in her direction. After they passed, she waited for a few additional moments to ensure that they were far enough away before she left her hiding spot and continued down the hall. As she moved into a hallway on her left she saw a row of several paintings lining the hall.

She paused when she saw a great depiction of a sorcerer battling winged demons on a mountain. The colors were striking overall and the painting was masterfully done. In the painting there was a second man who held an axe and shield and was covered in blood. At the warrior's feet lay four slain demons. She knew this scene very well without even looking down to the brass placard with the title upon it. The man with the battle axe was Janik, and the sorcerer was Cyrus.

This painting, though slightly different from the one hanging in her father's study, was a representation of the time Cyrus and Janik had saved her mother. Kyra's eyes flicked down to the brass plate on the bottom of the frame and read the words etched there in a voice barely above a whisper.

"The rescue of Lady Caspen, wife of Lord Mirnon Caspen." Kyra felt her stomach churn reading the words aloud. Never before had she been so bothered by the fact that her father had not gone to save her mother than she was at this time reading the placard on the painting. The one man who had pledged his life to her mother had left her there to suffer at the hands of a vampire. If her father had been imbued with a single speck of honor, it would be him in the painting. Even if he had to hire help to get the job done, he should have been there leading the charge.

Kyra glanced up and down the hall, making sure no one was around. She was not going to let this disgrace to her mother stand. Her mother was going to be remembered for who she was, and not by her cowardly husband's name.

The young sorceress placed her hand over the brass placard and concentrated. She felt the flush of warmth burn from her shoulder down through her elbow into her hand until finally her fingertips tingled and the faint sound of scraping metal could be heard. The heat in her palm grew intensely, almost to the same degree as when she held fireballs during battle. There was no pain, but she knew her spell was working.

When she pulled her hand away from the painting, she smiled wide and nodded with satisfaction.

"The rescue of lady Zana, daughter of Count Reginald Dimwater," Kyra read aloud from the newly changed brass plate. "That is much better," she whispered to herself. Kyra had never met her grandfather Reginald, but she knew his character from the stories that her mother had told her growing up and knew that he was a man of honor and a man that loved his family. Had he been alive when Kyra's mother was imprisoned by the vampire, he certainly would have led the charge to rescue her. This was a much more fitting way to remember her mother. Her cowardly father had been dropped from the historical record as far as she was concerned.

In that moment she almost felt sorry for Lord Caspen. She didn't hate the man, but neither did she feel love for him. Kyra realized then that over the last several weeks she had been blaming him for her mother's death as well, even if she had not consciously been aware of that fact. She allowed her mind to fully examine her feelings, and she admitted to herself that Lord Caspen should have been the one to die if the home were invaded. It should have been him to rush and fend off the intruder and protect the home, not her mother.

Kyra sighed heavily and began to cry. She knew that she didn't have time to waste, but her emotions wouldn't wait. With each tear that fell down her cheek she purged a portion of the sorrow and guilt she felt for not being there with her mother when the intruder came. Whatever it was this shade wanted, it seemed it was Kyra that he was after. She remembered Cyrus' words about the dagger, but those rang hollow for her and held little meaning. This did not feel like a robbery gone astray. Instead, it felt greatly personal. The more she thought of this, the anger returned and the tears subsided. She turned away from the painting and moved down the hall toward Janik's office.

When she eventually turned down the hall on the second floor where Janik's office was, she paused and peered around the corner. Janik was just leaving for the night, fumbling with his keys in his right hand, jiggling them into the lock and cranking them into place.

"Please don't come this way, please don't come this way," Kyra whispered.

Janik turned and started limping down the hall in her direction.

"Curses!" Kyra ducked back around the corner and glanced about for a place to hide. There was a window facing the courtyard from here, but if she were to open it and go out on the ledge, Janik would likely find her when he went to close and lock said window. Her other option was to dart to a room across the hall and go inside but she had no idea what was in that room. It could be an office or perhaps a dorm filled with apprentices. She glanced back down the hall toward the nearest exit. The hall was far too long for her to sprint down and escape from Janik's gaze before he would be able to round the corner and spot her. The door across from her was her best bet.

She darted across the hall, slipping her lock pick set out. She reached for the doorknob and gave it a small twist. To her great relief it was not locked. She opened the door just a crack. The hinges creaked and squeaked a bit, but not terribly loudly. She peered her head in, preparing a lie in her mind if she were to find anyone inside the room. No one was inside and the room was dark. She slipped in and gently closed the door behind her, making sure to lock it.

There were no windows in the room. The only light came from the space underneath the door. She summoned a small orb of light no bigger than her thumb and sent it a few feet in front of her face so she could find her way through the room.

She saw bookcases and chairs and finally a desk. The desk was large and bulky, the kind where the back of the desk was ornately made and extended all the way down to the floor to cover the feet and legs of whomever sat at it. She hurried around and ducked into the area where the chair tucked under the desk and extinguished her light. By this point she could hear a scraping limp as Janik turned the corner and began to walk down the hall connected to this room.

Pat scrape, Pat scrape, Pat scrape. The noise stopped. Kyra held her breath. The doorknob shook and rattled. Kyra's heart skipped a beat and she curled into the darkness under the desk as far as she could with her back and neck squished right up against the inside of the desk.

Boom boom boom.

"Feberik, are you in there?" Janik called from the other side of the room. Next Kyra heard keys jangling and she closed her eyes, wishing the man would just leave. Of all the rooms to choose, what cruel trick of fate was it that she would choose Feberik's office to hide in? Whatever Janik was looking for, the lock on the door was not going to stop him. Kyra heard the key scrape into the slot. It twisted the tumblers and snapped them back into their open position. The door opened and the hinges squeaked again. A flood of light washed into the room from the hall and Kyra remained absolutely still.

Pat scrape, Pat scrape, Pat scrape. Janik was moving into the room. *Pat scrape, Pat scrape, Pat Scrrraape, thump!* Janik's foot bumped into the base of the desk and Kyra had to bite her tongue to keep from crying out when she felt the vibration. She wedged her eyes ever so tightly shut and prayed that Janik would turn and leave.

Schlump! Something heavy dropped on the desk above her. Kyra placed her curled index finger in her mouth and bit it.

"I'll see you again tomorrow, little book," Janik said.

Kyra didn't breathe until she heard the final scraping drag of Janik's lame left leg on the floor, followed by the loud clicking of the door latch and the snap of the lock reengaging. She let out a sigh of relief when she heard Janik continue on down the hall. Still, for good measure she waited under the desk for a long time before she dared to move again. It was only when she was absolutely certain that Janik would be not only down the hall, but far, far away on a different floor, that she pushed the chair out from under the desk and crawled to the open space. She placed a hand over Feberik's desk and pulled herself up to her feet while summoning back a small flame of light to illuminate her way.

It was by chance that she saw the book in front of her. She had had no intention of grabbing it, but when she saw it was a simple black book with no title on the spine or the front cover, she was intrigued by it. What could possibly be so important that Janik would return it after Feberik was gone, and promised himself that he would come back for it the next day?

Kyra stretched her hand down and opened the front cover to discover that the book was Feberik's journal. She thumbed through a couple of pages, glancing only at the odd word here and there. She saw enough to understand that Feberik was an avid writer, with an entry written nearly every day. As one might expect upon reading a couple of the entries, she found the musings of Feberik's mind and a recounting of his emotions as he processed thoughts and events of each previous day. He wrote in such a way that it was obvious to her that Feberik used his journal each morning to reflect on the day before.

Though it intrigued her, she had something much more important on her mind tonight. She moved to set the book down and silently decided that she would come back sometime soon to see what kind of man she had been pledged to for marriage. She went to close the book, but several pages slipped out from her grasp, opening it to a different entry before she could close the cover. She saw her name written there on the page and paused. The date was shortly before her fifth birthday, a short while before Janik and Feberik had first come to Kyra's home to discuss the marriage. Kyra brought the book back up to her face and scanned through the entry.

Janik has again brought up the subject of marriage. I have told him before that I have no interest in it. I am only at the beginning of my career, and I have every intention of becoming a dragon slayer. He tells me that there is a young girl born of parents that owe our family a favor. He said her name is Kyra Caspen. I told him that if marriage was on his mind, then perhaps he should settle down and marry the girl himself. After all, his career has ended. There is no fighting left for a man who has a crippled leg and hand. Of course, I could not convince Janik of this. He became enraged at my expression of opinion, and ranted at me for several minutes before finally calming down and apologizing.

He has a good heart, but the man can be insufferable sometimes. I understand it, for I suppose I would act much the same way if my body became mangled in battle and I was no longer the man I had once been. Still, I sometimes catch myself longing for the brother I used to have before he rescued Lady Caspen. Everything changed then.

However, Janik is my brother. In an effort to make things right between us, he offered to discuss the matter one more time over drinks. I accepted, for I do not want him to be angry with me. So tonight, after I have finished my work for the day he and I will retire to the study room for drinks. I know he is hoping to ply me with alcohol, and get me to agree to something that he believes is in our family's best interest. I would be a liar if I did not confess that I was hoping to use the alcohol myself in an effort to help him see things my way. He's never been able to hold his liquor as well as I can, so I do believe the odds to be tipped in my favor.

There's nothing left to do now but wait. Tomorrow, I will make sure that the morning's entry describes the conversation we will have tonight over drinks.

Kyra scrunched her eyebrows together and looked at the words on the page for several moments. The man she saw in the entry did not reflect the man she knew. That was most curious to her, so she decided to read one more entry before going to find the rope. She had to know what Janik had said to convince Feberik. The man had always seemed so comforting to Kyra, she had a hard time imagining that he was actually the catalyst behind her arranged marriage. If that were true, then Kyra had to wonder whether she could trust Janik anymore.

Kyra gripped the page between her forefinger and thumb,

turning it slowly, almost afraid to see what was written on the next page.

> *Janik and I spoke over drinks last night. I now see that he was right all along. The union is good for our family, and he so eloquently pointed out other aspects that I had not even considered. Of course I am younger than he is, and therefore I am a closer match to the young lady. Also, as my body is whole and his is lame. I concede his point that I will be a more able father. Of the two of us, I will likely have a better earning potential and a much better ability to provide for and protect the family.*
>
> *Therefore, seeing the wisdom in my brother's designs, I have agreed to marry the young lady. Furthermore, I have made it known that instead of working part-time as an instructor at Kuldiga Academy, I will now switch to become a full professor. Janik said he can easily make that happen since he has been working there as a janitor for many years and is close to the right people. I see no issue with this, for I have taught there part-time for several years and have received nothing but the highest reviews during the annual evaluations. This will mean less adventure in the field for me, but as Janik pointed out, it falls to me to provide for the entire family now.*
>
> *Janik said he will soon arrange a meeting with the young lady's father. I hope with all of my being that this arrangement works out as well as Janik says it will.*

Kyra was stunned. The man who wrote this entry was so different from the man who wrote the previous day's entry. Even as a young girl she could see that there had been a marked shift in the man's thinking. On the first day Feberik had referred to her as a "girl" but then during the course of the second entry he referred her as a "young lady," showing a much greater degree of respect. Additionally, there was the complete and entire reversal of Feberik's feelings about marriage in general, and a dismissal of his previous career plans. What could Janik have said that would cause such a great change in only one night? The young apprentice questioned whether perhaps the alcohol they had consumed was of such a great quantity that Feberik had been inebriated well into the morning when he wrote the next entry as well.

Considering this she flipped to the next entry and scanned through it to see if he had second thoughts. She found only more affirmations of Feberik's plans to marry her. Whatever man wrote the first entry that she had read, it seemed he had disappeared entirely. Perhaps this was something she could talk to Cyrus about. She knew she couldn't speak with Janik about it, nor could she bring the subject up with Feberik. Even in an abstract sense, she did not wish to discuss marriage with her actual fiancé. Just the thought of it made her stomach flip. But Cyrus just might have some insight into this. More importantly, he had already told her that he was new to Kuldiga Academy. That meant he was not connected with anyone else in the same way that Janik or Feberik might be. The old wizard was the only logical choice. Besides, if she destroyed the shade tonight, he would owe her one.

Kyra set the book back on the desk and went for the door. She undid the lock and closed it behind her. She moved around the corner and down the hall to Janik's office. She put her lock pick set to work on Janik's lock, opening the door in a matter of seconds. She slipped inside and summoned the small light again to help her find the rope. She kept the light hovering low in front of her chest, to limit the amount of light that would shine out from the window that overlooked the courtyard below.

She went to a long counter along one of the walls and opened the top drawer. Inside she found a large, blue bottle. The only other things in the drawer were gauze bandages. She closed the drawer and moved to the next one and the next looking for the rope. When she found none in the drawers, she made her way toward a large cabinet that stretched from floor to ceiling. She pulled on the knob and a couple of long-handled tools caught on each other and rattled and jingled as the door opened. There were shears and brooms and mops and buckets, but no rope. She almost closed the door in a huff, but then her eyes caught sight of a cord dangling from the shelf in the top of the cupboard. She reached up to grab it and pulled down a coil of rope roughly twenty-five feet long. That was more than enough for what she needed. She stuffed the rope into her bag, closed the cupboard, and left the room.

She made her way back to her bedchamber and then dumped

the contents of the bag onto her floor. She removed her robes and left only a soft shirt on her torso before she slipped the feather mail shirt over her body. Over that she was going to put the padded leather tunic, but she noticed that the sleeves were very thick and would hamper her movement. This likely didn't make much of a difference for any Apprentice of the Sword, but she would need her hands as free as possible if she was going to be able to cast a spell quickly when needed. She went to her desk and pulled a small pair of scissors out and began ripping the seams at the shoulders to remove the sleeves from the leather tunic. When she was done she slipped it over herself, letting the excess length hang over her waist on the outside of her pants. Then she put her robes back on to conceal all of the armor beneath.

She hastily stuffed the rope back into the bag and opened the portal, stepping through to greet Leatherback for the second time that day.

CHAPTER FIFTEEN

Leatherback lazily opened an eye and watched her curiously as she came back through the portal. He purred and chirped, lifting his head from the ground. Kyra walked up to him and placed a hand on the tip of his snout, running it up the top of his face until she reached the point between his eyes and then she patted twice and gave him a large hug.

"Remember that I told you I would come back tonight?" Kyra asked. She looked up and pointed to the night sky which was filled with stars, but void of the moon. "I told you tonight we would play just like Boba and Aiden would, do you remember? Leatherback, my dear friend, I have something I need to ask of you."

The dragon pulled his head back from her, obviously sensing the trepidation in her voice. He cocked its head to the side slightly and then offered his high-pitched squeal. Kyra accepted that as a prompting for her to say what she needed.

"Like you, my mother is dead." A lump caught in Kyra's throat. This was much harder than she had anticipated. Previously she had tricked herself into thinking that because Leatherback was only an animal, it would be easy to command him to do what she wanted, but it was not so. Leatherback was not just an animal, he was her friend. Her most dear and precious friend. What she was going to ask him to do was dangerous for both of them.

Leatherback gently nuzzled her with the end of his snout and offered the high-pitched chirp again, encouraging her.

Kyra nodded and her eyes began to water as she thought of her mother.

"There is a shade that hunts us." The young apprentice shook her head and patted the dragon's snout with her hand and then she corrected herself. "I mean to say there is a shade that hunts me. It killed my mother and has been looking for me ever since. I am tired of hiding." She looked up to Leatherback's golden eye and smiled weakly. "I have been practicing my magic, and I think I am ready to change from being the hunted to being the hunter. I was doing some research today, and I believe I know how to find him," her words trailed off and she looked at her friend. Somehow she could no longer find the right way to ask him to come with her.

The dragon pulled away from Kyra and lazily pushed to its feet. It stood over her with his head held high into the air. He looked down at her and smiled. She could see the burning flames deep within his nostrils as wisps of smoke snaked out. Leatherback opened his mouth and in a deep, rumbling voice pronounced a single word that sent shivers down Kyra's spine.

"Boba."

Kyra stumbled back and looked up at her friend, reaching up with her left hand to cover her open mouth. He had spoken. His first word ever, and it came from a story she had told him. Did this mean that he understood what she needed?

Before she could ask anything, Leatherback lowered his head down so that it was level with hers and smiled again before saying his second word.

"F... Friend."

Kyra reached out and hugged the dragon's snout, laying her head upon his thick, strong scales and letting tears of joy and relief fall upon them.

"Will you come with me?" Kyra asked.

Leatherback pulled away from her and lifted his head high into the sky.

"Friend!" he shouted in a voice that shook the trees around him and was accompanied by a massive column of flame and sparks.

Before long the two were flying through the air. Kyra had used the rope to secure her staff behind Leatherback's crown of horns, and had used it to fashion a bridal of sorts for her to use as they careened through the sky. They traveled out beyond where they had been hunting some time ago when the satyr had warned them and sent them back. She was almost certain that the satyr had sensed the evil that was hunting her. With any luck, the shade would still be nearby.

The two of them searched the ground for hours with no luck. Leatherback glided below the clouds and over the tops of the trees, but they saw no monster. Kyra began to lose hope and was almost ready to give up the search for the night when she saw the mountain where the nest was located in which she had found Leatherback. She patted the dragon's neck and pointed toward the mountain. Leatherback needed no more instruction before turning and flying directly for it.

The two of them landed gently in the nest of rocks and Kyra dismounted from Leatherback. She smiled at seeing the old nest once more. It was almost like coming home, even though this was so different from the place where she had been raised. Leatherback kept watch, anxiously looking from side to side with his legs tensed and ready to jump.

Kyra moved toward the area where Leatherback's egg had been when she found it. The large, flat rock that had once covered the egg and concealed it now lay off to the side, discarded and forgotten. Kyra startled when a field mouse popped out of Guardian's hole. The little animal squeaked and squawked when it saw her and then disappeared back down into the hole. Upon remembering her little friend's death, she felt another wave of sadness and guilt come over her. Had she not been there at that time, that wraith would not have killed Guardian. It never would have found the nest if she had been anywhere else, because it had come for her.

She thought for a moment, wondering how it had known she was there. She rubbed her hands together and blew on them to keep them warm in the night. Her right index finger rubbed over a slightly raised scar on the back of her hand. Then she remembered she had cut the back of her hand on a thorny bush when she had been playing with Guardian earlier that day. If the wraith had been hunting her, then maybe it had come for the scent of her blood.

She hadn't read anything about that in the book that Cyrus had given her to read from, but then again, there had been a line saying that no one knew exactly how the wraiths were able to track their victims. It said that some attacks were purely happenstance and incidental, but that with others it seemed as if the wraiths knew exactly where their intended victims were and were able to attack without any warning whatsoever. Kyra wondered whether the wraith had indeed tracked her by scent.

Kyra moved back to Leatherback, motioning with her hand for him to come closer. As he did so she gave him instructions.

"Leatherback, if you fly above the clouds, can you hear me if I call for you?"

The dragon nodded its head.

"I have an idea to attract the shade that I am hunting. I will stay here and see if we can get him to come to me." Kyra looked up the mountainside, and noted with satisfaction that the peak was partially concealed by clouds on this night. "You fly up to the peak where you will be able to watch from above. You can circle in the air periodically, but be sure not to tire out. If you see him before I do, signal with a flame in the direction that the shade is coming from. I will move in to attack and you can come in from above. On the other hand, if I see him first I will call out for you to come and help. Stay close enough that you can hear me, but go above the clouds so that he cannot see you."

Leatherback chirped and launched into the air without hesitation.

Kyra walked around the nest until she finally found a bush with thorns like the one she had cut herself on before. She took one of the vines in her right hand, careful not to prick the inside of her palm, and stretched it out in front of her. She maneuvered her left hand underneath the thorny branch and then jerked her wrist so that it was cut shallowly in two places on the back side. The familiar sting came just as droplets of blood formed on the back of her wrist. Instead of sucking the blood or wiping it away, Kyra squeezed from the sides of the cuts until a few drops of blood fell to the stones below.

She moved away from the stones, putting her back to a large boulder that could conceal her and stared out over the rocky nest, waiting for the shade to arrive. She glanced up occasionally, looking for Leatherback, but she could see no sign of him. Even straining her ears, she couldn't tell that anything, much less a dragon, circled in the sky above. Kyra smiled, for if she could not see Leatherback even when she knew he was there, the shade would not be able to discover the dragon either.

Hours must have passed as the stars traveled on their courses through the night sky. For the longest time no one came. Not even the field mouse emerged from the hole. Everything was perfectly silent and still.

Without warning, something reached down from the boulder above and seized Kyra by the neck, yanking her up and holding her out over the rocky nest with one arm. She tried to call out, but the hand that held her squeezed so tight that she could not. She swatted at the hand that held her, but the creature laughed in her face.

"Where's the dagger?" the being asked in a low, gravelly voice.

Kyra looked down and saw a pale figure standing before her. He looked exactly like a man, except that his ears were pointed like those of an elf and he stood at least two feet taller than any man she had ever seen in her life. He was slender, but obviously imbued with unnatural strength as he was able to easily dangle her in the air with one hand. He wore dark colored clothes with a flowing over-cloak. His hair was long and silver in color, which only accentuated his prominent cheekbones that protruded out from his gaunt face. A pair of fangs became visible as he sneered at her and spoke again.

"Where's the dagger, half-blood?"

Kyra couldn't breathe and she knew she could not wrestle free with her strength alone. She let go with her hands and summoned two spells. In her left hand she called forth an orb of light and sent it streaking toward the shade's face. At the same time she formed a small javelin of fire in her right hand and sent it toward the creature's chest. The shade hissed and screeched loudly. Kyra never saw whether her spells hit their mark, for the shade flung her away, flailing end over end through the air until she crashed down on the rocks. Her left ankle twisted as it went down in between two boulders. The weight of her body continued on until the bones gave way and snapped. She only just managed to cover her head with her forearms before bouncing across several more rocks and coming to a stop against a large, round boulder. Her sides and back ached tremendously, and she knew that had she not been wearing the armor, she would likely have suffered many broken ribs as a result of the fall.

Crying out in pain, she reached down for her left ankle. She never saw the shade leap through the air toward her. A large streak of purple came down at her like a magical saber. It struck her square across the chest and knocked her to the side. She tumbled over the jagged rocks for several feet and gasped for breath. She looked down to see that her robes and the leather armor beneath had been split open. Her left hand came up to inspect the area and she fully expected to find a gash splitting her from left collarbone to below her lowest right rib, but luckily the feather mail had held together. She was most definitely hurt, but at least the spell had not cut her.

The shade walked toward her now, holding a purple fire in his left palm and summoning a mighty sword in his right hand. The wind blew his hair and cloak out to the side and he sneered at her wickedly.

"So this is the mighty daughter of Zana and Bhaltair?" the shade questioned in a mocking tone. "Pathetic."

Kyra tried to conjure another spell, but the pain in her leg prevented her from mustering any amount of focus, let alone casting an entire spell. The shade raised his sword high into the air and laughed at her.

"Tell me where the dagger is, or I will use your guts and innards to scry for it myself. I *will* be the one to deliver it!"

A great ball of fire crashed down from the sky with such force and speed that Kyra was knocked several feet away and the shade was engulfed entirely by flame. The shade's hissing and wailing was cut short as Leatherback crashed to the ground, shattering rocks and shaking the entire nest. Leatherback brought his jaws down and Kyra could hear them snap shut, ending the shade's cries of agony. Leatherback snapped his neck up and shook the shade's body violently before spitting it out on the ground. The great dragon looked back at her and went to her chirping and clicking.

"Friend," Leatherback said in a concerned tone.

Kyra looked up and raised her arm to meet Leatherback's snout.

"I'm alright."

Leatherback positioned his snout low enough that Kyra was able to drape her upper body over it so that he could scoop her from the ground. She was breathing heavily and her body was exhausted. She barely managed to center herself on the dragon's snout before going nearly completely limp. Leatherback moved back around to look at the shade's broken body. Despite the gaping holes that had nearly severed the shade's torso in half, there was no blood. Kyra peered over Leatherback's snout and looked down in disgust at the creature that had killed her mother.

A purple haze covered the body, then the bones began to right themselves. The holes closed and the shade opened his eyes. Leatherback snapped out with his left foreleg, bringing his claws down to bear where the shade was, but the shade disappeared and Leatherback stabbed only rock and dirt. Leatherback snarled and lowered his head, sliding Kyra down to rest on a boulder. He moved to stand over her, protecting her from all sides as his head turned every which way and his tail switched behind him.

The shade laughed with a taunting, echoing cackle. Kyra looked around from under her friend, peering around the massive legs that guarded her on every side like sentinels of scale and muscle. She could not find the shade.

"Your pet will do you no good here," the shade hissed.

Leatherback poured flame over the rocks and trees in the direction the voice came from. The forest began to burn and the shade continued to laugh. Now it called out from the other side of the nest.

"You will both die."

Kyra finally summoned enough strength to send a lightning bolt in the direction of the voice. It crashed into a rock harmlessly and dissipated without ever finding its mark. The laugh returned, teasing and taunting them. The ground began to shake and there was a great commotion a few yards away as rocks leapt up, stacking themselves upon one another. They formed into a bipedal humanoid shape and charged for Kyra. Leatherback stopped the creature with a swat of its tail, exploding the rocks out away from them.

The laugh returned. Leatherback snapped toward the direction of the sound and blew another great wave of fire into the forest. Now the fire rose all around them, casting the nest in an orange glow of death as thick smoke rose over them and blotted out the stars.

Kyra tried to stand, but the sharp pain shooting through her left leg brought her down in terrible agony. Something flew in from the side and Leatherback snarled as his whole body jolted. Kyra looked up, but she could not see what it was that was attacking her friend. The dragon danced and stamped around her, snarling and hissing as his tail flailed about and fire spewed from his mouth. He swung with his forelegs and there were screams and shrieks all around her.

Then there was a crash to her left. She looked up to see a great winged beast with the face of a bat, but much larger than a man. It growled at her to reveal fangs which were sharp and long. It fanned its wings and let out a shriek that nearly ripped her ears apart. She covered her ears and cried out. She could not concentrate or think of anything else but the sound. She was effectively paralyzed, and it seemed this time that Leatherback was too consumed fighting off other creatures to have noticed the one that approached Kyra now.

The shriek grew louder and louder as the beast ran toward her. It leapt up and glided the remaining ten feet between them, then dropped down on her with tremendous force. There were talons on its feet that now dug into her legs, piercing through the leather armor pants and crushing her thighs. She called out for help, but none came. The beast came down fast, seizing each of her arms and digging with its claws deep into her wrists. The screeching stopped and she looked up to see blood crazed eyes that shone red as firelight. The gaping snout hovered over her face, the nostrils flaring as it caught the scent of her blood. The wings wrapped around them, closing her in darkness. There was a flash of fangs as it opened its mouth and began to lurch downward toward her neck.

Just as she felt the hot, moist breath upon her skin, the beast was ripped away from her. Her body jolted as its claws and talons disengaged. She just barely caught sight of the giant bat creature flailing and clawing at Leatherback's snout before Leatherback flipped it out from under himself, then blasted it to smithereens in a wave of fire. All of the shrieking around her was gone and the dragon roared triumphantly.

"That was impressive," the shade commented. "Let's see how he does with me."

"Over there!" Kyra shouted when she caught sight of the shade off to her left. He held a great, gleaming scimitar in his hands and was walking calmly toward them.

"No, over here," the shade called out from the right. Kyra

turned around and saw another two forms, each identical to the first, and understood that he was using illusions.

"Kill them all!" Kyra shrieked.

Leatherback launched a furious assault. He drenched three of the forms in fire and used his tail to blast another two. He snatched out with his claws, seizing the gaunt figure in his grasp and bringing him up to his mouth, but the shade vanished into nothingness before he could finish the job. Kyra was unable to tell which one was the real shade. With focus born out of desperation, she was finally able to summon another javelin of flame and she sent it flying toward the closest shade. The javelin pierced through his chest and the form disappeared, turning into vapor.

For every one the duo destroyed, three more appeared. What was worse, each illusion seemed capable of casting spells. One of them threw a fireball at Kyra that blasted her in the side, disintegrating her robes and leather armor and blackening the feather mail beneath. In answer she sent a fire javelin at him just as Leatherback snapped down with his great sharp teeth. The shade turned into vapor as had each of the others they had managed to strike down up to this point.

Soon they were surrounded by more than one hundred shades, each of them launching spells and pummeling Leatherback with a barrage of assaults.

A great spray of blood erupted over the rocks near Kyra and she looked up to see jagged scales falling from Leatherback's left foreleg and an open gash over his unprotected skin. She knew she had to do something. She couldn't stand, so she crawled to get closer to the fight. She summoned the same whirlwind she had used on the wraith, trying to direct it and whisk away the illusions. It worked on a few, but then the other shades were able to counter the spell and they turned it back on Kyra. The tornado flew at her with tremendous force and power. It snaked beneath Leatherback and picked Kyra up and slammed her into Leatherback's belly and then dropped her back down to the rocks below. When she fell, her head cracked against a boulder and she heard a loud ringing sound. Her vision began to fade and her breathing slowed. It took great effort to reach her hand up toward her head, but when she finally managed to touch the spot that had hit the rock, all she felt was a great amount of warm liquid that smelled slightly of iron.

Leatherback's knees buckled above her. His hind legs failed and dropped and he roared in pain as his front legs quaked. He only barely managed to catch himself before crushing Kyra beneath him. His roars grew more and more frantic. There were too many enemies. Kyra tried to whisper an apology, but she had not the strength to make the words.

A great force shook the earth around them and a mighty thunder ripped the air apart over the nest. In her fading consciousness, Kyra was certain this was the end. The shade had tired of toying with them and would now devour them both.

A mighty wind rushed into the nest, carrying with it the flames from the forest. Mighty screams rose from the battle and it took some time for Kyra to realize that it was not Leatherback who was screaming. It was the shade.

Golden light swirled around Leatherback's feet and created a large shell over Kyra and her dragon. The shell protected them from all the spells that the shades threw at them, but also dampened the sound as if the battlefield was now far away from them. Kyra rolled over, and just before the darkness closed in on her vision, she saw a thin man with a long, gray beard walking through the nest, vaporizing the illusions as he made his way toward a single image of the shade, and pummeled it relentlessly with great bolts of lightning.

Her body went numb and her head fell to the ground.

CHAPTER SIXTEEN

Kyra awoke in her bed and startled when she saw several men hovering over her. Their hands weaved and danced over her body methodically as the men chanted in unison over her. She moved her head and looked at the nearest one. He was a red haired man with large, faded freckles covering his cheeks. He didn't take any notice of her as he continued to work.

"She's awake," one of them said suddenly.

"Move, move! Move away I said!" Cyrus bellowed. The men stepped back from her and the old wizard rushed up to the side of her bed and leaned down toward her face. His fierce, unflinching eyes bored down into hers as he studied her with a somber expression. He placed a thumb on her forehead and held it there for several seconds before moving his palm to cover her eyes. "Mhm, she's fine. Everyone out. Go tell the headmaster that I will bring her shortly. Have the tribunal prepared."

Kyra heard many footsteps leaving her room and the door closing behind them. Cyrus pulled his hand away from her face and held it out for her. She took it and started to rise as Cyrus scooped his other hand behind her back to prop her up.

She was awake, but not fully aware of where she was. She knew she was in her room, but she had no recollection of how she had gotten there. Worse than that, she had no idea what had happened to Leatherback. All she knew for certain was that Cyrus was the last thing she had seen before she had lost consciousness.

"Your friend is safe, if that is what you are wondering," Cyrus said.

Kyra looked around her room as if somehow expecting the giant dragon to be curled up in a corner somewhere.

"Where is he?"

"I sent him home," Cyrus said.

Home? What could Cyrus know about Leatherback's home? He had never been there.

"Where is he?" Kyra pressed.

Cyrus shook his head and waved a finger in the air. "It took some doing to convince him to let me take you," Cyrus said. "Once I persuaded him to believe that I would help you, I told him to go home. I told him that when you are better you would come back, that he should wait for you at home. He watched you for a long time and waited until I had created a portal to bring you back here before he finally leapt into the air. He was flying south from the mountain, but that is all I know. I assume you know where he is?"

Kyra nodded. "Who else knows?"

Cyrus smiled slyly and sat down on the bed next to her as he folded his arms and reached up with his right hand to place one finger alongside his right nostril.

"As far as Kuldiga Academy is concerned, you went out to a secluded place to study. You were there reading the book that I had assigned to you when you were attacked by the shade and did your best to defend yourself."

"And everybody believes that?"

Cyrus smiled wider and nodded his head.

"I hope you don't mind, but I took the liberty of tying it with the strange events that happened at your home. They were more than willing to believe that the same creature that had invaded your home was still wandering about the countryside. Given the time that has passed between the attack at your home and the fight you had near the mountain, it is extremely plausible the shade had moved to that area. Also, I told them that that was where you went when you got frustrated, or needed to be alone and reflect on things. So I let them draw the conclusion that perhaps the shade was a creature of opportunity and saw an easy fight in a single apprentice alone in the woods."

Kyra nodded and asked one more question.

"How did you know to find me?"

Cyrus' eyebrows shot up and he took in a deep breath as he nodded slowly.

"Let's just say when I saw a large fire rolling up the mountainside, I had a feeling you might be involved. Given the fact that I have instructed you not to practice your spells on trees, I knew that if it was you, you were in serious trouble. I know you are anxious to find the shade, and I had suspected that you might try and find him on your own. I must say that I share a great portion of the blame for what has happened. I am hoping we can put that behind us and move forward from here." Kyra nodded in agreement and the two were silent for a few moments before Cyrus spoke again.

"The other apprentices are busy spreading another rumor about you."

Kyra looked up, a puzzled expression on her face.

Cyrus smiled slyly. "Let's just say I don't think any of them are anxious to pester you anymore now that you have gone toe to toe with a shade and lived."

The two of them shared a laugh.

"What do you intend to do with Leatherback?" Kyra asked suddenly.

"So he has a name," Cyrus commented. The wizard offered a close-lipped smile and shrugged. "Keep him out of sight, and let's see if perhaps we can train him a little better. His fighting style was lacking, if you know what I mean."

"Will you tell the headmaster?" Kyra asked.

Cyrus shook his head. "No, but there is going to be a tribunal and you are expected to attend. As fortune would have it, or perhaps as misfortune would have it in this case, there are three priests from Valtuu Temple here. There are also several dragon slayers with them. I think it would be wise to make sure Leatherback, as you called him, stays hidden so long as they are here."

"The priests came to investigate what happened with Kathair," Kyra said.

Cyrus nodded. "That's why they came, but they have stayed for you. I can't tell you any more than that, other than to say you have been unconscious for a little over a week. They are anxious to speak with you."

Kyra's eyes went wide and she glanced to the center of the room.

"Leatherback is going to be worried," she said. "I have to get to him." She moved to swing her legs out over the bed, but stopped when a shooting pain stabbed up from her ankle to her hip. Then she remembered she had broken her left ankle.

"Keep still. You need your rest."

"I have to go, if I do not tell him that I am okay, he will come looking for me. If the dragon slayers were to find him, I fear for his safety."

Cyrus sighed and pushed off from the bed. "The last time I held you back, I had to rescue you from the shade. This time I'm going to help you, on the condition that you do exactly as I say and return here before the hour is out. Are we agreed?"

Kyra nodded emphatically. "Can you help me get to him?"

Cyrus pulled several strips of sturdy, thin wood from the folds of his robe. From another pocket he pulled a long roll of gauze. "I had a feeling that when you woke the first thing you would want to do would be to go back to him. I can place a splint on your ankle, and then cast a spell that will numb the pain for a short time. Do try not to walk on it. Try to hop as much as you can." Cyrus reached under the bed and pulled out a cane made of alder wood and set it next to Kyra.

"This will help you maintain your balance."

Cyrus braced her ankle with the splint and then cast a spell to numb her leg. He cautioned her again to be back as quickly as she could as he moved to the door, locked it, and exited the room.

Kyra rose gently at first until she knew for sure that the numbing spell had worked. Despite not feeling any pain, she did as Cyrus had instructed her and tried to keep off of her left foot. She cast the spell to open the portal and then went through.

Leatherback nearly jumped like a puppy when he saw her come through the portal. He bent his head down low and stopped just short of nuzzling her when his eyes saw her limping hop. He inspected the splint that was tied onto her leg and sniffed it.

"I'm alright," Kyra said. "I can't stay long, but are you okay?"

Leatherback smiled and with a twinkle in his eye he said, "I am okay, Dragon Friend."

"You can talk! I mean, you spoke to me before, but now you are using sentences. This is incredible!"

From around the other side, Njar approached her and came into view.

"He has made a good deal of progress in your absence," the

satyr said dryly. "What you did was extremely foolish." The satyr walked up to her with a harsh look in his eye. Kyra shrank back away from him, and even Leatherback retreated a few steps.

"You don't understand," Kyra started.

The satyr chief cut her off and stopped just inches short of her face so that she could smell his warm, moist breath.

"No, it is you who does not understand. That much was evident when you decided to attack a shade. If it was a creature that I thought you could defeat, I would not have made you run from it before. A creature of such power is not to be trifled with. Even I avoid them unless forced to confront one."

"That shade killed my mother," Kyra said. "What I did was foolish, but it will not happen again."

The satyr's expression did not soften. He folded his arms and studied her for quite a few moments before he spoke again. Kyra expected him to continue chiding her for foolish behavior, but what he said next was most unexpected.

"I have been able to catch a glimpse of your future," he said. "What you did with the shade was extremely foolish, and I am not sure how you survived, because Leatherback will not tell me everything that happened, but what I do know is that Leatherback does not suffer from the curse. More surprising than that were the glimpses of the future that I saw of you and him together; you were riding upon his back, chasing demons. I'm not saying the curse will never come to him, but I do believe now that you may just have enough of a chance to save him. Maybe you will fly north and find freedom for both of you. If that is a possibility within the grand designs of fate, then I will help you do that."

Kyra looked at him incredulously.

"You have changed," she commented.

The satyr smiled warmly for the first time since she had arrived in the aspenwood.

"I still seek balance," he said, "but now I see that helping the two of you will further that goal. If the two of you perform the things that I saw in the visions, then you will do much to protect the balance. You have me as an ally. Go back, rest your leg and heal. I will watch over Leatherback until your return."

Kyra hopped toward Leatherback and the dragon moved his head and softly nuzzled her right side, careful not to knock her off balance. Kyra reached out with her right arm and hugged him as best she could and placed a small kiss on the top of his head. When she pulled back she realized that there was a new color in the dragon's eyes. They were no longer dominated by the gold with green flecks she had seen before. The gold was still there, but it was a thin rim around a wide iris of sky-blue.

"His eyes have changed," Kyra noted.

"Apparently the magic of the glade and the spells that I have used to accelerate his maturity have had some effect on him." The satyr chief smiled and shrugged sheepishly. "When he began speaking more than just the odd word here and there, his eyes changed, starting to take on the color that you now see."

"I thought you said there would be no side effects," Kyra said.

"Then I am twice wrong," Njar said. "For apparently there is a minor side effect, and you do have a chance to protect him from the curse. All things considered, these are not such terrible things to have been incorrect about."

*****

Cyrus sat at the stone table in the cave and waited for the warlock to approach. This time he saw two others, dressed in the same robes and wearing the same golden amulet. They remained by the open door and did not come any closer.

"You were supposed to control the girl," the warlock said as he sat opposite Cyrus.

"I misjudged her tenacity, but that will not happen again." Cyrus took in a breath and folded his arms. "Severin has fled."

The warlock slammed his fist on the table. "Of course he has fled!" The warlock lifted a hand and pointed a finger at Cyrus. "You let the girl tip him off. When you stormed in to save her, he knew that he had been discovered. He has turned to hiding, and even we cannot scry his location."

"Have a little more faith," Cyrus said. "He will resurface again, for he does not have the dagger."

"How can you possibly know that?" the warlock hissed.

Cyrus sneered wickedly. "Because the shade was still looking for it."

The warlock reached up and pulled his hood back to reveal a

face of sharp, angular features. A long, thin, pointed nose sat between prominent cheekbones over a narrow mouth. The thin lips stretched into a smile and the warlock's eyes seemed to sparkle.

"Then finish it, Cyrus. Find him and kill him."

"I will. I have no doubt that I will be able to find him again." With this Cyrus paused for a moment, considering his next words. "I came to warn you about Severin, but you should also be made aware that Kyra is more powerful than you had first thought. Much more so. Also, there is a tribunal at the academy. I was invited to give my testimony of what happened, but I am not to be there when she receives her final judgment. You should be aware that there are priests from Valtuu Temple. They will be able to see what she is."

The warlock reached up and stroked his pointy chin.

"If they expel her, it would be easy to bring her into our fold. Then again, if the priests were to condemn her, that might complicate things."

Cyrus nodded his agreement. "If she were condemned, then she would be exiled. She would become hunted."

"Your task remains the same regardless," the warlock asserted. "Find Severin and kill him. If the girl is allowed to stay, then forge her into an ally for us. If she is exiled, then either ensure she will go so far away as to never interfere with us, or kill her."

"What of the dragon?" Cyrus asked. "I am not sure how, but he has grown and matured far beyond what he should have been able to in these last few months. He is the size of a dragon that is twenty or thirty years old. His fighting is rudimentary, but he has tremendous power and he is fiercely loyal to her."

The warlock dismissed the concern with a flick of his hand. "The dragon does not concern me. Given enough time, Nagar's Blight will consume his soul. Just be sure not to make an enemy out of him and let the curse do what it will on its own."

Cyrus nodded and then turned to leave.

"As soon as she is healed, I will resume training with her and we will find Severin."

CHAPTER SEVENTEEN

Kyra sat in a wide chair with her left foot propped up on a plush footstool. The headmaster sat behind his desk twiddling his thumbs, considering everything he had just heard. Three priests from the temple sat in chairs at the headmaster's left. Kyra's father sat in the chair next to her. The room was silent. The sconces flickered their light and the shadows danced around the room.

"Are you quite certain in what you see?" the headmaster asked one of the priests.

The priest nodded and continued looking at Kyra. The girl studied the priest, finding it rather unnerving that they asserted they could see anything of such a nature as what they claimed. All three of them had eyes that were cloudy and gray, void of all color and motionless.

The priest on the far right stood and pointed at Kyra. "As you know Headmaster, we do not see the way others see. We see the aura of a person, or that of any living creature, including plants. This is how we found the students responsible for attacking the young first-year Apprentice of the Sword in his sleep. This is also how we convicted their instructor of instigating the attack." The priest moved close and knelt next to Kyra. He wasn't old by the look of him, perhaps twenty, and yet he appeared to be the ranking priest among the three, despite the fact that the others both appeared older than he did, with wrinkles on their faces and one with graying hair.

"I can see the confusion in your aura," the priest told her. "You should know that your fiancé had nothing to do with the attack on your friend Kathair. We questioned him as well and found him to be entirely innocent of any wrongdoing."

Kyra knew for certain that the priest had in fact been telling the truth. As hard as it was for her to comprehend what this meant, she understood that the priest would not lie. As she thought on what he had just told the room a few moments ago, she remembered something that the shade had said.

"The vampire that imprisoned my mother, what was his name?" Kyra asked.

The priest stepped back and let the headmaster answer the question.

The headmaster cleared his throat and then spoke the name, "Bhaltair."

Kyra nodded and looked to the man that she had thought of as her father. It was a strange feeling. Just before encountering the shade, she had essentially begun distancing herself from her father, but now that she learned he was not her father, she wanted him back. Much better to be fathered by a coward than sired by a vampire.

Lord Caspen slapped his hands to his knees and rose to his feet.

"You do what you want," he said. "Whether she is expelled or not is not of my concern anymore. That thing is not my daughter." Lord Caspen turned abruptly and left the room before the headmaster had a chance to say anything in reply. The door slammed and Kyra startled in her chair.

The words *that thing* echoed over and over in her mind, threatening to tear her soul apart.

The young priest was quick to return to her side. He placed a hand upon her knee and the other upon her right forearm.

"Young Kyra, look at me," he pleaded. "It is better to know the truth than to hide in shadow. Had we not informed you of your heritage, you would have a more difficult time later in your life. Because you share blood with the vampire, you will have impulses that are against the laws of nature. You will not thirst for blood, for that is separate and a special curse that one vampire must choose to give to another being. But, there will be other things that will trouble you, and if you at least know they are coming, then you can fight them and conquer those impulses before they become a problem." He patted her leg and turned back to one of the older priests.

The older priest nodded his head in agreement and spoke.

"We meant what we said. We have searched your aura and found no ill intent. There is nothing in your character that suggests you will ever be anything but an honorable person. Therefore, we are recommending that you be allowed to stay at Kuldiga Academy. If you can tame the unnatural impulses thrust upon you by your blood, then you will be a mighty asset to the Middle Kingdom. You will have abilities that no other sorcerer or sorceress would ever be able to control. At fourteen you have already fought a shade. That much tells us your heart is in the right place. We know the attack was motivated by vengeance. Our gift of sight is such that we can see through the platitudes and lies that Cyrus gave the other masters here at the Academy. However, we have no interest in speaking with him. We feel confident that his lies were invented only to protect you and your dragon."

Kyra sucked in a breath and went rigid. They had not mentioned Leatherback before, and neither had she. Someone had broken the secret.

Before she could fret much more, the young priest patted her arm and spoke to her again.

"No one has betrayed you," he assured her. "In a person's aura we can see their thoughts and emotions. It isn't exactly reading a mind, but we can read the heart. We saw a few signs that led us to believe you have been harboring a dragon. Now, in the Middle Kingdom that is a grave offense. However, the priests of Valtuu Temple have a different opinion on the matter. You see, our order was founded by the Ancients - the Father of the Ancients to be precise. We know that dragons are not inherently evil, but that they suffer from a curse. We know that you are fighting this curse, and so far the dragon has shown no signs of the taint. If he did, we would be able to detect its presence even in your aura because of how close you are to him. You see, when a dragon bonds to a human, they exchange a portion of their energy with the human. It was very easy for us to see."

The priest pursed his lips anxiously and glanced back to the others behind him. Kyra watched the exchange and wondered what it was he wanted to tell her. The two older priests sat stoic and reserved, while he fidgeted with his thumb, tapping it against Kyra's forearm.

Finally he opened his mouth and shook his head as he spoke. "I have to tell you, that the sheer fact that there is a dragon in the Middle Kingdom that is not tainted by the curse is a miracle! We haven't seen anything like this before, and so we have taken a special interest in both you and the dragon."

One of the older priests cleared his throat, perhaps signaling the younger one to better control his tongue. The younger one paused for a moment, but then looked up and smiled at her. Even though she could not read any signs of emotion in the young man's gray eyes, she sensed that his smile was warm and as genuine as any expression she had ever seen.

"We spoke with the headmaster. Everything will work out alright, you'll see."

Again the older priest with the gray hair cleared his throat. He then glanced to the headmaster anxiously.

The headmaster rapped his knuckles on his desk and stood slowly. The young priest moved back to his chair and sat down respectfully.

"Kyra Caspen," the headmaster began. "After discussing the matter with the priests over the last week, I have been persuaded by those with more experience and authority in these matters that it will be of benefit to the future security of the Middle Kingdom to help you continue to work with this dragon. Therefore, it is the decision of this tribunal that there is nothing in your conduct, except of course the unfortunate event with Lady Priscilla, that merits any sort of punishment. Furthermore, this tribunal has decided that in so much as the dragon acted only to destroy the shade, which is a much greater enemy to the Middle Kingdom than a hatchling, there is no need to expose the dragon's existence at this point. If you will agree to allow the priests to visit with the dragon on a periodic basis to ensure that the taint has not found its way to his heart, he will never be spoken of again.

"Additionally, as your father has now abandoned you, you will be accepted as a ward of Kuldiga Academy. This means that I will allow you to stay here full-time until your graduation. Master Orres will be made known of your half blood and given the opportunity to break the betrothal if he so wishes, but that is a matter between you and him now. That is all, you may go."

Kyra nodded and then looked up to the headmaster. "I have a request of my own," she said. The headmaster narrowed his eyes on her and folded his arms. "Lord Caspen is not my father. I no longer wish to hold his name. From this point on, my name is Kyra Dimwater. I will take my mother's maiden name and carry that."

The headmaster nodded his agreement. "Very well, Miss Dimwater, you are most welcome here at Kuldiga Academy. Just make sure not to fling any more people into walls, and if you ever find another shade or shadowfiend, please take at least two instructors with you before you hunt it down."

Kyra smiled and nodded her head. "Of course."

"Good. Then return to your room. Please allow the priests to assist you so that you do not further damage your bones. Once you are healed you will resume your studies, and I am expecting great things from you in the future." The headmaster then turned to the three priests at his left. "As for the three of you, I will hold you responsible for Miss Dimwater's Dragon."

Keep your eyes open for the next installment of Kyra's adventures with Leatherback,

Dimwater's Demons.

Coming July 2016! And, as always, please leave a review on Amazon and Goodreads!

About the Author

Sam Ferguson is a fairly average guy.
That's it.
No, really, that's it.
Oh- you are actually reading this?

Well... the truth is that Sam is a very *lucky* guy. Now that he has become a full-time writer, it is easier than ever to juggle work in such a way that is able to spend time with his loving wife and five sons.

If he can carve out an extra hour for himself during the day, he'll hit the gym to try and regain the body he used to have in his youth (but he eats too much junk food to ever accomplish that goal).

He spent nearly five years serving as a U.S. Diplomat and absolutely loved the experience, but decided to move back home. Outside of the U.S. he has lived in Latvia, Hungary, and Armenia. He speaks Russian, Hungarian, and Armenian. (He used to speak some Latvian too, but he has no one to practice with anymore...)
He also has two dogs.
He plays the Elder Scrolls series.
His favorite superhero is Wolverine, but Batman is a close second.
If the kids go to bed at a reasonable hour, he will cuddle up with his wife to watch Scrubs reruns, the Big Bang Theory, Castle, or Burn Notice.
See, really just an average guy after all.

If you enjoyed this book, then join Sam Ferguson's Facebook page, sign up for alerts on his Amazon page, follow him on twitter and by all means leave a kind review!

You can also find new books and special deals each month by following Dragon Scale Publishing on Twitter @dragonscalebook, or by liking us on Facebook.

See the full collection of Dragon Scale Books by visiting:

WWW.DRAGONSCALEBOOKS.COM

The Netherworld Gate
Series:

The Tomni'Tai Scroll
The King's Ring
(Coming Soon)
Son of the Dragon
(Coming Soon)

The Dragon's
Champion Series

The Dragon's
Champion
The Warlock Senator
The Dragon's Test
Erik and the Dragon
The Immortal Mystic
Return of the Dragon

The Sorceress of
Aspenwood Series

Dimwater's Dragon
Dimwater's Demons
Dimwater's Dagger

The Fur Trader

Haymaker Adventures

Jonathan Haymaker
Brothers Haymaker

Kingdom of Denall

The Troven
The Secrets at the Keep
The Changing

Annals of Esparia

The Protector of
Esparia

www.ingramcontent.com/pod-product-compliance
Lightning Source LLC
Chambersburg PA
CBHW022100170626
46808CB00002B/526